PORTAL SLAYER

BENEATH THE SHADOWS

S.L. DOOLEY

TORN PARCHMENT

Contact the author: **www.SLDooley.com**

Cover design by Rob Williams, I Love My Cover

Map artwork by Matthew Robinson

Hardback ISBN: 978-1-956418-08-8

Paperback ISBN: 978-1-956418-07-1

For Wil

WHAT READERS ARE SAYING ABOUT PORTAL SLAYER: PATH OF DECEIT

The characters are compelling as are their varied reasons for being in Alnok. The unfolding events kept me engaged, excited to see what would happen next and how the Cord would handle the dangers and disagreements. Imperfect people doing what they think best. Not always pretty, either. A satisfying read, I appreciated that this book arrives at a natural conclusion yet holds open the door to more intrigue. -KS

***

Wow! Can't say that enough! Action packed, strong characters, deceit, anger, fear, self doubt, friendship, commitment, acceptance, forgiveness, love... a veritable Rollercoaster of emotions, ideas, life! **Very well done! Highly entertaining!** -MaD

***

The book is well-written, the plot moves it along smoothly, it is very entertaining and the characters are totally believable. **I will definitely [buy] the next book this author puts out.** -Sharon

BASTILLION CLIFFS
BORGAN RIVER
DURNOTH RUINS
MALVOK
TOR BARNOTH RUINS
SEOLFOR LAKE
TEGRE
BYDAN RIVER
KULUM
DESHIL RUINS
TUKLO MOUNTAINS
CHA-MAL LAKE
OLYAUND
THE MAP OF ALNOK
SHALHALA
ESIN RIVER
GALDOR RUINS
IKEALA
YUKOB RIVER
N
20 40 MI
THE KAIDILAS SEA

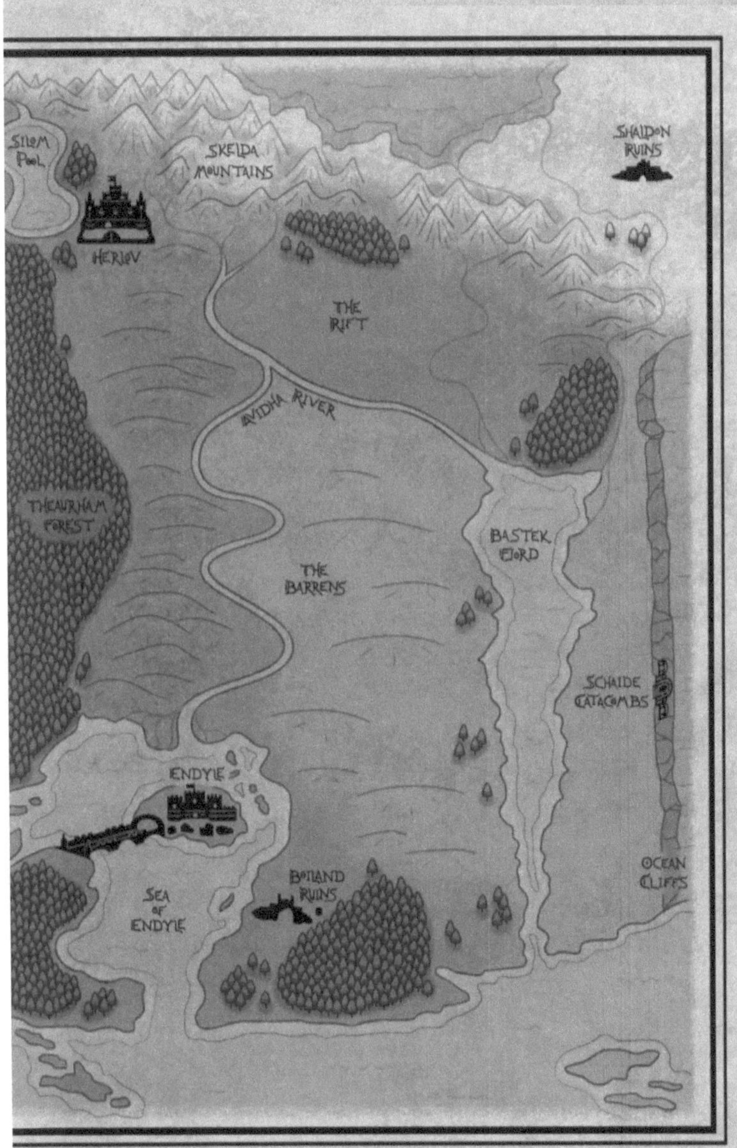

SILOM POOL
SKELDA MOUNTAINS
SHAIDON RUINS
HERJOV
THE RIFT
AVIDHA RIVER
THEAURHAM FOREST
BASTEK FJORD
THE BARRENS
SCHAIDE CATACOMBS
ENDYLE
BOLLAND RUINS
SEA OF ENDYLE
OCEAN CLIFFS

We need to reexamine what we think of as reality, because there is a world far more real than this one.

Governments have always loved crises. They provide the rationale for increased budgets and bureaucracies and subjugation of the population.
-Dr. Chuck Missler

For He rescued us from the domain of darkness, and transferred us to the kingdom of his beloved Son . . .
-Colossians 1:13

PROLOGUE

Smoke continued to fill the cold morning skies. Six distinct plumes, though Kade could only see two of them from his position on the Malvokian hilltop. All six temporal kingdoms were gone. It had been barely three sunsets since he had sent Moses and Nahor to Earth Apparent. Only two since he had discovered the prophecy.

"You are grieved," Lydia said.

Kade blinked, refocusing his gaze from the hazy horizon to the young Guardian. She gave him a gentle smile, her woven basket dangling from one hand, the berries inside forgotten.

"Many celebrate the temporals' expulsion from Alnok."

She had insisted he join her in this last harvest before winter. It had seemed a kind gesture to busy his mind after their loss. But perhaps she had more in mind.

Kade frowned. "The solemn memorials? Tearful tributes? All contrived?" He would not concede that all Guardians opposed Arkonai's rescue of the temporals hundreds of years ago.

Lydia smiled. "I said *many*, not all."

"And yet, the prophecy is real," he said, patting his canvas satchel where the parchment, rolled in a wax tube, was tucked safely at the bottom. He bent over a bush and plucked a handful of the ripe fruit.

Lydia held out the basket so he could deposit the berries into it.

"No one questions the significance of what you found at the top of the cliffs. But Kade, does it truly speak of the temporals' return?"

"I have no doubt."

"You understand if some see it as the reflection of a bereft heart?"

"I will not deny it is a salve to my sorrow," Kade conceded. "But it is a message of hope."

"When the kingdoms' leaders gather at Echelon Caverns, even if many arrive, they may not agree based solely on your interpretation of this . . . prophecy. Lord Talmond and Lady Ryla have said they will not attend."

"Will you?"

Lydia offered a small smile. "Of course. But Kade"—her smile slipped—"many are turning their attention to Cosyn." Her voice quieted as she mentioned his name. Most avoided speaking to Kade about his brother.

Kade swallowed the swelling anguish. It seemed his heartbreak would never mend. "All the more reason to consider the prophecy. We know Cosyn desired nothing more than to dominate the temporals while they were in Alnok. Is it so hard to believe he would continue his attacks in Earth Apparent?"

"No, I don't suppose—"

"Kade!" Ditimer, with long strides, hastened across the castle lawn. He smiled broadly as he approached, his teeth gleaming against his dark skin.

"We have completed our survey of Durnoth."

Kade shook his head. "I do not know what Lord Talmond hoped to find."

Ditimer shrugged. "Evidence of the enemy's departure." His eyes flitted west, toward Theurham Forest.

Kade clasped his hands at the small of his back and nodded. "Wise. But Cosyn's absence from the temporal kingdoms is not confirmation that he abandoned his purpose."

Ditimer and Lydia exchanged a glance.

Ditimer cocked his head. "Even so, does it change ours?"

"Of course not." Kade resisted the impulse to pace, but his urgency for the leaders of Alnok to heed the prophecy set a fire in his gut. How could he expect anyone to believe if his friends doubted?

Kade took a deep breath. "We are Guardians and protectors of the temporals above all else."

"Not the other way around." Ditimer's deep voice, though firm, held unwavering respect.

"We are so sure?" Kade said evenly. "Who are we to question what Arkonai commands?"

"Kade, I—"

Kade held up a hand and overlooked Ditimer's scowl.

"Do me the honor of hearing what the prophecy says."

"Of course." Ditimer bowed. "We serve the same Author. Our goals are forever aligned."

A smile tugged at Kade's mouth. "Though the means are not."

"I did not say so." Ditimer's eyes sparkled as he suppressed a grin. "No one questions your heart, my friend. Your love for the temporals was a testament to your dedication to Arkonai's directives."

"And continues to be."

"Indeed."

Lydia stepped up next to Ditimer. "What does the prophecy tell us regarding the temporals?"

Kade shook his head and began to pace. "The passage is . . . mysterious. It speaks of the temporals, of a lineage that will bring peace to the land."

"Temporals are hardly known for their peaceful nature," Ditimer scoffed.

Lydia set her basket on the ground. She touched Ditimer's arm. "It took a long time to overcome the division between the blessed kingdoms after the temporals arrived. But the agreement to stay out of their affairs brought peace."

"Not everyone was divided." Kade looked down at Lydia, affection swelling in his heart.

"No," she said, her expression soft and tears glittering in her eyes. "I shared your love for the temporals who came to Alnok. Many of us did," she added with a glance at Ditimer.

"Truth can unify," Kade responded. "Even if we do not understand its entire meaning, the prophecy is no less significant."

Ditimer's shoulders relaxed, and he nodded. "The implications remain to be seen."

Voices rose from the castle entrance and Lady Ryla emerged, giving instructions to attendants in her wake. She looked across the lawn and smiled. With one last command, she set out in their direction. Lydia gave Kade a wary look, but they were silent as the lady approached.

"Hello, Kade," Lady Ryla said, breathing heavily. "I was hoping to see you."

Kade bowed. "What can I do for you, m'lady?"

"After the recent events, the unfortunate passing on of our beloved temporals, I would not think of asking anything of you. I simply wished to convey my regret at not joining you at the caves."

"I understand. There is still much to settle after . . ." Kade's voice failed for a moment. ". . . the attacks," he finished.

"I am pleased you understand. And"—she slipped an arm through Ditimer's—"I hope you will forgive me for borrowing Ditimer. We will make for Deshill soon and we could use his discernment. We have no doubt Cosyn is scheming something."

Kade bowed again. "I will miss you both at the reading."

Lady Ryla smiled, gave Ditimer one last tug before releasing him and striding away.

"I am sorry, Kade," Ditimer said. His brow furrowed and his brown eyes filled with pity. He truly looked sorry.

"Of course, my friend." Kade put a reassuring hand on his shoulder. "I will share the prophecy with you when we both return."

"Perhaps you could wait. Give all Alnokians time to adapt to the temporals' absence. It may be too soon to declare any new developments."

Kade dropped his hand and shook his head. "If we are correct, and Cosyn is on the move, we cannot delay. It is imperative the leaders hear and incorporate the portents of the prophecy into any strategy they may devise."

Ditimer seemed as though he would say more, but simply nodded and touched his fingertips to his forehead. Kade and Lydia did likewise and watched in silence as Ditimer hurried after Lady Ryla, waiting at the castle entrance.

"His advice holds wisdom," she said, still looking at the gateway where Ditimer had disappeared. "We should pay heed to any of Cosyn's devices." She finally turned to Kade. "The Shalhalans have some insight into what his plans may involve."

"I do not believe making plans without all relevant information is wise. However,"—he glanced back at the castle—"I am eager to meet with the Shalhalans. There is more in the prophecy than the temporals' return to Alnok."

"Oh?"

"It lists what I believe to be a means to defeat whatever evil may lie in our realm. Perhaps some kind of defense. Or weapon. It speaks of a leader from the house of Micah accompanied by sword, light, shield, and sight. Five temporals."

Lydia squinted into the distance. "A sword and shield, I understand. But light and sight?"

Kade smiled. "I have some ideas. An enduring flame and an instrument to aid in discernment. All of which will require the most skilled craftsmen."

Lydia nodded in understanding. "Shalhalan craftsmen. But what about the fifth temporal? Nothing was specified?"

Kade's smile broadened. "An implement of old. A staff."

Lydia considered him for a moment, then strolled back to the bushes. "The prophecy was imparted to you," she said, gathering more berries and dropping them into her basket. "But open your heart to a meaning you might not fully understand." She straightened and looked at him. "And how others will support you in whatever quest you are called to. No single Periferial can carry Arkonai's message."

Kade plucked a few more berries. "We shall see."

CHAPTER ONE

Raelyn yanked the rotted blanket back from the open window and peered into the steel morning sky. The icy wind hinted at a fast-approaching snowstorm. A few sheep ambled close by, searching for a way out of the cold.

She glanced at Joshua, pitching a scrawny log into the tiny fireplace. The dilapidated hut barely held heat. The least of their problems. Even if it were perfectly insulated, it wouldn't hide them much longer. The Endylites were just delayed, fighting off the sea dragon. They would be in pursuit, if only out of allegiance to Cosyn.

She sighed and turned away from the window, working her numb fingers. Joshua winced as he sat on a blanket spread in front of the feeble fire. Most of his color had returned, but after nearly drowning in Endyle Bay, his movements were stiff and he tired easily. He seemed distracted. Nearly dying would do that.

Jinny, the Seon perched on her head, knelt on the floor, sorting through their meager supplies: a few ratty blankets, some roots and mushrooms she had scrounged from the nearby trees to "make a broth," Raelyn's bow, quiver, a few scavenged arrows and a rusted canteen. No seripyn.

"I don't know how long we'll be able to maintain without the tea," Raelyn said, pinching the bridge of her nose as the familiar headache prickled. They had only a general sense of where to go and what to do next. But without the seripyn to hold them in Alnok, they wouldn't get far.

"Do you know how to get to the Schade Catacombs?" Jinny asked, looking at Joshua.

He shrugged. "We left all but our smallest and least detailed map in Endyle. It shows a straight shot east. A body of water that has to be the Bastek Fjord, though it's not labeled. Then north. It looks pretty straightforward, but . . ." He shrugged again and gestured to the bench where they had laid out the map to dry.

Despite considering it so straightforward, Joshua had spent hours studying it.

Jinny smirked and rolled her eyes. "Sounds simple enough."

Joshua snorted. "Hasn't everything?"

Jinny took a deep breath. "The seripyn is one thing. We know we can resist fading for a week or more. But we will not get far without food and water."

"We'll need to risk going to shore for fish," Joshua said. "And fill that with water." He gestured to the canteen, as though the word for it escaped him.

Raelyn sat across from him, her back to the fire, and pulled her knees to her chest. "I want to find out if my brother's okay." She'd thought about it since coming to shore. But it was a risk she wouldn't take without his and Jinny's agreement.

Joshua met her gaze, the fire flickering in his gray eyes. "That'll probably happen soon enough."

Raelyn shook her head. "I can let it happen without waiting for the seripyn to wear off."

He frowned. "You can fade at will?"

"More or less. It's like I can think about Peter, and it makes it easier. I don't know how to explain it." She rubbed at her palm. A red mark, placed by Arkonai, had reassured her of her place in this quest. Until it had transferred to Peter's hand.

Joshua scratched at his beard. "Confirmation would be nice. I'd like to know everything's back to normal. The last I saw"—he looked from Raelyn to Jinny—"the last any of us saw . . . our homes were about to be engulfed in lava.

We closed the portal, but we don't know for sure what's happened. Lily might—" His voice caught. He cleared his throat. "I want to know everyone's safe."

"Of course." Raelyn offered a soft smile and squeezed his arm. Though a highly skilled soldier—talents that had been critical to getting them to the last plye—his tender heart was just as valuable. At least to her.

The front door, only wedged into the frame, creaked as a blast of wind battered the shelter. Dust stirred on the floor as the icy gust penetrated every crack and hole. The three froze. It subsided, and after a moment, it seemed no threat would accompany the turbulence. Raelyn let out a breath.

"We're in for some weather," Joshua said, rubbing his hands together. "Even if you could fade, can you get back? Without help?"

Raelyn chewed on her bottom lip. "I don't know." On only one occasion had she come back from fading without the critical tea. She looked at Jinny. "Remember in the forest? When we were hiding from the lushor?"

Jinny grimaced and blushed. "When I slapped you?"

"Exactly. We know that worked."

Jinny nodded as she abandoned her futile inventory and joined them, creating a circle. "Okay, but consider that Plan B. I am sure everyone is safe. But"—she fidgeted with the hem of her tunic—"we must assume they remain in danger. There is still the third plye."

"True," Raelyn said, but it was her dad about whom she was currently worried. He had to have made it to shore from his crazy trek out on the gulf. How he thought he could close the portal on that side . . .

"Okay," Joshua said, grunting as he stood. "While you pop in to see your brother, I'll keep watch. Might even catch a fish or two."

Jinny jumped up. "You are going to the bay?"

Raelyn frowned. "Are you sure you're—"

"I'll be fine. More worried about you than me. I'm just going down the hill. You're fading to Earth without a sure way back. You can't afford any surprises. Besides, a hike to the bay will be a walk in the park compared to where we're goin'." He stretched his back as he looked around the room. "Besides, I could use a change of scenery. Jinny, give her a smack if she's gone too long." He grinned and strode to the door, easing it open just enough to squeeze through.

"He is afraid," Jinny said after he'd gone.

Raelyn nodded. "Yeah."

"For you," Jinny clarified.

Raelyn smiled and nodded again. She took a deep breath. "Okay, here goes."

She closed her eyes and put all her thoughts on Peter. His kind blue eyes and crooked grin. Frying bacon in the kitchen; so excited to show her what he'd found.

Another gale of wind pummeled the hut. Raelyn squeezed her eyes.

Peter, standing at the bubble at the bottom of the bay, *in Alnok*.

Rain pattered against the roof. A roll of thunder grumbled in the distance. Raelyn huffed. It was no use. She opened her eyes . . .

. . . in Peter's room, kneeling near his bed. A storm raged outside the window. She scrambled to her feet.

"Peter!"

Footsteps thumped down the hall. "Rae!" Peter bolted through the doorway. "I knew it!"

"You did?"

Peter held out his hand to show Raelyn the red mark.

"This was on fire."

He took a step closer to her, his arm outstretched. Raelyn reached for his hand. His warm fingers brushed her's, but then passed through.

"It's okay," he said and then smiled. "You did it."

"*We* did it." Raelyn glanced at the window where sheets of water streaked down the panes. "The volcanoes have stopped?"

"Yes, but—"

"Is Dad okay?" Raelyn's heart pounded.

"He will be. The coast guard got out there as soon as things settled down. His boat had capsized, but he had held on. He's asleep—"

"Thank God," Raelyn breathed.

"Yeah, but Rae, it's like the volcanoes stirred something up. I mean, not a natural disaster. A political one. Everybody's at each other's throat. Riots in most major cities. National Guard's been deployed in New York City, L.A., *Salt Lake City*. I mean, Salt Lake! Like everybody's lost their minds."

Raelyn shook her head. "I don't know what it means. It might not have anything to do with Alnok and the last plye. It could just be a reaction. Everyone was so scared and confused. Probably still are. It might all settle down on its own. I don't know how Cosyn could spark riots." She rubbed her eyes and then sighed. "Even if it's not Cosyn, he's going to cause something to happen."

Peter frowned and looked her up and down. "How are you doing? Have you been able to rest? I mean, after the water . . ." Peter widened his eyes and shook his head.

Raelyn shrugged. "A little. But I had to see you before we travel to the next portal." She took a step closer to him. "I never could have closed the plye without you. I can't understand how you're doing it. Why you're so connected to me, to Alnok . . ."

"Just me? What about the others? Their families?"

"Nobody's even communicating with anyone back home. Much less interacting."

Peter folded his arms and cocked an eyebrow. "Weird." He chuckled. "I mean, it's all weird. But I don't know what would make us different. I haven't quizzed Dad on what he knows. He's still pretty weak. I wanted to let him recover. But I found this . . ."

He tugged at a chain around his neck, pulling a round amulet from his shirt. Though not as lustrous, and missing the gem-like flecks around the weeping tree, it was nearly identical to the Durinial.

"That was Mom's?" Raelyn asked, leaning in close.

Peter nodded. "Dad was wearing it when we found him."

"I don't know what to think about all this."

Thunder rolled, rattling the window.

"Right now, all that matters is you getting the last portal closed before everyone's torn . . ." Another grumble of thunder drowned out his words.

Something tugged at her elbow. She glanced down. Nothing.

She looked back at Peter, but his features were blurred.

"I'll get there as fast as I can . . ."

Peter mouthed words Raelyn couldn't hear.

Pounding thunder filled the room. Cold, musty air surrounded her. She blinked and Jinny came into focus, her dark eyes filled with fear. Joshua stood at the front door, his sword drawn.

"What's happening—?"

Banging came from the door.

Raelyn froze. Had someone followed Joshua back? The Endylites wouldn't bother knocking. But who else?

Joshua hurried to one side of the door, gesturing for Raelyn and Jinny to get behind him.

They rose to a crouch and hurried to Joshua. A shadow, visible through the cracks in the door, shifted.

"Can you sense anything?" Raelyn whispered in Jinny's ear.

Jinny shook her head. "I do not sense a threat. But whoever it is, they are blocking me."

The knocking came again, not as heavy, but insistent. They could wait to see if the stranger gave up. Or try to escape out the window . . .

"Your bow," Joshua whispered.

So Joshua thought confrontation their best option as well.

Raelyn tiptoed to her weapon and positioned herself in front of the door. She nocked an arrow and pulled back, giving him a nod.

Jinny yanked on the chain around her neck, drawing her push dagger and took a step back from Joshua to give him room.

He grabbed the edge of the door and pulled it away. It crashed to the floor in a cloud of dust as he scrambled back, brandishing his sword.

Raelyn blanched, blinded by the sudden daylight filling the dark room. A single shadow filled the doorway. Raelyn prepared to shoot. But Joshua moved in front of her, raising his arms, pointing his blade to the floor, as though in surrender.

Raelyn relaxed her bow and she and Jinny gathered around him.

Surrounded by new-fallen snow, a girl, not more than twelve or thirteen, watched them with a serene smile. Her ebony hair, from which a glowing lilac light radiated, set off her round, pale face and large, dark eyes. She took a step forward.

"I am Lima."

CHAPTER TWO

Frigid air blasted Kade's face as he galloped west across the empty landscape away from the Black River. He led his company of five: Avery, Othana, and the three Malvokian trainers: Altizara, Emaline, and Tilman. They had kept up this pace since daybreak. Crossing the hard, clay Rift, with no trees for cover, exposed them to an array of attacks. Hyram from the sky, dragons from the earth . . . betrayal from within.

He glanced at the crisp blue sky, the sun high and pale. Not even a cloud to blunt the light. They were an unmistakable target for anyone.

Kade leaned forward, pushing his horse faster. The movement sent a flare of pain across his chest. The gash from the dragon was not healing.

The mountains in the north could offer some protection. But that would require too great a diversion. The Schade Catacombs, where they would undoubtedly find Gabe, were in the southeast. This was the most direct route. They required haste over stealth.

The sun began its slow descent ahead of them. Kade squinted into the glaring light. They were now doubly vulnerable. Dangerously visible and, at least temporarily, blinded.

"Kade!" Avery drew up alongside him. "It's been hours!"

Kade ground his teeth, but nodded and tugged at his reins. There would be no satisfactory waypoints. They would have to risk any stops in the open. He winced as his horse slowed to a trot, jarring his wound. Avery took notice.

"Bloody dragon," he grumbled as he slowed his horse and pulled back.

Othana and Emaline trotted up next to Kade, but Tilman rode ahead several yards before pulling his horse to a stop, his head on a swivel, watching for danger. Altizara fell back, keeping watch on their western flank.

"Be on guard," Kade said, guiding his horse to a cluster of boulders. Othana dismounted and frowned as she led her horse nearer to Kade.

He eased out of his saddle. "Our rest must be brief."

His arms gave out just as he reached the ground. He stumbled backward. Othana caught his fall. With a steady grip, she guided him to the largest boulder. Kade patted her hand and sat with a grunt. She had suffered significant loss: two brothers, one an ally, the other an enemy. Though she could not mask the grief stifling her sunset-colored light, her instincts as a warrior remained in top form.

"Only a moment or two," Kade said, breathing hard. He studied Avery as the man dismounted and stretched his back.

Avery looked at Kade and frowned, taking a few cautious steps toward him.

"You all right, mate?" he asked, crouching next to Kade.

Kade nodded and took the canteen Emaline handed to him. "I will be." He did not remember so much gray in Avery's dark hair. He took one large gulp. "It will be some time before we reach a source of water. Drink sparingly."

"We should check your wound, Kade," Emaline said. She held a small pouch, likely filled with a treatment given to her by one of the healers.

Kade offered a weary smile and shook his head. "Not now. When we find a place to shelter. Here we are open to the eyes of the enemy."

Emaline nodded with a frown and tucked the pouch into her pack that was attached to her saddle. Tilman and Altizara trotted up from opposite directions.

"No one follows," Altizara said as she secured her bow to the pack on her back.

Tilman nodded. "The land ahead appears clear."

Neither of them dismounted. Ever the protectors. Tilman, trainer not only to Avery, but also to Joshua and Gabe, would break through any barrier to rescue them all. But Altizara's instincts and her affection for Raelyn went beyond teacher or even adviser. Perhaps her hand in crafting the Bokar had created a special bond, one rivaling Kade's own. She was not just Raelyn's trainer; she was her friend. A sister.

"The next troop will be some miles away," Othana said. "Much larger contingents. Nine total; each a day's ride apart."

Avery sat on the ground and took a couple of quick gulps from his canteen. He wiped his mouth with the back of his hand. "Do ye suppose Cosyn knows we're makin' our way to the catacombs?"

His tone was conversational, but his Yorkshire accent was thick, exposing his heightened anxiety. Since Cosyn's deception in luring Avery to Theurham Forest, promising to return him to his wife, the fear that was his constant companion had turned to all-out panic. He had been more determined than ever to return to Earth Apparent. That he was here now was a testament to his growth. And bravery.

"It is likely, Avery," Kade answered, watching him carefully.

Avery nodded and looked at the ground, frowning. "The prophecy, it mentioned the fire. That became obvious. But it also speaks of shadows. Any idea what that might mean?"

Kade took a deep breath, which was becoming more difficult. He glanced at the sky. Still clear. "Shadows could speak of a darkness over the land."

"Literal shadows."

"Aye. But darkness comes in many forms. There are shadows of the mind and heart."

"I can't fathom what my Penny might 'ave to face next. I dunno if she's better off in London or up north."

Othana fed her horse grain from her cupped hands. "What about your homestead persuades you to believe she would be unsafe there?"

Avery sniffed and looked west. "It's a backward little village. No resources to speak of."

"But Guardians have found cities to be unsafe. So many opportunities for threats."

Emaline sat next to Avery and offered him a grain cake. "Is it the village? Or the home?" she asked softly. Avery took the cake and nodded his thanks without meeting her eyes. He pinched off the corner and popped it into his mouth, chewing slowly and staring across the flat land. Finally, he swallowed.

"I grew up there. A little house outside o' town with a couple hundred acres. Dad worked for a shoe factory." His expression turned sour. "A bloody scoundrel. Hateful. He seemed to hate me most of all. I was an only child, so no one else to blame for his sorry life. Seemed to think I was the reason he wasn't a success. 'After the factory closed, he turned to drinking. I couldn't get away fast enough. Got a job with a financial firm and didn't look back."

He sighed and popped the rest of the cake into his mouth.

"After me mam died," he said around the mouthful, "I went back, and we had a huge row. Told me it didn't matter how much money I made, how expensive my shoes were, I'd never be worth nothin'."

Emaline reached out and placed a gentle hand on his arm. He gave her a bitter smile.

"Well, I showed him, didn't I? Made partner in me firm not ten years later. A 'ouse in London, one in New York. Beautiful wife."

"You are an overcomer." Kade chose his words carefully. In his zeal to encourage, he could also overwhelm and frustrate the man. "Remember—" Kade looked over Avery's shoulder. A plume of dust in the distance. He struggled to his feet. Encouragement would have to wait.

"Altizara?" Kade called as he stood. Avery was next to him in an instant.

She readied her bow and pulled an arrow. "Whatever it is, it must be moving at an incredible pace. There was no one there only moments ago."

Tilman stood in his saddle and drew his sword. Altizara nudged her horse without grabbing the reins. It complied by moving closer to Tilman, shifting and stamping.

Emaline stood to Kade's left and Othana drew close to Avery who was working his shield off his back.

It seemed Cosyn would make an appearance sooner rather than later.

"What is it?" Avery asked.

"I do not yet know," Kade said, training his eyes on the horizon.

"They approach from Herlov. Perhaps one of the soldiers," Emaline said.

"If so," Othana countered, "it can only be ill news."

"Kade?" Avery shifted on his feet, shield ready.

"Hold," Kade said, his voice barely above a whisper. A form took shape. Someone on horseback, galloping at full speed.

Kade took a deep breath and pressed his hand against his chest, preparing for the assault. But in that breath came a powerful certainty they were not in imminent danger.

"Somebody on a horse," Avery said, squinting into the distance. "Cosyn?"

"Nay," Kade said. "But remain on guard."

"Kade!" the rider yelled as he came into earshot.

Avery growled and stalked past Kade, planting himself next to Altizara's horse.

"Ditimer!" he shouted.

CHAPTER THREE

J oshua maneuvered around Raelyn, glowering at the girl. "Lachlor sent a kid?"

Lima held up her hands, shaking her head, eyes wide with shock. "I am not from Endyle!"

"Then where?" Raelyn demanded, looking past Lima into the cold twilight, left, then right. The hills, draped in snow, were empty.

"I am alone," she said and smiled.

Her serene expression spoke of timeless wisdom. Her eyes held Raelyn captive. Deep, erudite, safe. A few fluffy snowflakes clung to her long, dark hair. She looked roughly the same age as Lydia, and an elegiac twinge strummed Raelyn's heart. But, like Kade and most of the Guardians, her age was indiscernible. The girl's smile faltered and a ripple—confusion? anger?—passed over her face. It conjured a flash of Cosyn in his wrath as Raelyn had closed the plye in Endyle. But it was so subtle and brief, Raelyn dismissed the illusion.

The girl's clothes were clean and dry, and different from any in the other kingdoms. A cropped fur bolero covered the shoulders of a plain, jet-black dress. The full skirt nearly reached her black boots. She didn't have the look of a traveler, but in all of their scouting and supply gathering, they had come across neither town nor village. She had to have come from Endyle; sent to gain their trust. To draw them back; or keep them waiting until reinforcements arrived.

Raelyn glanced at Jinny, who stood on her right. She wasn't wearing her Seon, but she had proven the circlet was not always necessary for her to sense threats. She looked wary, but not afraid.

Joshua didn't relent. Though he kept his sword lowered, his grip tightened. Raelyn followed his example, keeping her arrow nocked, pointed at Lima's feet. The girl seemed harmless. But they had thought the same of Lord Lachlor.

"I live outside of Endyle," Lima said, her voice as clear as ringing bells. She laughed, shaking her head, then held out her plain skirt as though to prove her point. "Do I look like I belong in Endyle? Nay, that is where I came *from*." She paused, as though allowing them to consider her explanation. Her face turned serious. "I was banished when I would not adhere to their foolish and frivolous ways."

"Banished?" Jinny asked.

"Aye, others prefer Endyle to exile. Not me." Her voice grew husky, but Raelyn couldn't pin sadness to her demeanor. Lima stepped over the threshold, pulling her stole around her neck.

"I followed you," she continued, addressing Raelyn. "I saw you cross the sea. Unfortunately,"—she glanced over her shoulder—"so did others. You are not safe here. I can take you to a protected location."

No one responded. Lima tilted her head, patiently waiting for Raelyn's response. She had the air of a neighbor coming to borrow sugar.

"Why do you want to help us?" Joshua asked.

"Is that not what Periferals do?" Lima's eyes widened and the lilac aura pulsed. "Boiland has been deserted for hundreds of years. There are no resources. Food, heat . . . seripyn."

Raelyn's heart skipped. How did she know?

She had watched them leave the sea. She knew they were temporals. It was a reasonable assumption.

"That's right," Raelyn said evenly. "You have the tea?"

Lima nodded.

"How?" Jinny asked.

"In Endyle?" Joshua didn't hide his accusatory tone.

Lima nodded again and closed her eyes a moment, as though showing great patience and complete understanding. "It is an older variety from Endyle. It has been in my stores since I left. Why I took it with me . . ." She smiled and shrugged. "I only remembered it when I saw you on the shore."

"You must've been watchin' a while," Joshua said, sheathing his sword, but keeping his hand on the hilt. Either he was satisfied she could be trusted or wanted her to think so.

Likely the latter.

Lima drew her arms tight and shivered. "I have. Endyle may be altogether corrupt, but I was curious what business temporals would have there. Rumors of a group from Earth Apparent returning to Alnok reached me. I thought perhaps to rebuild some of the temporal kingdoms and villages. Even here, in ancient Boiland." She shivered again.

A shout echoed from the trees in the west.

Lima glanced left. She shook her head vigorously. "I am afraid time must be the crucible for your trust. I can lead you to safety."

Raelyn touched the Durinial, hoping for a nudge of intuition. But it was still.

Lima took another step inside, closer to Raelyn, holding her gaze with a calm, almost passive expression.

"I can lead you to a safe passage," she repeated, "but we must hurry." She reached out and touched Raelyn's hand, lowering the arrow so it pointed away from her. The bold move should have appeared impudent, but her warm, soft hand instantly put Raelyn at ease.

She nodded and looked at Joshua. His jaw tensed and he glanced out the door. He shook his head in frustration.

The shouting drew nearer. "Here! Boats!"

"It's a risk," Joshua said. "But we can't wait for them to find us."

Jinny nodded and rushed to their supplies. She folded a towel around the foraged food and thrust it at Joshua. With a second towel, she wrapped two water skins and the dried map. Another shout, closer, rang out as Raelyn strapped the quiver to her back and checked the buckle on the Bokar.

With no backpacks, they hugged their meager provisions to their chests and huddled around Lima in the doorway. She turned without a word and hurried across the crumbling ruin. Rushing past a few bleating sheep and to one of the other dilapidated structures, she ducked behind a decaying wall. They followed suit, Joshua wincing as he squatted next to Raelyn. It seemed he wasn't as healed as he let on.

"They must be here!" a soldier bellowed.

The sheep baaed their objection to the intrusion.

Lima held up a finger for them to wait. She peeked around the corner, her finger still raised. Then, with a curt nod, she gathered her skirt and dashed up a hill.

Raelyn pulled Joshua's arm around her shoulder as they followed Lima into a thick forest. A memory flashed across Raelyn's mind. She, Joshua, and Gabe following Kade as he led them away from the varga when they first entered Alnok. They had little understanding of what they would be called to do. It had taken some time before she trusted Kade. But he had proven himself. She tried to take comfort from their previous triumphs. But a creeping malaise circled Raelyn's thoughts.

***

"I don't feel good about this," Jinny whispered, as they followed Lima south just inside the tree line of a thick forest. The last of the daylight was melting away. She and Raelyn dropped back, allowing Joshua and Lima to drift ahead.

"A warning from the Seon?" Raelyn whispered back, gesturing to the circlet dangling from Jinny's belt.

"Nothing clear about her intentions. But . . . it is confusing." Jinny shook her head in frustration, tossing her once shiny black hair, now dull and tangled.

"How did you feel about Kade at first?" Raelyn asked. If Jinny could see some way to trust Lima, she might feel better. It's not like they had options. And Raelyn couldn't deny the relief in having someone else take the lead for a while. Someone with knowledge of Alnok and Earth Apparent. Someone like Kade.

Jinny continued staring ahead, frowning at Lima. Raelyn followed her gaze. The young girl passed nimbly around scraggly trees and over boulders, as though skipping through a park, the lavender light trailing her and lighting their way. She seemed confident they would follow. The shouts from Endyle had faded to silence as they traveled toward the sea.

"I did not have the Seon. But even then, I had a peace about his intentions. Ditimer, on the other hand . . ."

Raelyn pursed her lips and nodded. She had overlooked Jinny's misgivings about the Malvokian soldier. She shouldn't do that again.

"Let me know if you feel the smallest thing," she said. "We'll keep a watch for anything suspicious. But we need to get away from Endyle. And we need the seripyn."

Jinny nodded, but her frown deepened.

Raelyn jogged ahead, catching up with Joshua.

"How you doing?" she murmured.

"Maintaining," Joshua said, keeping his gaze on Lima. "Hopefully we're close," he added, loud enough for Lima to hear.

"Very close," she called back. "Just beyond that large tree," she added, pointing into the woods. All the trees looked the same.

As promised, they finally circled a massive fir-like tree and approached a structure, small and shadowed. A simple cabin; nothing like Endyle.

"Here," Lima said, tromping up two steps to a wooden door. She pulled it open and hurried into a dark room, sending purple shadows along the walls.

Joshua pulled on Raelyn's arm and went in ahead of her. She paused for a second before following him. When the door shut behind them, lanterns sputtered to life and lit up a small room with a bed in one corner, a stone fireplace and a wooden chair in the other. A workspace along one wall, next to a set of shelves, looked to be a makeshift kitchen. With living quarters so simple and sparse, an elaborate trunk at the foot of the bed seemed a red rose among daisies. Lima stood at the center of the room, smiling.

She glanced around as though just realizing the less-than-impressive nature of the dwelling.

"It is not much, but that is intentional." She bent over the fireplace and passed her hand over a pile of wood beneath a metal grate. Purple flames sprang to life before fading to yellow. "Endylites have passed within a stone's throw and not seen it. The rough-hewn planks blend completely with the surrounding trees, but we constructed them such that no light escapes. It is virtually invisible."

Joshua wandered to the far wall. "We?"

Lima blinked and shook her head. "My brother and I." She gave no other explanation, but her solemn, haunted expression said enough.

"Lima, I'm sorry," Raelyn said, stepping toward her. She put a hand on the girl's delicate shoulder.

Lima offered a strained smile and sniffed. "I have food," she said briskly and turned to the shelves, where baskets nestled next to jars of fruit. She pulled down a cloth-covered wooden bowl and handed it to Joshua, then continued to root past her supplies until she retrieved a small woven packet. She held it aloft.

"Here we are," she said triumphantly. "I knew I had a remaining supply of seripyn."

Jinny hugged her arms to her waist. "How is it you have this tea?"

Lima shrugged and handed it to Raelyn. "When I prepared to leave Endyle, I spent many months gathering supplies—"

"You and your brother," Joshua corrected.

Lima nodded. "Precisely."

She retrieved a kettle from the counter and placed it on the grate in the fireplace. "But *we*"—she shot Joshua a glance—"were forced to leave sooner than expected. I took everything I could carry from the kitchens." She held out her hand and Raelyn passed back the packet.

Lima opened it and took a pinch of crushed, dried leaves, carefully resealing the pouch. "I did not even know what it was." She lifted the lid of the kettle and sprinkled in the leaves.

"How did you find out?" Jinny asked, placing her towel of treasures on the counter.

Lima looked up from the fire. "Find out?"

"That it was seripyn."

Lima gave her a lopsided grin and took a deep breath, closing her eyes as she inhaled.

The scent of lavender and honeysuckle swirled through the room. Raelyn relaxed her shoulders. The tension and fear from days hiding in the ruin eased. There was no mistaking the aroma or the effect.

"I considered disposing of it many times." Lima eyed Jinny with a mixture of humor and magnanimity. "I am sure you are pleased I did not."

Jinny gave her a stiff nod. "Yes, quite serendipitous."

Lima handed each of them a wooden cup, which she filled with the brew from the kettle. Then she returned her attention to the shelves, opening jars and clanging pots.

Raelyn frowned at Jinny as the girl sniffed at the contents of her cup. Lima had just rescued them from oncoming soldiers, brought them to a warm, cozy hut, provided them with the essential elixir, and Jinny was treating her hospitality with disdain. Still eyeballing Jinny, she took an exaggerated swig, hoping to set an example of trust. It was the same oily seripyn from Endyle. But she relished the effects. The dizziness subsided and her stomach settled, revealing how hungry she was. Joshua handed Raelyn the cloth-covered bowl. As he drank, Raelyn peeked beneath the cloth covering the basket. A loaf of bread.

"I will have a stew ready soon," Lima said, hefting a pot onto the fire where the kettle had been. She added ingredients from tall baskets beneath the shelves. "Beyond that door is a washroom." She nodded to a darkened doorway next to the bed.

A washroom.

Raelyn grinned, glancing at Joshua, then Jinny. Who would get there first?

"You might find clothes that fit you in the trunk," Lima said, stirring in ingredients without looking up.

The only trunk was the carved, gilded chest by the bed.

"You go," Raelyn said to Joshua. "I'll see what I can find."

When Joshua had pulled a drape over the doorway, Raelyn lifted the lid to the trunk. A collection of mismatched tunics, shirts and pants lay crumpled atop what had to be spoils of Endyle. Silver goblets, rich velvety fabrics, and colored glass bottles collected at the bottom.

Raelyn selected a large black tunic and a pair of brown pants that looked like they may fit Joshua. Jinny helped her locate a small blouse and skirt and a second, smaller tunic and pants. It would do.

She passed the clothes to Joshua as he exited, his hair wet but still in his dirty clothes. He disappeared back into the washroom and returned wearing the baggy clothes. He propped the sheathed Ruah against the wall.

Jinny gathered the skirt and top and went next, then Raelyn. A simple lantern illuminated a bowl and pitcher full of water. Raelyn rinsed as best she could, toweling off with a thin cloth. Though ill-fitting, the clean clothes felt luxurious. She pulled the Bokar's holster over her head and rejoined the others.

When they had gathered back around the fire, Lima ladled a spoonful of broth into a bowl and handed it to Joshua.

"There is a well behind the house," she explained, retrieving two more bowls. She served Jinny and Raelyn.

"I am afraid I have no table."

"It's fine," Raelyn said. "Thank you. For everything."

Lima gave her a wide smile.

Soon they were sitting on the wooden floor, slurping a rich stew, dredging the bread through the bottom so not a drop was wasted.

Joshua heaved a deep, satisfied sigh as Lima gathered the bowls. "Thanks, Lima."

It seemed he and Jinny had relaxed with the comfort of clean clothes, a warm shelter and full bellies. But, even with immediate needs met, they still didn't know Lima's intentions.

Lima gave Joshua a warm smile. "I will locate some extra blankets . . ."

Raelyn stood. "Lima. It's not that I—we—don't appreciate all you've done. But . . ." She glanced at Joshua and then Jinny.

Joshua got to his feet. "You don't even know us."

Lima dropped her gaze for a moment, studying the floor. *Here it is. The catch.*

Lima met Raelyn's eyes. "Not everyone is allied with Lord Lachlor." She placed the stacked bowls on the wooden chair. "I was not entirely forthcoming when I told you about the rumors of the temporals."

Jinny sucked in a breath and jumped to her feet. Lima held out a defensive hand. "What I mean to say it, the rumors came to me from inside the Endyle walls."

"An ally?"

Jinny smiled for the first time since meeting Lima. "Ashford." The Endylite who had helped them escape.

Lima nodded, her eyes sparkling. "Yes. He dared not leave the castle, but he informed me of your arrival and of your intent to thwart Cosyn." A purple light flashed in her eyes.

"So Ashford was helping us all along," Raelyn said.

"Aye. Though he had planned a different escape."

Raelyn's face burned. She should have followed Joshua and Jinny's advice to wait. But she had barreled ahead, so sure they had to find the plye before testing Ashford's allegiance.

"That may have been partially my fault," Raelyn said, twisting the ends of her still-damp hair.

Lima raised her eyebrows, but she didn't seem surprised. "Oh?"

"I thought we were running out of time. Earth Apparent seemed to be about to explode. Our families were in danger. It was getting worse." A powerful reluctance stopped her from offering more details. Lima knew Ashford, knew something of their objective, but she still hadn't revealed her part in all of it. Kade had been more forthcoming about his plans. Lima had revealed nothing.

"We'll need to move on soon." Joshua said, drawing close to Raelyn and placing a hand on her shoulder. The warmth and weight of his touch settled her mind and gave her a deep comfort, not unlike the seripyn.

Lima took a deep breath and smiled. "I would like to help."

"Why?" This time it was Jinny who posed the question. Simple, to the point, and essential.

Lima's smile faltered. "I am also running out of time. I have avoided contact with Endyle for some time. But as they tend the sheep, they have wandered closer to my hideaway. And now, they will be searching for you." She sighed. "Besides, this"—she swept an arm over the room—"is not my purpose in Alnok. To simply survive on the outskirts of a castle full of fools." Her voice wavered and her cheeks flushed. "My calling is to the temporals."

Raelyn nodded. "I'm not as concerned with Endyle as I am with Cosyn."

Lima's face hardened. "Cosyn is a fool," she snarled with an unexpected vehemence. The lilac light brightened the room for a moment. As with Lydia, despite her youth, she transformed from innocent child to fierce warrior.

"We have no reason to fear Cosyn," Lima continued, her tone softer, but firm.

"Why not? You have a secret weapon?" Joshua asked.

"Perhaps," Lima said, cutting her eyes to Joshua with an impish grin. When she didn't elaborate, Raelyn pressed further, determined to assess her trustworthiness.

"How long have you lived away from Endyle?"

"Many years."

"Have you never tried to enter Keala?" Jinny asked.

Lima shook her head. "The battle between Endyle and Keala has driven a wedge that I could not hope to remove. Perhaps now, if the Kealans learn of how I have helped the temporals on their quest, they will accept me." She looked at Raelyn with bright eyes and a hopeful smile.

Lima, the innocuous child, had reemerged. A surge of shame shadowed Raelyn's irritation. The girl had been exiled from two warring communities and had survived on her own. The Periferals were powerful, but strength did not overcome loneliness.

"Thank you for helping us, Lima," Raelyn said softly.

Lima nodded. "I wish to know of your next plan. But first, sleep. We will discuss your strategy in the morning."

Raelyn opened her mouth to argue, but her eyelids became heavy. As though Lima had cast a spell.

They each took a quilt Lima offered them and spread out around the dwindling fire. Raelyn collapsed onto the soft blanket without a word. Lima was right. They could discuss their next move tomorrow. Joshua wadded his blanket beneath him as he sat propped up against the wall, his sword by his side. Jinny curled up close to Raelyn.

Comforted by Joshua's unspoken assurance that he would keep watch, Raelyn lay down and watched as Lima arranged the remaining blankets on her bed.

"Sleep well, my friends," she said.

Raelyn mumbled "good night" and as sleep overtook her, she watched Lima lie down, the lavender light glowing softly from her eyes as she surveyed her guests.

CHAPTER FOUR

Raelyn jerked awake to banging pots. She glanced at Jinny, who was sitting up, rubbing her eyes. Lima's bed was empty, and Joshua was gone.

Raelyn stood and squeezed her eyes against a sharp pain in her temples. The Endylite seripyn didn't eliminate all the symptoms.

"Joshua?" she called.

He stuck his head around the door from the washroom, shirtless and his hair dripping. "You okay?"

"Yeah. Where's Lima?"

"Rustling up breakfast." He nodded at the front door.

As though on cue, Lima opened the door, pink-nosed and ushering in a bitter wind. She shuffled inside with the large pot on her hip and a black cloak around her shoulders.

"Ah, good morning!" She struggled to close the door.

Jinny hopped up and helped her with the pot.

"Thank you! Just put it there." She gestured to the fireplace where coals shimmered. She dipped a large pitcher into the pot then flicked her hand and sent the coals crackling. She poured the water into the kettle, added more tea leaves, and put the kettle next to the pot.

"I thought I might use some of the roots you brought and make a soup for breakfast."

Raelyn pressed her palms to her forehead. With the headache came renewed anxiety. They didn't yet know how Cosyn was using the last portal, but they couldn't waste time.

"Lima, we need to—"

"I understand there is a journey to be undertaken. You can tell me about it while we eat. And"—she pointed to a ladder propped against the wall where their clothes hung on the rungs—"while your clothes dry." She must have washed them while they slept. It seemed her gestures of friendship had no bounds.

She motioned for Raelyn to sit in the lone chair and gave her a handful of roots and a knife.

Raelyn complied without arguing. But what to tell Lima? Or, more importantly, what should they keep from her?

Joshua sauntered out of the washroom. Raelyn avoided looking at his wide, bare shoulders with a towel thrown over one by helping Lima clean the roots as the girl cut them into the pot of simmering water.

"We need to get to the Schade Catacombs," he said.

So much for discretion.

"I thought as much," Lima said without looking up from the pot.

"You did?" Jinny asked, her arms full of the blankets she had folded from the floor.

Lima nodded and turned to face them, her knife in one hand, a large mushroom in the other.

"Although I am banished from Endyle and even separated from Alnok, I am well aware of Cosyn's disdain for the temporals. I am privy to his attacks. As a Periferal, my primary responsibility is to oversee the temporals. I have continued to carry out my responsibilities alone. But you are here"—her lips turned up, but her eyes were sad—"so I will continue to fulfill my commitment. Whatever may come, I will see you through to the end."

Raelyn let out a long, slow breath and with it, her remaining doubt. The thought of this young girl, alone, brushed aside by her people, living on roots and rumors, struck at Raelyn's heart. Lima had risked her own exposure by saving them from the Endylites and was now feeding them breakfast. With fewer allies than they might have realized, they couldn't afford to reject the help so readily offered.

Lima turned back to the pot of water, now at a rolling boil. "It is at least a two-day journey to the cliffs. From there, we can follow the shoreline east—"

"Why the coast?" Joshua interrupted.

Lima looked up. "It is the safest route."

"We have a map that says different." His gaze darted to Jinny, who was preparing their ratty blankets for travel, then to Raelyn. "It shows a path due east, through the forest."

"The map reveals a path," Lima said, going back to stirring the vegetables with the wooden ladle. "But it does not show the danger." She placed the spoon across the pot and turned, rubbing her hands together, very like Kade would do.

"The coast is a longer route but may save you from unnecessary confrontation."

"With what?" Jinny asked.

Lima gave her a humorless smile. "Any number of Cosyn's devices. But in those forests? Giants." She said the word casually, as though mentioning a spot of traffic.

Joshua scoffed. "Are we talkin' *Jack and the Beanstalk* or just oversized Alnokians?"

After everything they'd faced in Alnok, the thought of giants roaming the forests wasn't all that surprising.

"They're big enough," Lima countered. "But it is not only their size. Their numbers would overwhelm you."

"But no dangers on the way south?" Joshua pushed back.

"I cannot say. Perhaps. But I am sure about the giants. I have had many close encounters with them."

Joshua scratched at his beard and then rubbed the back of his neck.

Lima watched him for a moment before turning to Raelyn.

"Do you have a plan for entering the Schade Catacombs?" Though her tone was conversational, her expression was hard.

"What do you know about the catacombs?" Jinny stopped mid-fold.

"We all know of the prophecy," Lima replied, her eyes wide and innocent. "Kade saw to that. It is why Lord Lachlor was so determined for you to stay. He, like many others, questioned what Kade claimed." She smiled. "I am pleased the lord's devices failed."

"And Cosyn? You know about his attacks?" Joshua's sharp, direct question seemed to challenge Lima.

"I knew Cosyn was manipulating the inhabitants of Endyle. When I heard of your arrival, I wondered if your purpose was tied to the prophecy. Ashford relayed the rest." She shook her head. "But the catacombs, they contain creatures beyond any you have encountered."

"They're heavily guarded?" Joshua asked.

"Nay. There is no need. All who enter never escape."

No one had mentioned the reason they were making for the catacombs. The plye.

"We—" Raelyn began.

"Have a plan," Jinny rushed to finish, frowning at Raelyn.

"Of course," Lima said, and set about gathering bowls and spoons.

Jinny gave Raelyn a subtle shake of her head and then shared a look with Joshua. They were having second thoughts about trusting Lima. Why?

"We have a *map*," Raelyn said slowly, choosing her words so as not to override Joshua and Jinny's distrust. "But maybe a guide would be better."

Joshua pulled two tunics from the ladder rungs. He handed Jinny her beige one and pulled the gray one over his head.

"Look," he said. "We appreciate your help. Really."

Jinny plucked her pants from the ladder and draped the clothes over one arm. "I am sure Lachlor would have found us if you had not come to our rescue. But I believe we are to continue east from here."

"Of course it is your choice." Lima shrugged, and with a thin smile, handed Joshua a bowl. "But consider Kade's appointed leader"—she gestured to the amulet hanging from Raelyn's neck—"as you make your decision."

Raelyn's heart swelled. Lima's vote of confidence was as encouraging as if it had come from Kade. Lima ladled the soup into their bowls without comment. She hefted the pot from the fireplace and made her way to the door.

"Weigh your options carefully," she said and stepped out into the swirling snow, pulling the door closed behind her.

Raelyn turned on Joshua, who was blowing a spoonful of broth. "What is your problem?" she hissed. "Why are you so set against Lima's offer?"

Jinny touched her elbow. "Raelyn, though I do not sense animosity, I also do not discern benevolence. It is not like being shut out, as was the case in Endyle. I feel *nothing*."

"You're not even wearing the Seon." Raelyn gestured to the circlet hanging on Jinny's hip.

"Look," Joshua said, rubbing the back of his neck. "I'm not saying we're right—"

"Just that I'm wrong," Raelyn shot.

Joshua raised one eyebrow, which was more maddening than if he had glared. "We just need to be cautious," he said.

"We know where we need to go," Jinny said. "We have the weapons that gave us success in Endyle."

"But according to Lima, and I think she's right, by the way, we're heading to a place much worse than Endyle. Through a forest of *giants*. And we're even more vulnerable without Gabe's torch and Avery's shield. Why would we continue alone?" Angry tears stung Raelyn's eyes. She swallowed hard, determined to keep her emotions in check.

"We're not alone," Joshua said. He took a last swig of soup directly from the bowl and set it on the chair. "You've led us well." He grasped her shoulders and stared into her eyes. "Kade believed in you. So do I."

A tear slipped down Raelyn's cheek, despite her best efforts. She sniffed and cleared her throat. "If that's so, why can't you trust me? You were so keen to trust Ashford and I didn't listen. I won't make that same mistake."

He nodded and gave her arm a brusque stroke, his awkward way of consolation.

"If there's risk either way, why not take a chance on Lima?" Raelyn pressed. "I'll do anything to protect my brother and dad. Isn't Lily worth the risk?"

A muscle worked in Joshua's jaw, then he turned and stalked to the washroom.

"Raelyn," Jinny said, lowering her voice and shifting her gaze to the door. "We should not alter our course. I sense more of Lachlor than Kade in Lima. She is hiding something. Even Joshua senses it." She heaved a sigh. "If Lima wishes to join us, I will not object. But a diversion back to the sea is unwise. We should take the more direct route."

Joshua exited the washroom, buckling the Ruah to his waist. Jinny slipped inside. He nodded to Raelyn's clothes, still hanging on the ladder. "We should get ready to leave. The seripyn will dull our senses again. Before we know it, we could be here until spring's thaw."

Raelyn rolled her eyes and snatched her clothes from the ladder. "We have almost no supplies, no clear heading, and maybe a few more swallows of the tea. You really think ignoring Lima's guidance is wise?"

Joshua narrowed his eyes and looked at the floor. He took a deep breath. "Here's what I think: Lima came out of nowhere, just like Lachlor. She's offering to help, just like Lachlor. She's suggesting a different course than we agreed."

"Yes, but—"

New shouts rang in the distance, though it was impossible to discern from which direction or how far. They froze, eyes wide, listening.

Joshua shook his head. "And Jinny has a bad feeling," he whispered. "Since when do you ignore her advice?"

Jinny entered the room, dressed and her hair in a high ponytail, the push dagger hanging from its chain, and the Seon perched on her head. She gathered their towels with the last of their food.

"We should not delay. We will not remain hidden for long."

"Leave now?" Raelyn asked.

"Yes," Jinny said, keeping her voice even. "We must begin our journey east."

Raelyn growled, stomped past them into the washroom, and jerked the drapes closed.

Nothing's changed. However I lead, they want the opposite.

She pulled the Bokar's holster over her head and hung it on a nail in the wall. Yanking the pants over her hips and the tunic over her head, both clean but still damp, her hands shook. She cinched her belt and secured the Bokar back over her shoulder.

They'll just have to listen. I bet Lima's plan will make perfect sense when we get to the shoreline.

Shouts, now close enough to make out the words "here" and "go", echoed outside. Raelyn rushed back into the room, ready to rally Joshua and Jinny. But Lima stood in the middle of the room, facing them with a somber expression.

"We must leave now," Lima said. "No one from Endyle has come across this shelter. But no one was looking. It seems you are a higher priority than I guessed." With a determined look, she crossed the room to the trunk. She pulled up the lid and retrieved the soft swathes of fabric: three black cloaks like her own, but of varying sizes. She held them out and Raelyn took all three.

"How do you have—"

A look of impatience passed over Lima's face. "Ashford," she said, offering no other explanation.

Raelyn handed the longest cloak to Joshua and the smallest one to Jinny. Lima continued pulling items from the trunk. Three satchels, similar to the one Kade wore.

She then handed each of them a canteen of ornate silver, an obvious Endyle extravagance.

"Thank you again, Lima," Joshua said. He filled his canteen from the kettle before dropping it into his sack. "You've made our journey much easier." He slipped into the cloak.

Lima cocked her head. "But?"

"We're gonna stick to our plan." Joshua leveled his gaze at Lima. Jinny took Raelyn's canteen and filled both.

Lima nodded slowly. Then she flitted her gaze to Raelyn. "This is your choice?"

Raelyn shook her head. "No, we haven't decided," she said desperately. "Joshua, I really feel we should follow Lima to the shore. If she says there's danger in the forest to the east, we can't take a chance."

Joshua looked hard at Raelyn. "We're taking chances either way."

"Joshua, Jinny, please." Raelyn's voice quivered on the last word.

Lima pulled her satchel over her head and walked to the door. She opened it a crack and peered out.

Jinny, her brow knit, handed Raelyn her canteen but said nothing.

"It is clear," Lima said. "We should go now."

Raelyn's heart pounded. It was all moving too fast. They needed more time to discuss their next move. She couldn't separate from Joshua and Jinny, divide the Cord even more. But she couldn't *not* follow Lima, a Periferal. She would know the land and the path to the catacombs more than they would. She seemed to possess Kade's confidence and Altizara's fearlessness. How could they not see it? It seemed, against common sense, they were resolved to go their own way.

"We'll follow the map," Joshua said, his gray eyes unwavering.

Jinny, just as determined, planted her feet and raised her chin.

Raelyn opened her mouth and shook her head in disbelief. They couldn't possibly be so stubborn. If she went with them, told Lima no, maybe it would be okay. She glanced at Lima, whose lilac tendrils of light floated above her head, her arms, and her hands as the girl gripped the door handle.

Raelyn had to choose.

"We're wasting time," Joshua growled, taking a step toward the exit. "Are you coming with us?" he asked Raelyn, his eyebrows raised.

"I—I trust Lima," she said, whispering the girl's name.

She had more reason to trust her friends than this mysterious exile. But an inescapable urgency to follow Lima overtook her loyalty to the Cord. Joshua and Jinny were making a mistake. She couldn't stop them, but she would not risk her brother's safety, nor her victory in closing the plye, just because they had some vague reservations.

"I'm sorry, but this is my path," she said, her voice firmer, surer.

"Raelyn," Jinny said, grabbing her hand. "Are you sure?" She gave Lima an uncertain glance.

"Lima," Raelyn said, still holding onto Jinny. "How long will it take us to reach the catacombs?"

Lima glanced at Raelyn. "Five days for us, should all go well." Then she looked at Joshua with sad eyes. "For you . . ." she shrugged her shoulders and shook her head.

"Five days," Raelyn said, releasing Jinny and turning to Joshua. "If I don't find you at the catacombs, I'll come looking for you."

Joshua nodded but said nothing.

Raelyn hugged Jinny and kissed her forehead. "Please be careful." What else could she say?

Lima opened the door, and a blast of wind threatened to take it off the hinges. Raelyn started after Lima, but a rough hand gripped her own. Joshua pulled her close, his soft beard brushing her cheek, and whispered in her ear.

"Watch your back. I—" He pulled away, staring into her eyes, then shook his head and hurried out the door.

He and Jinny jogged around the shelter and disappeared into the falling snow. Lima trudged ahead, plowing a path south through the waiting trees. Hot tears ran down Raelyn's cheeks as she followed.

There was no reason not to trust the girl. She had protected them. Fed and clothed them. And, maybe as important as anything else, she had shown confidence in Raelyn's ability. Until Lima proved otherwise, Raelyn resolved to have faith in her.

CHAPTER FIVE

Kade lurched forward and grabbed Avery's shoulder. "His presence does not signify an attack."

Avery jerked away. "I don't give a rat's—"

"Kade! I bring news!" Ditimer shouted, still galloping at full speed. Kade could now see the man's face, dull and grim. He could not stop the lift in his spirit at seeing his friend. But he kept his joy in check. If Avery was correct, Ditimer had betrayed them. He seemed to be alone, but it could be a trap.

"Kade," Ditimer gasped as he pulled the reins, skidding to a stop directly in front of him. "Please"—his eyes shifted to Avery—"I have much to explain."

Kade continued to hold Avery at bay. "Indeed you do, old friend."

Altizara drew back her bow. "What makes you think for one moment we won't send you on to the next realm right here?"

Ditimer scrambled from his horse and approached Altizara with his head bowed. Tilman shifted his horse so that he and Altizara flanked him. Emaline and Othana stood next to a partially mollified Avery.

"Nothing is as you think," Ditimer said, stopping well short of his fellow Malvokians.

Avery wrenched from Kade's grasp. "You handed me off to Cosyn, you bloody bas—"

"No!" Ditimer shook his head and stepped back as Othana rushed to restrain Avery. "I would never join with Cosyn."

Altizara lowered her aim to Ditimer's feet, but Tilman's hand remained on the hilt of his sword. Emaline maintained a defensive stance.

"Please, you must listen." Ditimer took a step toward Avery. Kade advanced, ready to shield the temporal. The wounded look on Ditimer's face cut at Kade's heart. But he would not succumb to trust so easily. Not this time.

Ditimer cut a glance at Avery before meeting Kade's eyes. Gone was the stoic, obstinate soldier. His hands worked, clenching and releasing, his shoulders bunched, as though bearing a great weight. His dark, soulful eyes were full of remorse and torment. The pale golden light that had once shone like the sun was little more than a glint from his hands and face.

"I am grieved unto death," Ditimer breathed. He addressed Avery: "I am forever in your debt. I beg your forgiveness and I pray you allow me to prove myself trustworthy." His heart-felt apology seemed to take Avery off-guard.

"I—well, you," he stammered. "Look, you handed me over to Cosyn. You have nerve asking for forgiveness after that."

Kade strode past Altizara, Othana, and Avery, so he was eye-to-eye with his once-trusted ally.

"Speak quickly, Ditimer. What is it about your betrayal we do not understand?" The torment in Kade's heart gave his words a measure of force, overtaking his longing to welcome Ditimer back without reservation. He had allowed forgiveness to give way to blindness too many times. There would be no negotiating.

"You must know," Ditimer said vehemently, his nostrils flaring, "I was completely unaware Cosyn was involved."

"Bah, I don't believe that for a second," Avery spat and stalked back to his horse. Ditimer watched him go, his shoulders sagging.

"Tell me what happened, Ditimer," Kade repeated.

Ditimer nodded and glanced behind him. "Not here."

Kade cocked his head.

Ditimer scowled. "She is coming."

"She?" Kade's chest tightened.

"Lady Ryla."

Kade's mind raced through his encounters with Lady Ryla in the past months. Lord Talmond had been resistant to the temporals' arrival. But the lady had always stayed in the background, giving little input.

"I do not understand."

"I will tell you what I know. But we must hurry. I tried to reach you in Herlov, but you were already gone."

"You were with Lady Ryla?"

Ditimer nodded. "Aye. They tracked you through Theurham. I did all I could to lead them away."

After fleeing the forest, Kade and the company of Shalhalans had done everything to first avoid, then lure Cosyn's dragons. He had never considered other threats.

"Lead them . . ." Kade's eyes widened with realization. "The wagon trail. The tracks we discovered. They were yours."

Ditimer nodded.

"Kade, this is madness," Altizara pulled her horse around. "There is no reason to believe a word of what he says."

Emaline appeared on Kade's left. Of the troop, she had said nothing and her expression had been quizzical, but not angry.

"Ditimer," she said, her voice low and soft. "What you are saying goes against Arkonai's design. We are here to protect the temporals. Not attack them. Why would Lady Ryla choose to go against her Creator's directive?"

Ditimer tore his gaze from Kade's and looked at Emaline, his eyes glistening. "Design without the freedom to choose is empty. Lady Ryla has made her choice."

"What of Lord Talmond?" Kade asked.

Ditimer shot a glance over his shoulder. "If he is in league with Cosyn, I have not seen it."

"How do we know you speak the truth?" Tilman's deep voice resonated, his sword drawn, but at his side. Ever the strategic soldier, he was no doubt preparing to lead them away should Ditimer's appearance prove to be a trap.

"Perhaps now is not the time to determine his allegiance," Othana called, striding back to the horses. She took the reins to her and Kade's horses and led them back. She handed Kade his, giving him a meaningful look. Kade nodded and braced himself to mount without reacting to the pain he was sure to feel. Should Ditimer prove untrustworthy, it was best he were not privy to the injury.

Once on his horse, Othana swung into her saddle and gestured to Avery to do likewise. "If what Ditimer says is true," she continued, "we cannot risk an attack in the open."

Altizara glared at Ditimer. "Or he could be leading us directly to whoever pulls his strings."

Ditimer shook his head, stepping back to his horse. "I have been in increasing objection to Lady Ryla's course. At one time we agreed: the temporals were of no benefit to Alnok. But she has taken a new, hostile approach. When she realizes I am missing, she will see it as a betrayal. She will drop all pretense of friendship and will attack."

Ditimer hoisted himself into his saddle. The panic on his face seemed to have an effect on Altizara. Pursing her lips, she gave a curt nod and nudged her horse nearer to Kade and Othana.

Emaline took a step forward, looking up at Ditimer. "We will trust you once more, my brother," she said softly. "I am eager to welcome you back into our fold. But"—her expression hardened—"should you betray us again, I will see you are banished from Alnok forever."

Her rebuke found its mark as tears filled Ditimer's eyes. "I will earn your confidence."

Emaline strode to her horse without a word. When they were mounted and circled, Kade addressed them.

"We follow Ditimer."

"What about Gabe?" Avery asked.

"We cannot rescue Gabe if we are overtaken." Kade said, steadying his horse. "There is a pass that leads into the mountains. If the way remains open, we can follow it to the kingdom of Shaldon. From there, we make our way to the catacombs."

Ditimer steered his horse into the lead, but turned to face them. "She has soldiers to track us. I propose we split up to divert them."

Avery scowled his disapproval. "Not bloody likely."

"Will they not track both?" Othana asked.

"A diversion is wise," Tilman said. "We can camouflage one set of tracks and confuse the other." He unfurled his blanket and dangled it to one side of his horse. "We will increase our odds of escape. Kade, you should go with Ditimer. Take a northeastern route. Halfway to the mountain, double back before you continue. When you reach the mountains, go west. When the ground begins to harden, enter the mountains and find the pass. They will lose your tracks and believe you are traveling the easier route along the mountain base. We will take a direct route, masking our tracks. I can find the pass and we await you there."

"That'll work?" Avery asked.

Tilman shrugged. "I see no better options. The terrain is firmer here. But we should use our blankets to confuse any tracks we leave."

Avery, Othana, Altizara and Emaline followed Tilman's example, cinching their blankets to the back of their saddles.

"For the valor of Arkonai!" Tilman shouted as he spurred his horse and the five galloped away, kicking up sand.

Kade and Ditimer broke away north, following Tilman's instructions. Kade put his attention to their immediate task, forcing back fears of a second betrayal and what trap he may have sent the others into.

Betrayal or not, I may have doomed us either way.

***

"They were here!" a soldier called. He was so close to Kade and Ditimer's hiding place within a recess of trees and boulders, Kade could make out his furrowed brow even in the dying light. Kade's chest burned. His light had dwindled and was so weak, their pursuers would likely not see it.

Lady Ryla, her auburn hair matching her horse, nudged the beast forward and cantered to the soldier, dismounting before it came to a stop. Her crimson light seemed to diffuse from her wine-colored cloak as it spun around her. A troop of perhaps twenty soldiers spread out along the treeline. Some ventured further into the thickets, and Kade held his breath as one came so close he might have reached out and taken a swatch of fabric from his tunic.

The soldier who had called out was crouched, studying the ground. Ryla looked over his shoulder.

"There are many tracks. Multiple horses. But from here they seem to continue east." He looked up at her. "What course, m'lady?"

She was silent as she scanned the barren landscape, making a full turn until her gaze settled on the trees. She squinted up the mountainside, but it seemed the twilight had Kade at an advantage. He and Ditimer were virtually invisible, hidden among the shadows.

Kade's injury throbbed after their frantic flight to the mountains. They had doubled back as Tilman had suggested, then hidden their tracks before they led their horses into the mountains, concealing them within a shallow cave and returning just far enough to keep watch. But Lady Ryla was clever. Her eyes scanned the treeline, moving just over their hiding place.

"Here, m'lady!" another soldier shouted from several hundred yards to the west.

Lady Ryla whipped her head in his direction before giving the trees one last glance.

Kade poised himself for an attack. Ditimer could expose their position at any moment. Kade eased his hand to his boot, ready to withdraw the dagger Tilman had given him in Herlov.

Perhaps the others could reach Gabe in time. Their strategy might throw Ryla off their trail. But this moment tested Ditimer's loyalty.

Ditimer did not move or even seem to breathe as Lady Ryla mounted her horse and galloped ahead without a word. The soldiers rushed back to their horses and followed, disappearing into the darkness.

Kade slowly let out his breath.

"It worked," Ditimer whispered, sitting back and rubbing his face.

"For now," Kade countered. "I always felt she had an insight that rivaled Lord Talmond. He often deferred to her counsel."

"It was not insight she offered. It was deceit," Ditimer said, staring of in the direction their adversaries had gone.

"Indeed," Kade said, easing from the bushes. He remained crouched as he hurried back through the trees. Tilman, Altizara, Othana, Emaline—they were all fully capable. Even Avery was rising to his full potential. But Ryla had lingered longer than Kade expected. She might still return and follow them up the mountain. If the others had continued, they may have made the prudent choice.

"Kade," Ditimer said, catching up. "I need you to understand. Though I have not always agreed with the role of the temporals in the Periferie, I never meant them harm. I only wanted them returned to Earth Apparent. Lady Ryla promised to work to that end. If I had known Cosyn . . ."

Kade glanced at Ditimer. His heart ached to put his full trust in his friend. But there were now too many occasions in which putting his trust in the wrong places, even trusting in his own understanding, had proved catastrophic. He would not make that mistake again. For anyone.

"We are all vulnerable to deception," Kade offered as they reached the cave where the horses were waiting patiently. "Particularly when looking to serve our own agendas."

Ditimer did not reply.

They made their way on foot through thick brush and clumps of scraggly trees in silence. The temperature dropped as a full moon peeked through the leafless branches. Finally, the trees thinned, and they came to a narrow clearing.

"Tilman?" Kade whispered.

"Kade," Othana breathed as she crept from the trees, Avery right behind her. "It is good to see you."

"The plan worked, then?" Altizara leaped from atop a flat boulder, behind which she had apparently been hiding.

Avery gave Ditimer a wide berth; Altizara and Othana ignored him completely.

"Where are Emaline and Tilman?" Kade asked.

Altizara gestured with her chin. "Ahead, with the horses. They are setting up camp in a protected crevice in the mountainside."

Kade nodded. "Very good. Lead on."

The campsite was further than Kade had expected and by the time they reached the crackling fire, hidden within a slot canyon, he could only take sips of breath as he tried to minimize movement in his chest. He wiped a sheen of sweat from his brow.

"Kade!" Tilman strode to him, reaching for his horse's reins. He stopped and frowned. "You are unwell."

"What?" Ditimer moved toward Kade, but Tilman blocked his way.

Othana rushed to Kade. "Why did you not say?" She eased her shoulder beneath his arm.

Kade tried to smile. "Indulging my injury would serve no one."

"Bloody hell, Kade," Avery said, handing him a canteen. "Who does it serve if you pass out cold?"

Kade chuckled, then grunted at the fresh wave of pain across his chest.

"Who says wisdom cannot come from temporals?"

Othana eased him to the ground, and Emaline rushed to his side with a pouch of healing herbs. Altizara scrambled up the cliff side and disappeared over the edge, a good place to keep watch.

"Not so injured you can't engage in a little sarcasm, heh?" Avery said as he helped Emaline remove Kade's cloak.

Kade could only nod as he watched Tilman take his and Ditimer's horses to join the others. His gaze sought out Ditimer and found him standing against the far cliff, beyond the firelight.

There would be time to explore forgiveness. For now, it was enough that they were safe.

Emaline redressed his wound. The oozing, bright-red gash showed no sign of healing. They finally settled around the fire. Ditimer drew nearer, staying close to Kade's side.

"Wasn't sure we'd make it this far," Avery said, his eyes glazed as he stared into the flames. A thick, umber beard had grown in, lighter than his dark hair. His prior insistence on maintaining a shave and haircut was well beyond practical. Paired with his scruffy appearance, dark shadows gathered beneath his eyes.

Kade shifted to include Ditimer in the circle. "It is as Ditimer said. Lady Ryla is in pursuit, accompanied by a troop of Malvokian soldiers. We were successful in leading her away from this path. For the time being."

"The time being?" Othana dropped a handful of sticks into the fire, sending embers drifting up. She brushed off her hands and took a seat next to Tilman.

"She is clever and resourceful," Ditimer said, rubbing at his arm. "I have no doubt she will realize her mistake and make for the mountains."

"Why is she so bloody keen on catching us?" Avery asked.

Kade looked at Ditimer, raising one eyebrow. Ditimer cleared his throat.

"There is a sect of Periferals who do not want temporals in Alnok."

Kade fought the impulse to glance at Othana. She would understand Ditimer's actions more than anyone. She had only recently admitted to not believing the prophecy, though she had shown remarkable dedication despite her disbelief.

Ditimer continued. "When Kade relayed the prophecy and his belief that temporals would once again enter the Periferie, this time with a call to close the plyes opened by Cosyn, many issued objections."

"Lord Talmond and Lady Ryla most vehemently," Tilman said.

"They were wrong," Ditimer said firmly. "We all were. I understand that now. Lord Talmond followed Kade's guidance. But when Lady Ryla came to me with a plan to return the temporals to Earth Apparent, it seemed reasonable."

Emaline cocked her head. "Even after Cosyn's plyes were discovered?"

Ditimer shrugged. "We did not see the need for temporals in our battle against Cosyn."

"And after they arrived?" Tilman asked, his tone curious rather than accusatory.

"It wasn't only the frailty of the temporals," Othana said, her voice barely above a whisper. "Many felt Kade's affections influenced the meaning of the prophecy."

Emaline gasped. "You believed Kade lied?"

Kade chuckled. "My honesty was not in question, but my intensions were. It is true, my heart grieved the loss of Jeannetta, Reeder, and so many others. Sending Moses and Nahor to Earth Apparent pierced my heart to the point of despair. A prophecy speaking of their return seemed too . . ."

"Convenient," Avery said.

Kade nodded.

"But Ryla doesn't just want us out of the Periferie," Avery continued.

"Nay," Ditimer murmured. "She wishes you destroyed." He leaned toward Kade, catching his eye. "She was promised dominion over Earth Apparent with Cosyn."

Avery shook his head. "So she's hot on our heels."

"And Cosyn likely has his horde seeking our whereabouts," Tilman added.

Avery scoffed. "Do we even have a chance?"

"You forget the greater power to which we have access." Kade leaned to one side and dug his hand into his satchel, retrieving the canteen of seripyn. He handed it to Avery, who met his eye as he took it. He opened the container and swirled the contents.

"I haven't forgotten. But since the river . . . since I, you know"—he moved his middle and index fingers in a walking motion—"I haven't really been aware of . . . or felt . . ." He shrugged his shoulders and took a gulp of the tea.

Even now, Avery could not find words to describe his encounter with Arkonai on the water. But the motion for "walking" was close enough. He knew only power far greater than his own could have set his feet on the surface of the river.

"You must trust. Even when your feelings do not match the circumstances. Trust *truth* apart from emotion."

Kade sighed. *My own trust put us in this position.*

But it was not the same. In fact, he must trust in their path even more. The prophecy had thus far been fulfilled. And they would not abandon Gabe. They only had a little further to go.

CHAPTER SIX

"We have lost much time," Kade said as he mounted his horse. Fresh pain radiated from the center of his chest and, settling into his saddle, he let out a slow breath. Despite Emaline's best care, the wound continued to fester. He insisted Tilman take the lead. Avery rode next to Kade, Othana and Emaline flanked Ditimer, and Altizara brought up the rear.

They had risen before dawn and scattered all traces of their camp. Now, as a pale yellow morning light rose, the mountains sprang to life. Birds chirped, celebrating the sun's arrival. Dazzling blue topaz glittered within the gray canyon walls. Lofty evergreens creaked and swayed as though protecting the mountain's inhabitants from a frigid wind. Tall, frost-covered grasses flanked their path. Winter's hard chill had settled in, forcing them to layer cloaks and blankets over their shoulders.

"The pass will narrow," Kade said. "The deeper we travel into the mountains, the harder it will be for the horses to manage the trail. We will continue until nightfall, then our horses will need to return to Herlov."

"We are already delayed," Altizara called. "Without horses . . ."

Kade nodded. "Yes, and if we encounter Ryla and her men, we may not arrive at all."

"The troops leaving from Herlov?" Othana asked as she nudged her horse nearer to Kade. "Will they not thwart the lady?"

Tilman shifted his shoulders to turn halfway and shook his head. "No one will question the Lady of Malvok. Even if they have suspicions."

"Lady Ryla will likely keep up her pretense," Ditimer added. "She will offer her help, joining the march east."

Tilman nodded. "You say her contingent had fewer than thirty?"

"There will be more," Ditimer grumbled.

"In the meantime," Avery said, turning and glaring at Ditimer. "We will keep a close watch on you."

Kade did not argue. Avery was right to doubt Ditimer. His prudence would balance Kade's own desire to seek restoration for the soldier.

"Let us make as much time as possible while we have the horses," Kade said, nodding to Tilman to increase their pace. He spurred his horse and they set off in single file.

They wound between high cliffs, first ascending until they could see the flat plains of the Rift through the trees, then a steep descent, before climbing once more. The horses showed no fatigue. The group saw no evidence of Ryla and her soldiers, but Ditimer grew more anxious.

The sun climbed high in the sky until low, gray clouds crowded out the light and swathed the mountains in shadow. A few soft snowflakes caught up in Kade's beard and the temperature continued to drop.

Kade pushed them as fast as he dared, but even if the horses could maintain their course along the tight twists and turns, the burning wound across his chest would not allow it. He forced deep breaths in time with the rhythm of the hoof falls. Despite the cold air, a thin sweat broke out over his forehead. He leaned forward to ease the pain. A roll of distant thunder joined the snow.

"Kade?" Ditimer called.

Kade tried to wave to reassure him, but he could not move his arm.

"Kade!" Avery shouted, and Kade jerked, pulling his horse to a stop.

"What?" Kade mumbled, scanning the dark trees flanking their path, looking for the source of Avery's panic.

"You need to rest," Ditimer said.

Kade shook his head. "A little further. Night will be upon us soon."

"Kade, it is just past mid-day," Ditimer said, his voice thick with concern.

Could the clouds block so much of the afternoon sun? Kade took another gasping breath. He felt hands tugging at his cloak and he allowed himself to be eased from his horse.

"Over here," Tilman whispered.

"Emaline, prepare a treatment . . ." Altizara said.

More voices, hushed but urgent, then silence . . . darkness . . .

***

Crackling flames and the smell of campfire forced Kade's heavy eyelids open. Blurred faces surrounded him.

"I must look near death," he croaked and then coughed. The expected dagger of pain was dulled.

"Help him sit up," Emaline said.

Tilman and Ditimer propped Kade against a fallen tree. Kade took a deep breath, his chest constrained by tightened bandages.

"Emaline?" He touched his tunic.

She nodded. "I redressed the wound." Her grim expression did not instill confidence in his recovery. She brought a spoon to his lips, tipping a bitter broth into his mouth.

Kade swallowed and coughed again. But his vision cleared. The fire in the wound abated.

"How long—"

"'Tis nearly nightfall," Tilman said.

He and Ditimer crouched in front of Kade. Emaline sat to his right, adjusting his blanket over his lap. Avery paced near the fire. Othana and Altizara were stationed a few paces away, watching the trail to the east and west.

"I am better. You have a knack for healing, Emaline."

"Hopefully better than her skills in combat," Tilman said, grinning at the diminutive girl.

Emaline launched toward Tilman, who scrambled backward with a yelp. He stood and took another step back, his eyes wide with shock.

With a shift of her shoulders and quick footwork, Emaline had Tilman off his feet and then on his belly. She forced his right arm behind his back.

"I yield!" Tilman chuckled.

She stood and brushed off her hands. "Let that be a lesson to you." She took up her position next to Kade and gave him an impish grin.

Tilman stood and bowed. "I will never question your skills again, m'lady." Their cheer seemed a release from an afternoon of worry.

Tilman turned to Kade. "I stand corrected. Emaline will no doubt restore your health."

Kade gave him a weak smile. "I fear the wound may share a fate similar to that of the dragon egg stolen away to the catacombs." He shifted, so he was sitting taller.

"How do you mean?" Avery asked.

"Just as the dragons could produce no other eggs as long as the single egg remained safe and intact, so it seems this wound will continue to deteriorate as long as the dragon breathes."

"How do you know this?" Ditimer asked.

Kade shook his head. "I do not. But after the treatment from the Herlovian healer, and now with Emaline's attentive care, I should be improving."

"I heard of similar maladies when the dragons attacked the Echelon Cavern," Othana called as she continued to watch the path.

Kade took another breath and nodded.

Avery stopped pacing. "Did they get better?" He stared down at Kade with a deep frown.

"Some did," Kade said. "Even so, we have already lost time diverting to the mountains. There may be a choice to make soon."

"What's that supposed to mean?" Avery narrowed his eyes.

"I fear I may endanger Gabe if I continue to hamper our progress."

Avery threw up his hands. "You're the only reason we've made it this far. Whatcha mean you're endangering Gabe?"

"Speed is of greater value now."

"Oh, no, no, no," Avery shook his head, waving his arms as he strode to Kade. "I don't know what you're playing at, but we're getting you back on that horse and we're going on with you."

"You underestimate your abilities once again," Kade sighed, staring into Avery's wide hazel eyes.

"Do I, now?" Avery squared his shoulders. He glowered at Kade with fierce resolve. Gone was his ever-present fear. His eyes shone with the determination of a warrior. Of a leader.

"I would say it is *you* who underestimates *your* abilities," Avery continued.

A knot formed in Kade's throat. No one spoke. Tilman exchanged a glance with Emaline. Othana and Altizara drifted closer, watching Kade warily. Ditimer fell back, as though unsure of his place.

Snow fell in larger flakes, landing and melting on their cloaks. Even the bare trees stilled and seemed to maintain a watchful tension. A cold silence fell over the mountain pass.

Kade could not stop the smile tugging at the corner of his mouth. "Perhaps I have—"

"Bet your bollocks you have. Now, if you've had enough of a lie down, we should be off." Avery continued to stare Kade down.

Kade blinked away tears. He shook his head and chuckled. "It seems I have taught you well." He struggled to his feet. Tilman and Emaline rushed to help him. He gestured to the horses, huddled just off the road. "Lead on," he said to Avery.

The Yorkshire man looked uncertain but gave a curt nod and strode to his horse. Everyone followed suit except Ditimer, who was standing at the center of the path, hands on hips, head cocked. When the others were all mounted, Avery nudged his horse toward Kade.

"You suppose Gabe is okay?" he whispered, his previous confidence gone.

Kade did not answer right away. Though he could always discern the danger or well-being of Alnokians and temporals alike, Gabe's status was hidden. This gave him hope. Gabe was likely being held as bait. His captivity would serve as a lure. One they would never deny. Cosyn craved power. But in his vanity, he relished an audience. This would satisfy his appetite for both. But, in the meantime, Gabe would suffer.

"I am confident he lives. For now."

Kade nudged his horse forward. If they maintained a steady pace, they might reach Shaldon in two days.

"Kade!" Ditimer hissed, rushing back from the road, sliding across the gravel.

Kade pulled up and gave his startled horse a pat.

"We must find an alternate route," he said, continuing to look over his shoulder.

Kade glanced up and down the empty path.

"You have seen evidence of Ryla's soldiers?"

"There is something . . ." Ditimer shifted on his feet, looking from Kade to the others, then back to the road.

"Ditimer!" Kade said. They could afford no time for riddles or ambiguity.

"I knew we could only divert her for a time," Ditimer said. The fear that had plagued Avery during the quest now had Ditimer floundering.

"You believe she has found us?"

"Not 'believe' Kade. I *know*."

"How?"

Ditimer glanced past Kade again, his jaw working, as though coming to some decision. He shook his head brusquely.

"With this." He held his arm out to Kade and pulled up his sleeve. Along the inner portion of his forearm, just above his wrist, was an angry red mark, scar-like and crude. As though a brand.

Kade looked into Ditimer eyes, tortured, pleading.

"I was barely aware of it at first. But the longer I . . . worked with Lady Ryla, the more distinct the mark became. When I was not near her, it would fade, until it almost disappeared. But when it would burn, redden, I knew she was close. It became more than a signal of her presence. It connects us somehow. Binds us."

"Binds?"

"I fear I will never be free of her." Ditimer jogged to his horse, mounted, and spurred it back to the road. "She draws near."

"From the east or the west?"

Ditimer swallowed. "Both," he whispered.

CHAPTER SEVEN

"This place you're taking me," Raelyn panted. "We'll be safe?" She had heard no voices from the forest in some time, but Lima hadn't slowed her pace.

"Aye, you will be safe," Lima said, giving Raelyn a quick glance. She didn't seem the least bit tired. "A little further and we can take a brief rest."

The cloak Lima had provided was warm, but didn't block all the snowfall. Despite having the hood pulled tight, Raelyn's hair was wet and stringy, her fingers, damp and cold. Thankfully, her feet were warm and dry.

At Lima's insistence, they had traveled south through the morning and into the afternoon without stopping. As soon as they left Boiland, a tether of remorse latched onto Raelyn, pulling tighter and tighter the further they went. Every step hammered a nail of guilt into her chest. Joshua and Jinny were completely unprotected. Facing giants on their own. She shouldn't have left them.

But she kept her mouth shut and followed Lima. No matter what, she had to get to the plye. She had to close it. She had to save her brother and father.

A smattering of evergreens, their branches laden with drooping yellowed pine needles, hid the duo from unfriendly eyes. But the clumps of trees were growing thinner, giving way to short, frosty grasses. There were no sheep this far from the hills. It seemed even the animals didn't want to go this way.

Raelyn slipped on a patch of snow, her back pinching where she had fallen so long ago outside Malvok. She steadied herself and tromped on, wiping her nose before pulling her cloak tighter. It didn't matter that her legs were burning and her face was numb. She had promised to meet Joshua in five days. According to the map, his way was undoubtedly shorter. The only way she and Lima might beat them to the catacombs would involve an unexpected delay for him and Jinny. Any delays they might face could only mean they ran into trouble. They came against the giants. Or worse.

"I don't need a rest," Raelyn grumbled.

Lima wiped the melted snow from her face. "Even so, soon we will lose the protection of the trees. Before traveling in the open, we need to confirm no one from Endyle follows. We must make the next leg of our journey without stopping."

Raelyn nodded, too winded to respond.

The anemic forest ended abruptly with a trio of tall evergreens huddled together as though holding council. Lima slipped into their center and Raelyn followed. The ground, though damp, was free of snow within the quiet, pine-scented enclosure. Despite her compulsion to continue, Raelyn sank to the ground to relieve her cramping legs.

Lima, however, peered around a tree, back the way they had come. She waited without a word. Raelyn's heart slowly stopped pounding and her breathing returned to normal. Finally, Lima stepped back, seemingly satisfied they were not being followed.

Raelyn struggled to her feet. "We're in the clear?"

Lima nodded. "It seems so."

"Would the scouts have given up?" Raelyn tried to swallow, but her mouth was dry.

"Perhaps." Lima met Raelyn's gaze.

"You think they followed Joshua and Jinny?"

"I cannot say. It could be they did not see my shelter at all. In that case, they would have no direction to follow. But that was the risk the others took." Lima's flat tone pricked Raelyn's heart. Whether out of pragmatism or callousness, it seemed Lima had abandoned any concern for the others' safety.

"Take some water. We will rest here until nightfall. Can you endure the cold without a fire?"

Raelyn nodded as she dug her water skin from her sack. She took a swig, re-stowed it, and leaned against a tree, shivering. Pulling her cloak tighter and the hood lower did nothing against the cold. She sank back to the ground and closed her eyes.

Crackling and a warmth on her toes woke her. She blinked her eyes open to a small fire at the center of their refuge. She found Lima sitting across from it, watching her, the flames reflecting in her ebony eyes.

"Your fingers were turning blue," she said, nodding to Raelyn's hands.

"Will it expose us?"

Lima shrugged and poked a stray branch into the fire. "It will be night soon and we will make for the shore. But I have heard nothing from the scouts."

Raelyn's stomach clenched. Maybe because they had gone after Joshua and Jinny. Another wave of regret pounded her.

She drew back her hood and closed her eyes as the fire warmed her face. Would Joshua and Jinny be able to risk a fire? Was she going to ponder their fate at every step?

Without a doubt.

Raelyn adjusted the Bokar so it wasn't wedged against her ribs. There didn't seem to be a comfortable position. Where would Joshua and Jinny—

Raelyn shook her head and took a shaky breath as she looked across the fire at Lima. "I think I made a mistake leaving them."

"*You* left *them*?" Lima's dark eyes glittered as she stared intently at Raelyn.

"I, well, we shouldn't have split up."

"You assessed your situation and each of you made a choice. You should not doubt your decision. Or theirs. You have developed many skills since you came to Alnok."

"Skills?" Raelyn hugged her knees to her. "Maybe. Not sure if they'll be enough. I thought our biggest advantage would be working as a team. But from the beginning, we were divided. And now . . ." She shook her head again, fighting back tears.

"Kade recognizes the potential in others. He bestowed the role of leader on you for a reason. The prophecy specified the descendant from Earth Apparent would be such a leader," Lima said.

"Why not Joshua? Or any of the others?"

Kade, Altizara, Othana, Kala, they had all encouraged her, shown unwavering confidence in her abilities. But this young girl, rejected by her people, or she having rejected them, had a unique perspective. Her view was even more trustworthy without Alnokian influence. She wasn't trying to convince Raelyn to close any portals. They hadn't even discussed the plye. Lima hadn't insisted Raelyn recognize her value or embrace her leadership skills. She was just a girl trying to help. Without an agenda, her honesty was worth something. Maybe worth more.

Lima took a deep breath. "When Kade discovered the prophecy, he set about trying to convince every Guardian in Alnok the temporals would return. Even those who believed, did so begrudgingly—"

"Did you? Believe?"

The corners of Lima's mouth turned up. "Without question."

Relief and a new affection surged through Raelyn, warming even the coldest parts of her body. Lima's confidence in the prophecy was enough confirmation that Raelyn had made the correct choice. Joshua and Jinny should have opted to follow.

"Moreover," Lima continued, "I knew I would have a part in seeing the quest to its end."

A gust of wind found its way into their shelter, and the fire flickered. Lima shifted her gaze beyond the trees.

"We should leave soon." She looked back at Raelyn. "The prophecy was clear. A child of Micah would enter Alnok once again."

"A child . . . of Micah—"

"Come." Lima stood and began nudging dirt onto the fire with her toe. "We should hasten on while it is dark. Remember to take some seripyn before we begin."

Raelyn joined Lima in putting out the fire. Kade had never divulged details of the prophecy. What did Lima know?

But the girl seemed eager to begin their trek to the sea. Questions would have to wait.

Soon they were bundled up and leaving the protection of the trees. A blast of wind buffeted Raelyn, sweeping her hood off her head. She tugged it back in place, leaned forward and followed Lima and her pale-purple light as the last of the hazy twilight dwindled away.

Brittle grass crunched beneath Raelyn's feet. The snowfall had stopped, but the night air was frigid. The wind made conversation not just impractical, but impossible.

Raelyn hunched her shoulders and focused on Lima's light as they continued for hours. Her eyes watered and she wiped at her nose until it was raw. A headache bit at her temples and she gasped. She hadn't taken the seripyn.

"Lima!" she called.

Even in the dark, she could see Lima shake her head. "Just a little further, Raelyn!" she called over her shoulder.

Raelyn pulled her cloak tighter. She could hold out. She'd gone without it for longer in Shalhala. And even if she faded, Lima was here to protect her and make sure she returned. It had been some time since she'd had an update from Peter. Riots, chaos . . . whatever was happening, Cosyn may well throw everything he had through the last plye. Even more reason to rely on an Alnokian ally rather than brave it alone. An ache surged through Raelyn's heart.

If anything happened to Joshua or Jinny, she wouldn't know until it was too late.

Please protect them. Keep them safe. Bring us together again.

The prayer had to be enough.

Raelyn lost track of time, but as promised, they didn't stop. Neither did the wind, but the grass gave way to sharp, gravelly rock. Lima trudged ahead, her light getting brighter the further they were from Endyle. A gust of wind brought the briny scent of the sea. Raelyn increased her pace and walked alongside Lima as a desperate vigor sent painful tingles of feeling to her toes and fingertips.

"Lima, are we—"

The distant crash of waves answered her question. They were close. A hazy gray daylight rose, revealing heavy clouds, threatening more snow. Pain pierced Raelyn's temples, and she tripped on a rock. Though she regained her balance, when she glanced at Lima, the girl's upturned face blurred. Raelyn tried to explain she had forgotten to take the tea, but Lima swam out of focus and all went dark.

***

"Raelyn!" Peter's face hovered over her. "Are you safe?"

"I am for now," Raelyn smiled, getting to her feet in Peter's bedroom. "Are you?"

"Yeah." Peter scratched his neck. The gesture made her think of Joshua. "But I don't know how long it'll last. We have a curfew, but most everyone stays in. Everything's closed." He shrugged. "Wouldn't matter anyway. There's been a run on everything. Shelves are empty." He frowned and shook his head. "I can't make out Cosyn's next play."

A chill ran up Raelyn's spine. Peter saying that name sparked a deeper sense of reality. Beyond her presence in Alnok. Or even her conversations with Peter. She wasn't just saving him; they were both saving the world.

"You said there were riots. Why?"

Peter shook his head as a hardness entered his eyes. "You name it. Americans blaming China for the volcanoes. China accusing America of sending spies. Every day there's some new catastrophe and people are just getting angrier and angrier."

"How's Dad?"

"Better. He's up and around."

"Did he explain why he went nuts and sailed out over the gulf?"

Peter chuckled. "Yeah." He looked Raelyn up and down. "How much time you got?"

"No telling. Give me the Cliff's Notes."

Peter took a deep breath and nodded, squinting at the ground as though looking for a place to start. "Mom and Dad knew about our connection to the fifth dimension." He looked at Raelyn. "Our heritage in Alnok. The talisman I showed you? It's been passed down for decades through Mom's family. She wore it as a sort of protection when things got bad."

Raelyn flinched and looked away. "It didn't seem to work . . ."

"Rae." Peter's gruff voice forced her to look back at him. "It's not a magic talisma —"

"Dad seemed to think so."

"Right, so it didn't impact anything *here*. But apparently it proved useful when strange things would happen. Things Mom couldn't explain. Dad said at first he thought she was just being wonky. But there were times when she was able to ward off strange shadows, threats that had no explanation."

"Threats from Alnok."

Peter nodded. "Knowing what we know, that's exactly what it was."

"So Dad thought he could do the same thing with the volcanoes."

"Yeah, he knew what was happening made no earthly sense. He figured it was worth a try. If it meant protecting you."

Tears sprung in Raelyn's eyes. "The mark," she managed to say and cleared her throat, nodding at Peter's hand.

Peter opened his palm where the red mark, bright and well-defined, remained. "Still a mystery."

"More a mystery is how you're able to see Alnok. Take part in what's happening."

A descendant from Micah . . .

Lima's voice whispered to Raelyn. Pieces were falling into place and a dread sank into Raelyn's gut.

"Where's the next plye?" Peter asked.

Raelyn shook her head. She'd never get used to it. Peter talking about Alnok almost as though he was part of the Cord.

"The Schade Catacombs. I'm on my way there now."

"From the ocean?"

Raelyn frowned. "Yeah, why?" She looked over her shoulder.

Peter drifted past her, squinting out his window. "I can see the waves."

"Really?" Raelyn joined him. But she could only see the house across the street.

"A cliff and"—he shivered—"cold."

He turned back to her. "What does it mean? My connection?"

"No idea. No one in Alnok knows why. Joshua's family, Jinny's father, they don't interact the way we do. Maybe something to do with acceptance?"

Peter frowned. "Acceptance of what?"

"Of something you can't understand, but you believe. It's kind of looking past your own understanding and logic and being open, and accepting, even if it doesn't make sense." Raelyn paused while Peter considered her explanation.

"You know," she continued, "if it hadn't been me . . ."

Liquid trickled down Raelyn's throat. Peter reached out and touched her hand as he faded from sight.

She was sitting on the ground, Lima holding the canister to her lips.

"Welcome back," she said, but she looked troubled.

"Is everything okay?" Raelyn grunted as she struggled to her feet, gravel grinding into her hands. Just as Peter had said, they stood on the edge of a cliff overlooking a slate sea. The Kaidilas. The wind howled off the waters.

"We are safe for now!" Lima shouted over a gust and walked to the edge of the cliff. The clouds parted in the distance so that her small silhouette was outlined against a pink sunrise peeking out on their left and lighting a vast ocean.

A wave of loneliness took Raelyn's breath away. First Avery, then Gabe, now Joshua and Jinny. They had to get to the catacombs. Only then would all of this be worth it.

CHAPTER EIGHT

"Come," Lima said, grabbing Raelyn's hand as she traversed the cliff's edge. "The easiest place to climb down is this way. It is not difficult, but we must time our descent with the tide."

"You're not worried about Cosyn? Kade always told us to travel at night."

Lima gave her a cool glance. "I am not worried."

Raelyn grimaced. Of course, Lima wouldn't want to be compared to Kade. How often did her dad compare her to Peter? To Harlan? But Lima was a Periferal. Even as a young girl, it seemed she should be above such things as jealousy or resentment. There was something comforting about sharing basic feelings with a Guardian. Kade always seemed so above human emotion. Wise, temperate, stoic . . . Lima, she seemed to understand her without expectation.

Raelyn let out a slow breath, releasing thoughts of Joshua and Jinny. Of Kade and Altizara. Of plyes and Cosyn. Lima knew what to do and where to go. Finally, someone who would take the lead and let her . . . follow. Like one of the sheep from Boiland. Completely dependent on Lima.

Raelyn slowed her pace, allowing some distance between her and the girl. Rather than providing comfort, the thought of Lima taking over brought a measure of unease. From the moment they'd left Lima's shelter, the girl's encouraging, nurturing demeanor had become indifferent, even harsh.

Raelyn shook her head. What did she expect? Lima had to focus on their escape and concealment. How long had she been alone? And now, she was risking everything to play guide to a temporal. How would anyone behave? She had to be focused and shrewd if they had any hope of getting to the catacombs in time.

A rising rock formation along the cliffside forced them away from the edge blocking their view of the sea but bringing relief from the wind. It cast a cold shadow over their path. Lima hurried ahead, scrambling along the cobbled base.

"This way," she called, waving at Raelyn to follow before disappearing behind a craggy protrusion.

A camouflaged opening led to a cramped tunnel. Lima was already bent over, making her way inside. Light filtering from the opposite end and a consistent briny breeze promised a short jaunt. Shorter than the one Larken had led them on when they escaped Shalhala through the mountain. Here, there was no soft sand to crawl through. Instead, Raelyn struggled not to twist an ankle on the sharp, loose stones. The low, uneven ceiling made her head a constant target. But the anticipation of seeing that beautiful teal lagoon into which Larken had dove without hesitation made the assault easier to bear.

Lima was nothing like Larken. The jovial Shalhalan turned fierce guide and leader had been lost to this very sea. There'd been no time to grieve. Their quest from Shalhala to Keala and on to Endyle without pause had left no time for such indulgences. But now, following a similar tunnel to the Kaidilas, a sharp twinge made her heart ache. What would he have said in the face of her choice to follow a stranger from Endyle, leaving her friends to an unknown fate? Guilt compounded her grief. If an Alnokian as capable as Larken could fall, what chance did Joshua and Jinny have? The tunnel ceiling seemed to bear down.

If anything happened to them, it would be her fault.

She tripped on another stone.

Two more people she would have led to their demise.

Lima's pale-purple light flickered off the ashen walls as the tunnel widened to a narrow cave. Here, they could stand upright, and Raelyn stretched her aching back. The sound of crashing waves buffeted the cavern as though the ocean were just ahead and not at the bottom of a cliff.

Lima brushed her hair from her face and gazed around. "We can take a moment to rest here, protected from the cold. The tide will be lowest late in the day."

Raelyn nodded and shivered. Ignoring the cold was easier when they were moving. "Do you think Joshua and Jinny can get around the giants?"

Lima shrugged and peered down the tunnel toward the light. "Unlikely. It is a dangerous route." Lima turned and gave her a firm stare. "You made a wise choice, Raelyn." Her brown eyes gleamed and her light swelled, casting strange shadows into the corners of the cave.

"They didn't?"

Lima frowned. "They took a different path. It may well have been the best choice for them."

"I hope so." Raelyn sighed and sat against the wall on a spot clear of rocks. She picked up a pebble and inspected it; like black glass, smooth and shiny. "I feel like I abandoned them." She tossed the stone. "I let them wander into some unknown danger."

"Your experience should tell you all roads hold the potential for danger."

Raelyn squinted up at Lima. "But you still think this was the best option? Us splitting up?"

Lima sat next to her. "Not the best option, but the one with fewer risks, given the circumstances. I maintain this is the best route."

"But they have a better chance of getting past the giants, just the two of them."

"Certainly."

Raelyn shivered again. She should have pressed harder for them to follow Lima.

"They'll reach the catacombs in five days?"

"Perhaps sooner."

"But you don't know."

Lima shook her head. "I do not."

She offered no words of consolation and Raelyn found this strangely comforting. As though Lima trusted her ability to accept uncertainty without baseless encouragement. That she was strong enough to withstand hard truth. Whether this was Lima's opinion of her or not, the idea strengthened her determination. Kade would say Arkonai would work the outcome for good.

She looked at her hand and rubbed the spot on her palm where the mark had been. The mark that now belonged to Peter. What did that say of Arkonai's plan for her?

Raelyn listened to the rhythm of the waves as the day wore away. Lima offered no conversation, leaving Raelyn to play out scenarios from home. How might her dad try to help this time? How could a geologist offer aid in a riot? In political upheaval?

She touched the Durinial, tracing the tree with her fingertips. It had been silent for so long she had almost forgotten to anticipate its warnings. Its direction. Kade had never mentioned a family heirloom from Alnok. But her dad had used a similar amulet belonging to her mom to help close the plye from Earth. Who knows? Maybe it was his efforts that gave her and Peter the strength needed to complete the task.

Lima stood and brushed her hands off. "I believe it will be safe enough to make our way to the beach."

Raelyn blinked and looked around. The daylight seeping in from either side had diminished. She followed in silence until they reached the mouth of the cave where she breathed in the cold, salty air and took in the view. Unlike the expansive beach and lazy lagoon where Larken had first led them, today, foamy white waves crashed against the cliffside. They roared, surged and sprayed against the rocks before withdrawing into the sea, then swelling again.

It was equally beautiful in its power as when calm, but slightly sullied by the fact a sea dragon called the waters home. In the distance, low cloud cover rendered the waters a pensive gray.

"Follow my lead," Lima said and eased her foot over the edge.

As they descended, the waves subsided, crashing lower and lower on the cliff. Lima was right, they had to time their climb perfectly. Too fast, the water would wash them out to sea. Too slow, they wouldn't have time to traverse the shore before the next tide.

Lima had assured her the climb wasn't "difficult", but that opinion turned out to be highly subjective. Aside from a few straggly roots from some distant trees, there were few handholds and the sliding pebbles made footholds treacherous. Raelyn slid and skidded as Lima climbed below, showing her where to go.

The sun never made an appearance, but the daylight faded into a cold, gray twilight. Raelyn's hood fell away, and the wind sent needles of cold ocean spray buffeting the cliff, freezing Raelyn's sweat to her forehead. The wounds she sustained in her lower back and shoulder sprang to life, aching in different but equally painful ways. She slid her foot down to find the next outcrop and her legs trembled. Her fingers burned. She couldn't go much further.

But she did; lower and lower as daylight fizzled completely, plunging them into complete darkness. With no way to judge how far they were from the bottom, Raelyn began counting each step. They could only have another fifty or so.

At fifty, she started over.

Her muscles screamed objections. She couldn't keep going. She couldn't hold on.

"Lima."

Silence. Even the waves were quiet.

"Lima!"

Her foot came down on level ground, sinking into wet sand and holding her boots in place.

"Very good," Lima breathed.

She took Raelyn's sweaty hand and pulled her along the narrow beach, her lavender light reflecting off the wet sand and cliff. The waves were close, sloshing up to their feet. An icy wind blew off the sea and whipped Raelyn's hair around, pelting her face with drops of water.

Lima released Raelyn's hand as they reached a shallow divot in the cliffside. The sound of the rumbling waves reverberated off the walls in a low murmur.

"We can rest here only a moment," Lima said, scooping up bits of soggy driftwood. She tossed them into a pile and passed her hand over them until they flickered to life. Dark smoke rose from the purple flames until they turned yellow.

Raelyn dropped her satchel and sank to the ground. She huddled close to the fire, shivering so hard her muscles cramped. She was too tired to talk. Too tired to think.

Lima stood at the cleft's opening, her back to Raelyn. Slowly, the small space warmed. Raelyn's chills subsided. Lima returned to the fire and sat next to her.

Raelyn took off her cloak and spread it out to dry. "What do you know about the catacombs?"

Lima stared into the flickering flames. "I know it is where the deepest evil resides." Her voice turned harsh, almost angry. "A place abandoned by all of Alnok. Given up for lost. Forsaken."

"Have you been there?"

Lima nodded. "Once. Long ago. I would never have imagined a temporal entering."

"Which is why Cosyn created his portal there."

Lima leaned back, considering Raelyn. "What do you know of this plye?"

Raelyn chewed her lip for a moment, frowning. "Nothing. But I didn't really know anything about the other two, either."

"And yet, you were victorious." Lima smiled and nodded, apparently impressed.

Raelyn returned the smile, then it faded and her shoulders sagged. "But I wasn't alone."

"Neither are you now alone."

"Right. I have—you." *Peter*, she had meant to say. But an overwhelming reluctance redirected her statement.

"You have me." Lima's smile broadened as she nodded. "And you will need all of your strength to combat what is there. We will continue soon."

Lima stood and wandered to the mouth of the cave. She paused a moment before she turned and circled the fire, sitting across from Raelyn just out of the light. The fire licked at her feet and her face remained in shadow.

"At lowest tide, just before dawn, we will follow the shore to a safe place out of reach of the waves. You should sleep if you can."

"All this to avoid the giants?"

"Aye."

"It means a lot that you have confidence in my ability."

Lima leaned forward and smiled. "Of course. It is as the prophecy says, ' . . . a child of Micah will defeat the shadows.'"

"Have you seen the prophecy?"

"Nay, I have not encountered Kade in many hundreds of years."

Raelyn frowned and pulled her legs to her chest. Something about the word 'encounter' seemed out of place.

"I do not need to see the prophecy," Lima continued. "I understand its meaning. Although . . ."

"Although?"

Lima chuckled. "Well, of course Kade would have given you some reason *why* a second-born was chosen to enter Alnok."

Raelyn's mouth went dry. The warmth left her hands and feet. "What do you mean?"

Lima drew closer to the fire. The flames seemed to come from her eyes, not just a reflection in them. She cocked her head. "Your brother?" She seemed uncertain, but a gleam shone through the innocent confusion. "He would be the first child of Micah."

"I . . . don't understand. He couldn't come."

"That is true."

"He was sick. That's why I came. To save him. From Cosyn."

"Of course." Lima gave her a sympathetic smile.

"Are you saying . . . the prophecy . . ."

Raelyn's chest tightened. Peter's uncanny way of seeing and even appearing in Alnok. His assistance at the plye in Endyle. The mark that transferred from her to him . . .

"The prophecy . . ." Raelyn tried again, but her voice failed.

Lima again seemed confused. "But of course, the Cord comprises firstborns. All but you. The prophecy referred to your brother. To Peter."

CHAPTER NINE

A very stood in his saddle, peering over Kade's shoulder at Ditimer's arm. "So, this is like, what? A Periferal walkie-talkie?"

"Why have you not spoken of this before?" Kade demanded.

Ditimer swallowed, his eyes darting to Avery, then Altizara, Tilman, and Emaline. As the last of the daylight faded away, each of their lights seemed a glaring beacon.

"I had not considered she might use the mark to track my position."

Tilman spurred his horse nearer to Ditimer, glowering at the man.

Ditimer cowered.

"Even now," he said quickly, "I do not know this"—he raised his arm—"is how she found us." He gave Tilman a pleading look. "But we cannot tarry."

Altizara trotted her horse up next to Tilman and stared at Ditimer. "Could it be you are leading us to Ryla?" She leaned forward, glaring, as though attempting to extract the truth with her stare.

"I do not fault you for doubting me," Ditimer said, his voice rough with emotion. He rubbed at his arm. "If I wished to betray you—"

"Again," Avery interjected.

"I would not have wasted the effort to evade Lady Ryla to reach this pass. Please trust me once more."

Kade nodded, but hesitated. It was not just Ditimer he did not trust. He did not trust himself. Too much was at stake to put his faith in the wrong person—as Avery said—again.

A roll of thunder shook the ground and a whisper of cold wind blew through the treetops. The storm was coming.

"Kade . . ." Ditimer held Kade's gaze, his eyes begging him to follow his lead. Then he yanked his sleeve down and pulled his horse off the path. His pale light dwindled.

"We have no more time." He gestured for Kade to cross to the other side of the trail. "Leave the trail. Head north, further into the mountains."

The air changed. A sudden drop in pressure. Kade struggled to take his next breath. It was not only Ryla who drew near. He doused what remained of his golden light. The others did likewise.

"Kade?" Avery asked in a low voice. He felt it too. Having been in the company of Cosyn, he would recognize the shift when the enemy drew near.

"Kade, we must go," Othana said, nudging her horse into the dense leaves north of the trail and disappearing into the darkness.

Kade nodded. Othana spurred her horse on, and Avery followed without question. Then Altizara and Tilman. Emaline lingered, gazing at Ditimer with sad eyes.

She touched her forehead. "For the valor of Arkonai."

Ditimer nodded. Emaline glanced at Kade as she took out after the others.

A company of soldiers rounded the corner to the east. Then another from the west. Kade glimpsed Lady Ryla as he spurred his horse and left the path. He glanced back once to see if Ditimer followed. But the man remained on the trail, his horse pawing at the ground. Kade's heart lurched. He pulled to a stop behind a tree.

Ditimer shook his head as the first soldier reached him with sword drawn. Ditimer drew his own sword and blocked the blow. Kade blanched as a bright flash exploded from their connection. Shouts seemed to come from all directions. He could do nothing for Ditimer.

He spun his horse and continued his flight without looking back. Ditimer would hold them off for as long as he could. Kade would not waste his sacrifice. He pushed his horse faster, ignoring his throbbing chest.

He ducked under a low-hanging branch. Skirting around a tree, he overtook the others one by one—dark, quick-moving shadows. When he finally approached Othana, sweat was running down his back and his legs were shaking. She glanced at him and slowed enough for him to take the lead. Another growl of thunder was followed by a few needles of icy rain.

"We will cross to the far side of the mountain range," he called over his shoulder.

"That's completely out of the way," Avery shouted between gasping breaths.

"We must escape Ryla and her men," Othana said.

Kade led them up a steep incline. He cut back to the west and, as the forest grew thicker, rain poured from a slate sky. Kade spared a glance up, squinting against the deluge as they all gathered around.

"We will go just far enough to release the horses," he shouted, "then continue on foot. There is a passageway, one I used to visit Shaldon. It is well hidden, but we must reach it before Lady Ryla closes the gap."

He pushed his horse faster, steadying himself as best he could, scrambling over loose stones and around trees. He could hear, just beneath the patter, Othana's horse following close. But the pressure in the air continued.

Their narrow trail became slick with ice as night took over. Finally, the storm broke and a shy, waning moon peered between the trees. Thankfully, it did little to penetrate the darkness. But circling, like dark specks in the sky, yet unmistakable, hyram stalked them from above.

This was not Ryla's doing.

Kade kept the group moving, despite the fire in his chest. The detour, first into the mountains and now to his secret pass, would cause an impossible delay.

The birds were hidden against the night sky. Kade could only hope his group were equally camouflaged.

Blessedly, he had heard nothing of Ryla's pursuit. It seemed Ditimer had redirected them, either by combat or deceit. Either way, the man had proved himself faithful, likely paid with his life, joining Olmund, Lydia, and countless others. The thought sparked grief for Ryla more than Ditimer. She had allied herself with Cosyn, rejecting her people and her Creator. While there was always hope, a hope that her eyes would be opened, nothing indicated she wanted anything more than the same power Cosyn craved. What was she promised? What could have turned her heart black?

There was nothing he could do for her. She had made her choice. Kade redirected his thoughts to Arkonai, staving off despair.

The mountain rose, steeper and steeper. The horses stayed the course as Kade led them through an ever-narrowing, steadily climbing rift. If Ryla or the hyram attacked them here, there would be no escape.

Kade hunkered over his reins, blocking his face from the sharp cold. The pain had returned. It was no longer Gabe needing rescue. If he was correct, his own time in Alnok would draw to a close if they did not destroy the dragon.

"Kade," Othana called. "The soldiers are close."

Kade nodded. They could go no faster. *He* could go no faster.

Just as the first glimmer of morning light rose, a shout echoed from behind and a caw screeched from above. Then another. Still at a distance but closing. Kade scanned the trees to his left and then right, searching for familiar markings. A boulder, perfectly round, made of a glittering white quartz, appeared ahead.

They were close.

The trees gave way, allowing Kade to lead them faster. Visible in the full light of morning, soft grasses, glittering with ice, broke through more quartz. Ahead, a tall yellow tree grew from the base of a rock formation jutting like a pointed finger from the mountainside. Kade pulled his horse to a stop and gritted his teeth when dismounting. He put his finger to his lips as Othana and Avery followed suit. Altizara, Tilman, and Emaline were not far behind and dismounted.

As they gathered around Kade, shouts came from behind. Kade frantically searched the area. A fallen log obscured the next marker, a grouping of black rocks, unremarkable to anyone else not looking for signs of the hidden pathway.

Kade continued, leading his horse to another quartz boulder and a massive tree stump. Lady Ryla and company drew closer, the hooves of their horses now echoing through the mountain gap.

"Here is where we part ways with our trusty steeds." Kade pulled his satchel from his saddle and, from beneath a blanket, withdrew a staff. Othana took his satchel and glanced at the staff. She cocked her head at him but went to gather her own supplies without questioning him.

Tilman had barely unloaded his horse when a black bomb hurtled from the sky and crashed into his back, sending him sprawling. Kade slapped his horse's rear, causing it to dart up the rift, and rushed to Tilman's aid. The man jumped to his feet, his face red, scanning the sky while Othana and Avery drove the other horses away.

Another bird dove at them, missing Emaline by inches. Tilman pulled her out of the way, his slate light flashing.

But if the birds had wanted to strike, nothing would stop them from hitting their mark. The hyram were not attacking. They were flushing them out.

"Quickly," Kade whispered. He stooped over, hurrying past the stump. Using the staff, he pushed aside a clump of drooping branches from a yellow tree. He waded through thickets that pulled at his cloak and tangled in his hair.

The hyram cawed and screeched above. At a sheer wall, Kade looked over his shoulder and waved for the others to follow. Hidden in the folds of the rock was a cleft, only wide enough to shimmy through sideways. Cobwebs tickled Kade's face, and he pressed his hand against his mouth to suppress a cough. He paused, listening. The shouts came at a greater distance. Despite the efforts of the demonic birds, Ryla and her men were moving on.

Finally, the crevice widened and opened to a sun-dappled clearing. Kade clenched his chest and leaned against the wall as, one by one, the others exited the passageway.

Altizara stood at the opening, bow in hand, braced for any followers.

"I believe we will be safe to rest for the moment," Kade said.

Avery, red-faced and gasping for breath, dropped to the soft grass. He dug through his pack and withdrew his canteen, taking a swig.

"You don't think they'll figure out we gave them the slip?" he asked once he had caught his breath.

"If they follow the horses," Tilman said, "it will buy us time."

"This path is unknown to Lady Ryla," Kade said. "Even to Cosyn. He believes all roads to Shaldon were destroyed."

Avery frowned and looked around. "What happened to Ditimer?"

Kade shook his head. "He held them off."

"Forgiveness is hard," Altizara said, shaking her head as she stowed her bow and joined them.

"But should be freely given," Emaline added.

"Indeed," Tilman said.

"I understand your struggle," Othana offered. "I, too, was greatly betrayed."

"But you offered forgiveness?" Emaline asked.

"Aye." She handed Kade his bag. When he took hold of it, she paused for a moment, her eyes flitting to the staff, before letting go. She turned to Emaline.

"It did not stop me from sending him on from this realm. Forgiveness may still require recompense."

Tilman raised his eyebrows and considered Othana for a moment, but did not respond. Altizara squeezed Othana's shoulder as she passed by her.

"You suppose Ditimer is deserving of Ryla's vengeance?"

Othana shook her head. "That is not for me to pronounce."

Kade pulled his satchel over his head, then patted the contents: his canteen of water, a smaller canteen of seripyn, some food provisions, and the prophecy. They were silent for several long minutes.

Avery finally stood and caught sight of the staff. Now the queries would come.

"What you got there?" He nodded to the staff with a frown.

"A walking stick," Kade replied. There would be time for explanations later.

Altizara, who was closest, inspected it. "Is that so?"

Kade smiled. "It will have other uses, I am sure. But I am glad to have it"—he touched his chest—"for now."

They all watched Kade for a moment. When it was clear, he would reveal nothing more, they set about preparing for their upcoming trek.

"How long will it take us to reach the catacombs?" Avery asked.

"We should reach Shaldon in three days," Kade said, peering into the trees ahead. "If we limit our breaks."

"Kade, you should rest now," Emaline said.

Kade did not argue. Tilman lit a fire.

"It has been many years since I have traveled this path," Kade said as they settled around the flames. "I can only hope it remains open to us."

"If it isn't?" Avery asked.

Kade sighed. "We will press on until we can go no further. But the prophecy states the Cord will overcome the shadows."

"The shadows in the catacombs."

"Shadows come in many forms. Some are in caves. Some are in our very hearts. Where the battle lies, we do not know."

***

Kade followed a way he knew by heart, though no path was visible. Soaring trees rose from the mountainside, their multi-colored trunks devoid of branches except at the tops where glittering sunbeams passed through, dappling the forest floor. Kade knew every tree. Every stone. Even after so much time, nothing had changed. Even the air—richer, denser—told Kade he was on the correct course. With the staff, he no longer required assistance.

"She won't find us here?" Avery asked as he walked alongside.

"The path is well hidden. I do not know what we will find on the other side."

"No one knew of this path," Tilman said from behind. He wiped at his cheek where blood still ran freely from a gash left by the hyram ambush. He had staved off Emaline's attempts to clean it.

"What business did anyone from Malvok have in Shaldon?" Altizara called. She and Othana were keeping watch at the back of the line.

Avery cocked an eyebrow at Kade.

Kade shrugged. "Shaldon, or what once was Shaldon, lies north of the tombs. It was a great kingdom led by a supremely brave leader, Mistress Thamsyn."

"Mistress?"

Kade shrugged again. "She did not wish to take a royal title. She ruled her kingdom as an equal."

"Alone?"

"For some time, yes. Her husband was lost long before Cosyn began his attacks. But not before their lovely daughter was born."

"Even in alternate dimensions, single moms exist."

"Indeed. But her lineage saw the prophecy fulfilled."

"Oh?"

"Her daughter was Nahor."

"Ohh," Avery breathed.

Kade couldn't help but smile.

"Kade?"

"Yes?" When there was no answer, Kade stopped and turned. Avery was at a dead stop ten feet away, holding up Emaline, Tilman, Altizara and Othana, all of whom grinned at Avery.

"A foa," Kade called

"Looks like a fox," Avery retorted, then cocked his head. "Crossed with a lion."

"But entirely harmless," Kade said. He approached the foa and held out his hand. It trotted to him and allowed Kade to stroke the top of its head. Avery closed the distance.

"Go ahead." Kade gestured for him to stroke the animal's soft fur. Avery plunged a hand deep into its coat. The foa shook its body before bounding away. Kade laughed and then sighed.

"Even in the direst of circumstances, joy comes unlooked for."

Heartened, despite the icy wind and his throbbing chest, Kade continued to lead the troop around trees and through tall brush into a narrowing canyon. The mountains closed in until it appeared they had come to a dead end. Kade cut to his right and scrambled up an opaque stone outcropping. He eased down the other side and continued up a hill. At the top, his wound pulsed in time with his heartbeat. His breath came in quick puffs of vapor. They stayed under the cover of the trees as the hyram circled high in the gray sky.

Kade scanned the horizon.

"There is our first stop." He pointed to a glittering stream in the distance. Thus far, their journey had been a success.

Kade touched his forehead and raised his hand to the sky. A prayer of thanks.

They worked their way down the opposite side of the hill and continued to tromp through the trees in silence as dense clouds moved over the sun, stealing their shadows, their warmth, and some of Kade's cheer. Darkness bore down, and a rumble of thunder signaled yet another storm. An icy blast of wind tore past them and Kade pulled his cloak tight around him, glancing back at Avery doing the same.

A bloated raindrop splashed on Kade's nose.

"A bit faster, my friends," Kade called and pressed on.

Ahead, the trees gathered closer, standing nearly trunk to trunk. Another rumble of thunder shook the branches. Kade felt the hyram before he saw them. Even darker than the storm clouds, black specks soared above them.

"The hyram will see to Lady Ryla finding us if we do not find cover." Kade glanced back. But not only had Avery and Othana fallen behind, even Tilman and Emaline struggled through the dense forest. Altizara lagged even further back.

"Just through there." Kade pointed at two trees, that formed a 'V' between a pair of boulders.

Avery stumbled and squinted at Kade as though fighting to focus. He was fading.

"Avery, you need the seripyn."

"No, no, I'm okay," Avery panted.

"Here." Kade grappled with his bag to find the canteen of tea.

"I'll be fine, I'll be . . ." Avery fell face forward. If Othana had not caught him before he hit the ground, he would have busted his nose.

"Kade!" Altizara shouted.

Kade spun to see one of the hyram streaking from the sky. Othana let go of Avery and grabbed her bow, scrambling to Kade.

Tilman and Emaline caught up. He drew his sword while Emaline knelt next to the unconscious temporal, protecting his body with her own. Altizara joined Othana with her bow. They both nocked arrows and aimed at the sky.

The first bird dove past the trees and Othana let an arrow fly, piercing the hyram's wing and sending it careening to the ground. Altizara took out the next. One after another, they interrupted the assault.

Between the forked trees, they would have some protection. But another bird, nearly as big as Tilman, was leading a group of a dozen more.

"Tilman!" Kade shouted. "Get Avery!"

Tilman nodded, sheathing his sword, and threw Avery over his shoulder.

He ushered Tilman and Emaline through the tree fork and turned back. Othana and Altizara were nearly out of arrows. Another bird plunged through the tree line.

Its talons lashed at Othana before it disengaged, circling around with two more birds taking its place. Kade roared, anger overtaking the pain.

He stalked back to the women.

The trees were filled with the black ravens, blocking the last of the feeble light.

"Through here!" Kade shouted, ushering Altizara and finally Othana to the other side of the trees. The hyram were too large to follow. But Kade could not bring himself to dart away and skitter to safety.

He planted his feet, ignoring the fire in his chest, and faced the ravens. For too long, the creatures had watched from the skies, shadowing the group's every move. Kade's golden light rose, creating a halo around his feet. The tree trunks nearest him appeared gilded. Kade clenched the staff, channeling the heat to his palms. Icy rain broke free of the gray clouds and the birds descended, showering Kade with feathers, sharp beaks, and slashing claws. He felt a nip at his ear and a slash at his side.

"Kade!" Tilman shouted from what seemed a great distance.

Kade could only see a chaos of beating wings. The cries of the birds filled his ears.

His halo faded. The rain stole the warmth from his hands. He beat at the birds with the staff. Without thinking, he forced the last of the heat building in his chest to his free hand, stretched out his fingers and clutched one of the ravens by the neck. Its threatening caw cut off with a surprised squawk. Kade stared into its beady eye. The remaining murder of crows halted their attack, as though startled at such a defense.

Kade brought the bird close, its wings flapping against his shoulders and its foul breath nearly intolerable as it struggled to break free. Then it stopped, hung limp for a moment, and dissolved into a black powder that fell at Kade's feet.

Kade jerked his head up, holding out his glowing palm to the remaining birds. The light spread like a wave, rushing to the treetops and overtaking the rest of the birds. Black powder mingled with the rain, creating a sooty downpour. Kade watched the sky until it ran clear, then stumbled through the tree fork.

"Come, we cannot tarry," he said without stopping.

Avery lay at Emaline's feet. Tilman wiped blood from his cheek and hoisted Avery up. Othana slid up under Kade's arm and supported his weight.

"We must hurry," Kade said. "Ryla will not be far behind."

"Just point the way," Altizara said.

Kade nodded and stumbled forward. He could barely grip the staff and dragged it on the ground as he leaned heavily on Othana.

"We must give Avery the seripyn soon," he gasped.

"Soon," Othana agreed. "But we must put distance between us and Ryla's soldiers."

Kade focused on the forest ahead of them. As his vision tunneled in, he prayed he could lead them to the stream in time.

CHAPTER TEN

No words would pass from Raelyn's numb lips. She tried to take a breath, but her chest felt bound.

Lima frowned. "I thought you knew."

Raelyn shook her head, but her throat closed over the jumble of questions buffeting her mind. Her eyes burned with tears of confusion and dread.

Lima stood and circled around the fire, sinking next to Raelyn with a frown of concern. She took one of Raelyn's hands between her own.

"I am sure Kade had his reasons for not telling you," she said, patting her hand. "Even Ashford expressed surprise." She shook her head. "You have proven yourself quite worthy."

"But Peter was sick," Raelyn croaked.

"Of course." Lima continued to stroke her hand. "You had no choice." She tutted. "Perhaps Kade was afraid you would not come if you knew . . ." She took a deep breath and straightened. "You are here now," she said, a bright optimism in her tone. "You should not discount your success thus far."

She gave Raelyn's hand one last squeeze and then stood. "You should get some sleep. Fatigue will always distort understanding. I will keep watch."

Lima disappeared from the cave, her light fading into the night.

Raelyn couldn't move. Her throat ached. The fire did nothing to warm the cold seeping through her body. Peter had been chosen. Not her.

She looked at her hand. The seed Arkonai had given her that had become the red mark was meant for her brother all along. Peter could see Alnok, interact with her, help her, because he was supposed to be here.

She leaned to her left, unbuckled the Bokar and held it in her lap, watching the firelight flicker across its leather cover. She ran her hand over the intricate leaf-and-flower pattern. The book, given to her as an empty cover, had seemed an inditement. A confirmation of her lack of worth. Her inability reflected in that unwritten story. But she had gathered four pages. Chosen them herself. A sob escaped her lips.

But the book was Peter's.

She drew the Bokar to her chest and let the tears come, crying in bitter whispers. Why was it given to her?

Still hitching, she wiped her eyes and looked at the book again. It may be Peter's, but she *had* chosen the pages.

She closed the first plye in Olyaund. Then the second beneath the waters in Endyle. She had led a group of four across a realm she never knew existed. Could Peter have done it all better? According to their dad, Peter was better at everything else. Unlike her own fumbling, he might have stridden through the forest outside the Olyaund wall and marched right up to the portal. He might have read the words without hesitation.

He even helped her close the second portal, showing her to use the sword instead of the book. Could she have done it on her own?

Tears spilled from her eyes, and she sniffed.

Fraud.

Second-rate.

Worthless.

The words beat against her until she was so weary, she slumped onto her side and drew her legs up. She closed her eyes.

Peter should have entered Alnok. This had not been her quest all along.

***

The smell of cooking fish drew Raelyn from a deep sleep. She forced her puffy eyes open. Lima was crouched over the fire, turning a skewered fish in the flames. She glanced up and gave Raelyn a sympathetic smile.

"I hope you are hungry. You must eat quickly. The tide will be low enough to travel soon. It is imperative we reach the cove to the east where we can climb back up the cliff before the sea rises. There, we will be well past the forest and out of the giants' territory."

Raelyn pushed herself to sitting. Her face was swollen, her throat dry.

The Bokar was still in her hand. She buckled it back into its holster and took the stick Lima offered her.

She wasn't hungry, but she picked at the fish, peeling away the scales to get at the white, flaky meat. She would need the energy. And that was something she sorely needed. Right now, she didn't feel like moving from the spot.

She tried to muster the urgency to continue. The chaos going on at home would only get worse. There could be mobs beating down the door to get to Peter and Dad. Whatever Cosyn was sending through the plye in the catacombs had to be worse. If it was worse than illness and volcanoes, how could she do anything if she wasn't even supposed to be here? She had barely closed the first portal and wouldn't have closed the second one without Peter.

You still have Joshua and Jinny counting on you.

Raelyn took a sharp breath and choked on the bite she was chewing. As she coughed, Lima handed her a water skin.

Raelyn took a gulp.

"Lima," she said.

"Yes?" the girl answered as she kicked out the fire, preparing for their departure.

"Are you sure Joshua and Jinny will be okay?"

As much as Raelyn wanted to believe she had proven herself a worthy leader, it was now clear she wasn't. Now that she knew why, her friends might be on their own more than they realized.

Lima was silent as she pushed her foot through the remaining soot. She stopped and looked at Raelyn, her dark eyes shrewd.

"I do not know what Cosyn might release on them. Or if Cosyn himself will choose to thwart them. But they will encounter opposition. Of that, there is no doubt."

"Can they defeat what's coming?" Fresh tears stung Raelyn's eyes.

"Are you asking if they can overcome the evil? Or overcome that evil without you?"

It was as though Lima had given her a sharp slap. Of course, Joshua and Jinny were more than capable of making it to the catacombs. In fact, their chances were probably better without her. But no assurance assuaged her guilt. She had left them to fend for themselves.

"I think they have just as much strength with or without me," she said. She sounded like a defiant teenager, arguing against an elder's critique. She cleared her throat. "Kade .. . Arkonai appointed me leader. But it took all of us working together to close the plyes."

"Did it now?" Lima nodded, but she looked distracted. She draped her cloak over her shoulders and strode to the edge of the cave, looking left, then right, before turning back to Raelyn.

"You were never the only one shouldering this burden. Each of you has something to fight and something to fight for. You must let them go. They must overcome their own challenges. Face their own . . . giants, as it were. As for us, we must go. We have little time to beat the tide."

Raelyn stood and looked at the half-eaten fish on her stick. She tossed it into the pile of ash. She pulled the satchel over her shoulder, then the Bokar's holster as Lima watched silently, her eyes lingering on the book.

Raelyn slung her cloak around her and pulled the hood low over her face. She followed Lima, trudging across the soggy beach, barely twenty feet wide. The waves pounded onto shore and ate away at the rest.

A cold, wet wind blew off the sea. The clouds continued to bear down. It seemed all the words had been said and they traveled in silence. But one word echoed in Raelyn's mind.

Burden.

It felt exactly right. Joshua's burden for his daughter. Jinny's for her family, and now for Gabe, who had come to Alnok to save his dad. Avery had his wife.

Who would Peter have fought for? Dad? Her? Why was *he* in the hospital?

Because he was a greater threat.

Cosyn attacked Peter to keep him out of Alnok.

Raelyn's shoulders sagged. She glanced up and realized Lima had pulled ahead. Raelyn bent her head and jogged a few steps to close the distance, following the girl's disappearing footprints before the wet sand swallowed them up.

During treks she'd made with Kade, traveling from Malvok and on to the Tulum outpost, he had patiently answered her questions, encouraged her, declared her worth. But he had lied. At least hadn't told her the whole truth. Which was the same as lying. Even Larken had bolstered her confidence as they fled Shalhala and made their plans to reach Endyle. Raelyn surveyed the Kaidilas Sea. He was somewhere out there, lost when the sea dragon attacked their boat. In the distance, white caps rumbled across the steel ocean, gaining steam and breaking well before the shore, but closer than when they had begun.

"Lima," Raelyn said, striding up next to her.

"Yes?" Lima glanced at her as though surprised she was still following.

"You're sure we'll reach the cove before the tide comes in?"

Lima glanced out at the sea. "We can afford no delays, but yes, I am sure."

"What could delay us? That's why we came this way, right? It's Joshua and Jinny we need to worry about."

"They seemed confident in their ability to overcome the giants."

"Are *you?* Confident in their ability?"

Lima sighed. "They have a chance . . ."

"But?"

Lima squinted ahead, then slowed to a stop and faced Raelyn. "Understand this: I wish to see Joshua and Jinny at the catacombs. But you are the one to face the plye, not them."

Raelyn searched Lima's dark-brown eyes, gentle with compassion. She was saying Joshua and Jinny weren't necessary because Raelyn had been chosen to destroy the portal. But that wasn't exactly true.

"I can't do it without them," Raelyn said and wiped the salty spray from her eyes. "If we travel even faster, could we intercept them sooner? Find them before we reach the catacombs?"

The urgency that had been absent when they began came on at full force. She had worked so hard to lead them well, only to realize the importance of working together. But now, she needed them more than ever.

Lima's expression turned impassive. "I do not think that would be wise." Her tone was flat. She resumed her march.

"Why not? We could beat the tide and join forces before we head for the catacombs."

Now, nothing seemed more important than reuniting the Cord. If she had any idea where to find Gabe and Avery, she'd strike out after them, too.

"Why did you not remain with the others?" Lima asked without looking at her. "If your unity was so important?"

Raelyn's heart skipped. She shook her head and opened her mouth. But the harsh question jolted any retort from her mind. She had followed Lima because the girl had promised this was the better path. The right path.

"Because they were wrong."

"Because you made a different choice," Lima corrected. "You walk the same course, even on different paths."

"I don't understand."

"You assume they are wrong, because it is not the path you chose."

"But you said—"

Lima closed her eyes and shook her head, as though drawing on a deep reservoir of patience. It was a familiar expression. Chillingly similar to Cosyn's mocking composure.

"On this path, you will avoid their obstacles."

"But I'll have my own."

"Precisely."

"Any idea what those might be?"

"Perhaps. But our immediate concern is the tide." She strode ahead, leaving Raelyn to stumble in her wake, scolded and torn.

She gripped the Durinial, hoping for direction, assurance, something. Lima seemed unable, or unwilling, to offer those things. The amulet was silent and cold. The waves drew closer with each swell.

Kade had advised Raelyn similarly, telling her he would only reveal as much as the temporals were ready to handle. But this was different. Kade answered her questions directly, honestly. Lima spoke in riddles. Kade encouraged. Lima patronized. Kade loved. Lima . . . used.

CHAPTER ELEVEN

"Joshua, wait!"

The crowded trees blunted Jinny's cry, but she was still too loud. Joshua shot a frown over his shoulder. She wasn't far behind. She could catch up. He needed to set the pace. Lima had given them five days. They had made little headway the first night, threading their way through the dense forest. The frequent need to check the map didn't help. And the terrain had already forced them inland more than he wanted to go.

"Joshua," Jinny gasped, as she reached him. "We must wait."

Joshua took a deep breath and stopped, rubbing the back of his neck. He spun, ready to chastise Jinny for falling behind, but her flushed cheeks, deep frown, and clenched fists cut off his reprimand. Nimble as she was, she was no match for his longer strides.

She took a deep, steadying breath. "Are you trying to lose me?" she snapped, her accent heavy in her anger.

"No, sorry, Jinny." Joshua helped her take off her satchel, which she dropped to the ground and dug through, yanking out her water skin. She took a violent swig and glared at him. The Seon had slipped, resting lopsidedly on her head.

Joshua checked the sun, straining behind bloated clouds. Rain would come soon.

"The map doesn't exactly spell out how far we need to go," he said. "If we're gonna reach Raelyn in time, we have to push ourselves harder."

Jinny knew their peril as well as he did. But articulating his objective, offering a reminder as to why he was doing what he was doing, was sometimes necessary to spur on the troops.

Jinny stood. "I know, but—"

"We both saw something in Lima Raelyn couldn't," Joshua continued.

"Yes, but—"

"We can only hope she makes it to the catacombs, but if she doesn't, we'll need to be ready to finish the job."

"Okay, there's just—"

"So, if you want to—"

"Listen to me!" Jinny shouted.

Joshua snapped his mouth shut and blinked at the rare outburst.

She took a deep breath. "I could discern nothing from Lima. No good. No bad. Just empty. I do not know if Raelyn is in danger. But that way"—she gestured ahead of them—"has always been darkest."

"I know. We've always known that. Since Endyle. Can you sense more?"

Jinny swallowed and took another shuddering breath. "I am not falling behind because I am tired. What lies ahead is a terrible weight. The air, the ground, it is all . . . heavy." She tossed her water skin on top of her pack.

"Heavy?"

Jinny pursed her lips and stared at the ground. She fiddled with the hem of her tunic.

"As though an evil is making the air thick. The ground feels as soft as deep sand. Every step carries an unnatural weight." She looked up and met Joshua's gaze. "Something is pushing back."

Joshua nodded slowly. "Okay . . . would it help to take that off?" He gestured to the Seon.

Jinny touched it, shaking her head. "It is not only the east. There is something closer. That is why we must wait."

Joshua shifted his gaze to the trees. "The giants?"

Jinny nodded. "It is a raw, untamed rage. Unfocused but strong. My guess would be the giants."

"I know you hate this question, but can you estimate how close?"

Jinny heaved a sigh and squinted into the trees to the east and then north.

"I estimate they are drawing nearer, closing in from the north. But there could be more in the east." She shrugged. "They're giants. I suspect we will see them before too long."

"We can't stay here. But we're strugglin' to move ahead. What do you suggest?" He gave her a smile to soften the question.

Jinny put her hands on her hips and turned in a slow circle, scanning the trees. She faced Joshua again. "Let me lead."

Joshua cocked his head. "Oh? Thought you were having trouble with forward motion."

Jinny scowled and rolled her eyes. "Think of me as scouting ahead. I can keep us from running into danger."

Joshua pulled the satchel over his head and rooted inside for the map. He rolled it open and studied the portion where they most likely were. The forest west of the Endyle Bay, maybe not more than ten miles or so. But according to the sun, they were ten miles further north than they should be.

Maybe.

Everything was a guess.

He returned the map, grabbed the fancy canteen, and sloshed the seripyn around. They'd agreed to wait until they saw Raelyn again before they drank any. He dropped it back into the bag, pulled out the water skin, and took a drink.

"You're sure you'll sense the danger before we run into it?"

Jinny nodded.

"Okay." He adjusted the sack over his shoulder. Grasping the strap, he rolled his shoulders, trying to ease the tension in them. They needed to hurry, but if they were caught by the giants, they might not make it to the catacombs at all. He stepped to one side.

"Lead the way."

Jinny nodded and squared her shoulders. She strode past him, nimbly darting around the trees. What she lacked in speed, she made up in agility.

Joshua took out after her, keeping close on her heels.

"Holler if you think we need to switch gears. But I'd like to push our way south if we can."

Jinny nodded. "I hope Raelyn is making progress."

"Yeah. You think we shoulda gone with her?"

Jinny was quiet for a moment. Finally, she shook her head as she ducked beneath a branch without breaking stride.

"No. Raelyn saw something in Lima that compelled her to follow. It may have been the path she needed to take. But not for me."

"There was something off about that girl. I kept thinkin' about Kade. What he woulda said. All his talk about purpose, workin' together, trust. I didn't see that in Lima."

"Kade would have advised the opposite of everything she did. But, I will admit, I thought she might have told us about the giants just to scare us into following her."

Joshua sighed. "Same thought crossed my mind."

Jinny pushed aside a dry tree branch but stopped and cocked her head, like a rabbit sensing danger.

Joshua slowed his breathing, listening hard for whatever Jinny was hearing.

"Jinny what—"

She jerked and let go of the branch, smacking Joshua in the face.

"Arrggh! Jinny—"

But she jerked her head around and stared at him with wide eyes, then shook her head firmly with a finger to her lips. She crouched low and gestured for Joshua to follow.

She led them due south, darting from tree to tree, taking care to avoid stepping on the dead leaves. But their pace slowed as they hit a sharp incline. Evening was creeping up on them.

They couldn't have gone more than a couple of miles before Jinny paused again. She peered around a tree, searching the forest back the way they had come. Whatever she sensed, Joshua couldn't see or hear a thing. But she sure was searching for something. The hill they'd climbed gave them a good view of the forest. A blanket of dry, tangled branches dusted with snow mingled with a few evergreens. It was like the forest he'd gone to with his dad to cut down the tree for Lily's first Christmas. Same wet cold, same quiet. If they got home for Christmas, he'd get an even bigger tree. She'd be old enough to hang a few of the ornaments . . .

Jinny bolted forward and dove behind two wide trees. Joshua scrambled after her. When they were crouched between the trees, tall enough to be redwoods, Joshua opened his mouth to ask what he should be listening for. She clapped a hand over his mouth. He nodded his understanding. She eased her hand away and pointed up.

The treetops to their north swayed, as though caught in a blustering wind, the branches scraping and clicking. But there wasn't any wind. It was dead still.

In the distance, a dark clump of trees parted. It had grown too dark to see the forest floor. A violent creak was followed by a ground-shaking thump.

Something was edging closer. They couldn't wait here.

Joshua tugged on Jinny's arm. They had to keep moving south. Jinny followed without objection. Darkness was gathering much faster than their pace. But they seemed to create some distance. The wind noise quieted. But Joshua's vision was getting worse. The fading was coming faster than the darkness.

As the remaining light faded, Joshua spied a small clearing between two tall, juniper-like evergreens. His vision blurred as he rushed toward them and tumbled into the soft branches, landing on his hands and knees. Jinny collapsed next to him. The trees seemed to huddle in close, leaning in on them, protecting them. Joshua sat back on his heels and looked into the shadowy treetops, a headache pulsing in time with his heartbeat. The clearing was a good place to rest for the night. The boughs would keep them hidden and would muffle any sound. They might even keep warm. They couldn't risk a fire.

"You think we're in the clear for now?" he whispered.

"I think so. Hopefully, they'll stay well north of us."

Joshua nodded and dug into his pack as he swallowed back vomit. He couldn't wait any longer. He found the elaborate canteen Lima had given him and unscrewed the top, offering Jinny a drink.

Jinny shook her head and sat next to him, digging through her own pack and withdrawing the skin.

Joshua stared into the canteen. He could wait and leave open an opportunity to check on Lily. Though he'd relied on Raelyn's view of Earth until now, her assessment didn't mean his baby girl was safe. But if he continued on like this, he was compromising himself and Jinny. Which ultimately threatened Lily's safety.

He'd have to put off seeing his daughter.

He took a swig of the seripyn, forcing himself to swallow as his throat threatened to close up. He let out a long, shaky breath, part relief, part lament, and closed his eyes. His head cleared and the worst of the nausea passed. He eyed Jinny.

"You okay without the tea?"

"I think so. Another day maybe." Jinny drank from her water skin and propped herself against one of the trees, drawing her cloak around her. "You think I should? You know, fade? I have not seen my family since we left the ruin."

Joshua scratched at his beard and shook his head. "I couldn't risk it. I don't think you should either. If we get out of this forest and out of reach of the giants, we can reconsider."

He listened for anything out of the ordinary, but it seemed the giants had moved away or also stopped for the night. The darkness in their hiding spot was complete. No fire, no moon, no light from a Guardian, whether gold, blue, or purple.

Joshua shifted, adjusting his sword. He laid his head against the tree, but then sat up straighter. Jinny sighed and then cleared her throat.

"What d'ya suppose these giants look like?" Joshua whispered. Silence might be hard for Jinny to tolerate.

"I suppose I imagined a troll or something. Big, hairy, ugly."

"Yeah, me too. Kinda like bigfoot or something."

"I hope we do not find out."

"We made some good progress today. Gotta do better tomorrow though."

Finally, a rising moon set the clouds aglow. He could see Jinny, head rested on her arms which were crossed against her knees.

"Get some sleep," Joshua said. "I'll take first watch."

Jinny looked up and smiled weakly. "Thanks."

She adjusted the Seon and curled up with her head on her sack. Joshua settled in, forcing his thoughts away from his aching back and heavy eyelids. Aside from an occasional rustle or creak, the forest was silent. But that didn't mean Jinny wouldn't be able to sense something.

When Joshua's eyelids would no longer cooperate, sliding closed over and over, he nudged Jinny.

"Swap you out."

Jinny sat up and rubbed her eyes. She stretched and yawned. "Okay," she whispered.

"We still in the clear?"

Jinny paused, then nodded. "I feel nothing closer."

"Good deal." Joshua stretched out on his back and put his hand behind his head. As he drifted off, another rustling sound came. Loud enough for his arm hair to stand on end. He snapped his eyes open.

Jinny was on her feet.

"We need to move on," she whispered as she grabbed her pack. Joshua jumped up and pulled his sack over his shoulder. The trees were silhouetted against an ever-brightening sky.

Musta slept longer than it felt.

"We'll keep going south," he whispered, shaking the drowsiness from his head.

Another creak resounded through the forest, still some distance away, but definitely closer.

Jinny took point. Joshua steered them west as best he could.

Maybe Lima was right. The coast might have been a safer choice. Joshua's chest tightened at the thought. Nope, something was off. No matter how bad the giants were, Lima had the potential to be worse.

Raelyn shouldn't have gone. He should have tried harder to dissuade her. Why'd she have to be so damned hard headed?

His throat suddenly ached.

She thinks she can handle anything. And what she believes she can't handle, she deals with better than she thinks. She wants to protect everyone, ignoring her own safety. Then she goes and does the least safe thi—

Joshua's legs stiffened, nearly coming to a halt with his realization: Maybe Raelyn went with Lima to lead her away. Raelyn's smart. She had to know the girl was bad news. She was trying to protect him and Jinny. Which meant she was in more danger than any of them ever realized.

Even if the giants disappeared, allowing them to keep to the north, they had to go south. Straight south. To Raelyn.

Please keep her safe.

Hopefully Arkonai, or whoever, heard that.

He bolted forward, catching Jinny and pulling her by the elbow.

"Wha—"

"Raelyn, we have to find her."

"What do you mean?" Jinny followed him without dispute.

"We thought Rae knew what she was doin'."

"What makes you think she did not? What changed?" Jinny panted.

"That's the problem. I think she did know. I think she tried to protect us and put herself in danger."

Jinny was silent, her brow furrowed. "She wanted to get Lima away from us?"

"Yep." Joshua's frown deepened. His stomach was knotted.

"Okay, let's find her."

If they could just clear the giants' territory, they might reach the shore soon enough. If they couldn't, they'd have to be prepared to do battle.

CHAPTER TWELVE

Leaning heavily on Othana, Kade took one labored step after another, as though slogging through thick mud; each breath a desperate gasp to force cold air into his lungs. Frozen droplets pelted his face. A light snow had begun.

Kade wanted to get clear of the path entrance, but they had made little progress. No one had followed. It seemed his pathway was well concealed. For now.

"Kade!" Tilman called.

Kade stuttered to a stop and craned his head, trying not to disturb his torso.

Tilman eased an unconscious Avery to the ground.

"Yes, of course," Kade murmured. Othana helped him limp to Avery.

Fading was dangerous. But Kade had learned. The temporals could withstand much more than he ever thought possible. Gabe, Jinny, Joshua, and Raelyn had previously gone ten days or more without the tea. And they had closed the plye. Even so, he should have insisted Avery drink. This was not good timing.

He reached for his satchel.

"Kade," Othana said softly, and held up his bag. He sighed and smiled. She had taken it when they left the horses.

"Thank you. If you could administer the seripyn?"

"Of course." Othana eased out from under Kade's arm, and Altizara was there to take her place. The movement caused a flare of pain that sent spots in front of his eyes.

He should have insisted they leave him. Now that they were on the hidden path, they could. Emaline could carry the staff from here.

Emaline dropped next to Avery and lifted his head into her lap. Othana dribbled some of the seripyn between his parted lips. As soon as the liquid hit his throat, he sat up, coughing violently. He grappled with Emaline, as though fighting to get away.

"Avery!" Kade's one-word command was enough to jerk Avery to attention.

"The entire world's gone bonkers!" he yelled, jumping to his feet, nearly knocking Othana over. "She's hiding out at the Yorkshire house!"

"Avery!" Othana hissed, as she stood. "Quiet!"

Avery shook his head, his hazel eyes wide with fear, but he lowered his voice. "She couldn't get to London if she tried."

Tilman gripped Avery's shoulders. "Calm down."

Avery nodded and swallowed.

Altizara coaxed Kade to a clump of downed trees and settled him on a log.

"What is happening?" Emaline asked, ushering Avery closer to Kade.

Avery took a deep breath and studied the ground. "Penny wor sit-tin' at t'living room window. All t'lights off. Outside there was shoutin'. People runnin' here 'n there. Gunshots . . ."

"Here." Emaline handed him her canteen.

Avery took a quick swallow. "I couldn't tell what wor goin' on, but"—he looked at Kade, tears filling his eyes—"she wor scared. Never seen 'er so scared," he finished in a whisper.

His Yorkshire accent had come on fully. The carefully curated illusion of the smart London banker, the smooth financier, gone. All the money in the world could not mollify the outright terror for his wife. Severing his connection with a despised father from whom he had spent a lifetime striving to escape, even after the man was long dead, no longer mattered. Penny was, once more, in dire danger.

"Was it the volcanoes?" Othana asked.

Avery shook his head. "I dunno. I don't think so. They were evacuatin', tryin' to get away from t'explosions, the last I saw. The town wor virtually empty. Now"—he shook his head—"there's too many folks runnin' about. Breakin' windows, marching. It was anger, not fear."

"Cosyn will not have been idle," Kade said and grimaced when Emaline raised his arm and began removing his cloak. "Whatever evil now plagues Earth Apparent, we can be sure Cosyn means it as his last and greatest effort."

"If this truly is his last plye," Tilman said, brushing away a pile of snow with his boot to create a space for Altizara to dump a handful of kindling.

Kade shook his head. "We were unaware of his deeds before."

Emaline lifted his tunic, exposing his chest to the icy cold air. He sucked in through his teeth and closed his eyes.

"We have kept a careful watch," he grunted.

Othana shook her head. "Kade—"

He waved away her objection. "We know what to look for."

Emaline removed Kade's dressing, peeling away the last strip from the oozing gash. "Kade . . ." she whispered. But she went to work preparing the herbs.

Altizara passed her hand over the pile of sticks. Her yellow light glowed and a few flames sputtered to life. She frowned and poked at the wet wood, too stubborn to light properly. When she managed to coax the fire to small but steady flames she shrugged and stood.

"We thought we knew what to look for," Othana persisted. "But we were caught off guard by the second dragon. There could be more we do not know."

They were silent as Emaline spread the ointment and herbs over Kade's chest. As the balm took effect and the pain subsided, Kade took a deep breath.

"You are right, Othana. There could be more. For now, we must focus on rescuing Gabe. What good is it to worry about events over which we have no control? Does it provide aid? Relief? Comfort?"

"Of course not," Othana said, her shoulders drooping.

Emaline wrapped the wound and helped Kade lower his tunic. He eased back into his cloak then took hold of the staff.

He smiled at her and touched her cheek. "Thank you. That will see me through to the catacombs."

"If you need—"

Kade shook his head. "It must."

Emaline nodded and moved to Tilman, swatting away his hands as she inspected his cheek. Most of the snow around the fire had melted away by the time she had applied a yellow paste to the gash from the hyram's talon and the bleeding had stopped. The troop huddled around the flames.

"Was there anything else, Avery?" Kade asked. "Something that might suggest what is threatening the temporals?"

Avery shrugged, deflated. "Just seemed like chaos."

Tilman cocked an eyebrow. "That might be all it takes."

Avery frowned and looked at Tilman. "For what?"

"For the temporals to destroy each other."

"What Cosyn set in motion," Othana said as she passed around some bread and dried fruit, "might be enough for them to do his work for him."

Avery scoffed. "We been doin' that for years."

"Which makes our duties all the more crucial," Altizara said. "Not just this"—she gestured to the path—"but our calling to protect, guide, serve those Arkonai loves."

Kade caught Avery's eye. "You understand now why destroying the portals is more important than anything?"

Avery nodded but looked back into the fire. "I just feel so . . . useless."

"But you know that you are not."

"Aye," Avery sighed.

"Good. Now that you understand your value and the urgency of your quest, you will continue without me."

"What?" Avery jumped to his feet.

Tilman and Altizara strode to him, speaking objections over each other.

Even Emaline put her hands on her hips. "Kade, we have made clear—"

"What is clear," Kade interrupted, "is my part in this quest is over. These delays, they will only ensure Gabe's demise. The quest, Gabe's safety, Cosyn's defeat, all circumvent my involvement."

"So," Avery said, scratching his face, "what you're saying is you feel useless . . ."

Kade frowned. "I did not say—"

"But you know you are not."

"It is not the same."

"Your value to this quest cannot be measured in miles." Avery knelt in front of Kade. "Arkonai called you, too, mate," he said softly.

Tears stung Kade's eyes. For so long, he had sought to teach Avery this very lesson. Longed to have him grow in his calling, understand his worth, lean on the guidance of his Creator. They were the very lessons he should have been attending himself.

Introspection, it seemed, was a trait he had yet to develop. He had allowed the prophecy, revealed to him alone, to obscure stumbling blocks. It could be his role was not only to teach and mentor the temporals. It seemed he could learn from them as well.

Kade sighed and nodded. "Aye."

His thoughts cleared. And with the pain subsided, a renewed energy surged through him. Unless Arkonai called him on, he would see to it Gabe would not spend one more day in the catacombs.

"Besides," Avery said with a grin as he stood. "You have this new walking stick to help you along." He gestured to the staff at Kade's feet.

Judging by the curious stares from each of them, there would be no avoiding an explanation. He picked up the staff, running a finger over the vine-and-flower pattern.

"I retrieved this in Herlov before we embarked. I had it placed there for safekeeping just before the Cord entered Alnok."

"For whom?" Altizara asked. "Who crafted it?"

"It was crafted for the Cord by Shalhalans, just like the Cieskild, the Ruah, the Seon, the Bokar, and the Leohfaet. It is the Staebor."

"Someone stayed behind? In Earth?" Avery asked.

Kade nodded. "In a sense. That is all I will say. For now."

Tilman shook his head. "Why carry it now? If a temporal refused the call, what is the benefit of an unmatched weapon?"

"Perhaps none." He met Tilman's gaze. "But much time and skill went into its creation." He swept a glance over each of them before resting on Avery. "Nothing is wasted. No object too inscrutable, no effort too small, no role too mundane. All creation has purpose. The Staebor has yet to play a part in this quest. But that does not mean it will not."

"Now, we have rested long enough." He stood, using the staff and ignoring Emaline and Othana's offers to help. "I would like to think Ryla and her soldiers could never find this route. But the hyram attack makes that unlikely. We should not stop again until we reach Shaldon."

Tilman was already kicking out the fire. Kade strode ahead, unaided. Avery matched his pace with Othana directly behind. Emaline and Altizara marched side-by-side. Tilman passed Kade, rushing ahead to assure their path was clear. They made no sound but for the crunching snow beneath their footsteps.

As evening approached, the snow subsided, leaving them in an ethereal twilight of silvery white. Should Ryla come from behind, there would be no hiding. Kade increased his pace.

"What's at Shaldon?" Avery's breath came in hard gasps.

"One of the first temporal cities to fall."

"A ruin, like Deshill and Durnoth?"

"Aye, but I have not returned since its destruction."

"So, you don't know what we'll find?"

"I do not. But if the way remains open, we will have an advantage over Ryla and her soldiers."

"You believe it is still there?" Tilman asked as he strode past them to take point.

"I have no reason to believe it is not."

"The dragons . . ." Othana argued.

"Attacked Shaldon, yes," Kade conceded. "But many escaped. Hinson rescued Nahor. He was a brilliant stone mason and I will trust the way remains open."

"What way?" Avery asked.

"A passage even more secret than this mountain pass."

"It'll get us to the catacombs?"

"It will. And it may make up some of the time we have lost."

"Jolly good. I can't imagine what Gabe must be going through."

Kade's chest tightened, and his wound twinged in protest. He could only trust Arkonai with the boy's protection. That would be enough.

Deep into a frigid night, they continued until they reached a gurgling stream. They paused long enough for a drink. The clouds parted, exposing stars like chips of ice.

They had only one chance to pull ahead of Ryla. If the passage was blocked, they would have no choice but to fight to the finish.

CHAPTER THIRTEEN

Joshua swore under his breath. Jinny was leading well, her Seon firmly on her head, but they were definitely on the defensive.

It's like trying to get past the lushor after the shipwreck.

The little gremlins had hemmed them in until they had run right into Lord Lachlor. No plan. Just reacting. Somehow, they'd been successful. Raelyn had closed the portal. He hadn't been on his A game then. He wasn't now.

Thankfully, the giants didn't seem to be herding them as much as tracking them. But they were doing a good job with one coming so close, Joshua got a good look at it, standing at least fifteen feet tall and towering over the smaller trees. Its lanky arms ended in sharp claws. Beady eyes peered from a face disturbingly human-like though elongated with a wide mouth full of sharp teeth. Course, woolly hair covering its body served as good camouflage, and it nearly disappeared in the shadows. Though this one was stealthier, the others were easily heard, lumbering and tearing up saplings. Joshua and Jinny had been close on the bigfoot image, though blurred photos didn't capture the wild savageness of their growls and roars.

He and Jinny had avoided the creatures by hiding in clumps of trees and following a zigzag pattern southeast, even doubling back north, but always making their way to the sea.

"Shhh," Jinny stopped and crouched in the undergrowth, holding up one hand. A flash of pride bloomed in Joshua's chest. She was a soldier in her own right.

"Something—"

A thunderous roar resounded through the trees to their left, followed by a crack as a small tree was thrust aside. A giant, seemingly alone, charged around a wide evergreen, gaining speed as it approached, its eyes laser-focused on Jinny. Matted black hair covered its face, shoulders and abdomen. Joshua blinked, trying to piece together what to do next. How'd they miss this one? His brain was slipping gears, slowing him down. He couldn't make connections . . .

Protect Jinny.

"Behind me!" Joshua shouted as he drew his sword.

Jinny scrambled backward. The giant lumbered forward, closing the distance. Joshua rushed toward it. He ducked as it swiped at him. With a clumsy step to the left, he stabbed at its exposed ribs. Not even enough to cut through the skin. Only tick it off.

It shrieked and gave a backhanded swing. Joshua dodged, so it smacked his shoulder rather than taking off his head. But it was enough. He spun as he went down, his sword landing somewhere in the brush nearby. Before he could get to his feet, the giant was on him.

"Over here!" Jinny cried. The giant, its arms still stretched out for Joshua, jerked its head around, searching for the noise.

"Here!" Jinny shouted louder, demanding.

The giant snorted and adjusted its bulk to chase its new prey. Joshua got to his knees, desperately searching for the Ruah. The creature turned its back on him and started after Jinny. As it took its first couple of steps, Joshua ran his hand across the hilt of the sword. He grabbed it and jumped to his feet, racing toward the giant, gaining ground.

It was right up on Jinny. Joshua raised the sword and pulled back. This had to find its mark.

Using his momentum, he rammed the sword into the giant's lower back. But he rebounded and the beast spun around. It raised both arms, roaring. Joshua took another run at its chest. He missed, but the sword sank into the soft flesh under its arm. The giant stopped moving. Joshua twisted the sword.

The giant took a few gasping breaths and staggered to its knees. Joshua yanked his sword back as the giant fell forward and was still.

Jinny looked over the dead body, gasping for breath, her eyes wide.

"We gotta move," Joshua said, striding to her. He grabbed her elbow and prodded her forward. "No chance the others didn't hear that."

Jinny nodded and raced ahead. Joshua kept his sword drawn. The acrid stench of the giant's blood drying on the blade turned his stomach.

More snapping branches and a few distant howls kept the pair moving until just before sunset, when all went quiet. As the sun's orange glow gleamed between the tree trunks in a blinding glare on their right, Jinny slowed their pace.

She stopped and put her hands on her thighs as she caught her breath. "I have to rest. We can't keep going after dark, anyway."

Joshua nodded, the motion punctuating a creeping headache. He blinked to clear his vision. No obvious hiding spots, no tree clusters to crouch between. Two trees, growing side by side, with intertwined branches that were mostly bare but for a few stubborn leaves, created a thick, scraggly canopy. If they could make it up to the boughs, they might be able to see something coming, not just hear it.

"Can you climb?" Joshua asked, nodding at the treetops.

Jinny squinted up, then pressed her lips together, strode to the closest tree, and hoisted herself onto a thick lower branch. "You coming?" she called.

Joshua sheathed his sword, adjusted his satchel, and followed Jinny.

It was the perfect climbing tree with thick, sturdy branches and coarse bark. Not unlike the trees he'd climbed with Ford in the field near their childhood home. The intense memory of his twin brother tightened his chest. Joshua gritted his teeth. He'd never been emotional before coming to Alnok. Now, everything triggered sappy reflection.

This is why you're sloppy.

He grunted and forced his legs to move faster. The shoulder the giant had struck ached each time Joshua grasped a branch. But he ignored the pain . . . and his sentimental memories.

Within minutes, they were twenty feet off the ground. Jinny reached a thick branch growing horizontally from the opposite tree and shimmied across. She settled into a crook made by a second branch and the trunk. Joshua removed his bag and hung it on a shoot above his head. He found a comfortable spot—at least somewhat comfortable—against the trunk, facing Jinny. With no fire and little to block the wind, it would be a cold night. And sleep would be next to impossible. But they wouldn't be caught off guard. Hopefully, they would be hidden enough. But something else brought deep relief to Joshua. As the last of the daylight faded, he saw the dark edge of the forest. They were almost through. The first leg of their journey was complete. They were that much closer to Raelyn. And the Schade Catacombs.

***

Joshua dozed to the gentle chirruping of crickets, but kept himself on the edge of sleep, so that he heard every creaking branch, each rustle from below. He kept an eye on Jinny, but she fared better. Bolstered by the tree and surrounding branches, she seemed to sleep soundly. At the first gray haze of dawn, she stirred.

"There are a few just north of us," she said in a low voice, stretching and shivering.

Joshua sighed. "How's your head?"

Jinny shrugged. "Hurts. But I can manage."

"Good deal." He wouldn't mention his throbbing temples and churning stomach. "I'd say we might reach the tree line by midday if we hoof it."

Jinny cocked her head.

"If we *hurry*."

Jinny nodded. "What then?"

"We'll figure it out. Right now, we need to focus on getting outside their territory."

"You sure it is a boundary these creatures will not cross?" Jinny dug out her water skin and sipped.

"We can only hope." Joshua struggled to his feet, his shoulder stiff and sore. He pulled his pack from the makeshift hook. "Everything has its own turf. Not hard boundaries, but basic instinct may keep them to this forest. Otherwise, we would have encountered them before."

It sounded plausible, but he had no clue. None. These things could come after them until the catacombs were no longer an option, leaving Raelyn and Lima to close the plye alone. If that's what Lima had planned.

Dark anger licked at the edges of his mind and Jinny's image slipped sideways. Joshua shook his head, clearing the emotion and bringing his sight back into focus. Anger toward Lima or toward Raelyn and her stupid choice wouldn't help their situation. It wasn't just aggravation that coiled tight in his stomach. It was a deep fear that Raelyn's choice had put her in terrible danger. The same dread he had felt for Lily every day she was missing. He had entered an alternate dimension to rescue his daughter. And he would go just as far for Raelyn. He growled.

More stupid emotion.

"What is wrong?" Jinny asked as she tiptoed across the branch to Joshua, arms outstretched.

"Nothin'" he grumbled and took a swig of water. He pulled a strip of jerky from his pack and tore off a bite as Jinny began her descent.

Help us get through this, he prayed to no one in particular. But an answer whispered through his mind, like a sigh through the treetops.

Do not lean on your own understanding.

Joshua looked down. Jinny was only halfway to the forest floor. Always easier going up than down.

The sun had broken over the horizon by the time they were at the base of the tree, ready to set off.

"You good?" he asked.

Jinny did a slow turn, rubbing her hands together in a very Kade-esque way. "Yes," she said and resumed their trek southwest.

The trees thinned as midday approached. But rather than providing warmth, the sun exposed them to whatever might be nearby. Birds seemed oblivious to the cold, twittering and calling from above. A gust of icy wind rattled the treetops. For the first time since leaving their makeshift treehouse, the hair on the back of Joshua's neck prickled. The giants seemed to prefer dusk, but that didn't mean they wouldn't take advantage of an afternoon snack.

Jinny stopped and put a finger to her lips as she glanced over her shoulder.

Joshua held his breath and listened. A steady rustle; heavy footsteps from the north.

"Go," Joshua whispered, but Jinny was already moving, adjusting their course south. As the day wore on, a glimmer of hope kept Joshua's headache at bay. They covered more ground than he would have thought possible. The trees gave way, and the ground went from a springy path of dead leaves to coarse rock and gravel. They had to be getting close to the cliff. Ahead, the sun shone on a clearing. Though tempting, Joshua knew better than to risk being exposed in an open glade. Especially one that backed up to a sheer cliff.

"Jinny," Joshua whispered. "We can't risk getting hemmed in."

"We don't have many options," she snapped.

Though out of character, her frustration was justified. But it wasn't just that. They *didn't* have options. Joshua raised his eyebrows and watched Jinny jog around a rotted tree stump. *Don't.* He'd never heard the girl use a contraction.

Somehow, the shift in her language opened his eyes to an air of confidence that went above her willingness to lead, her ability to sense danger. He hadn't noticed it until now, but she seemed to have finally embraced her role in Alnok.

A low snarl came from behind them. Joshua searched frantically for a place to hide or escape to. But there were only scrubby bushes and craggy boulders.

Joshua drew his sword without breaking stride, and Jinny yanked her dagger from its chain around her neck. The distant whoosh of waves crashing onto the shore drifted across the frigid air. They'd come further south than he thought.

"Here's where we put your territory theory to the test," Jinny gasped as they jogged over larger and larger rocks. A stack of boulders rose on their left, shadows pooling at the base. Then a darker shadow. A hole.

A cave.

"This way," Joshua shouted and started for the opening.

"Joshua! Wait!"

He turned to see a giant rush toward Jinny. Joshua skidded to a stop and reversed course. Then a second giant lumbered from the now-distant forest.

Joshua intercepted the first and swiped his sword up, missing the giant as it jumped back, roaring. It charged again and Joshua let out a guttural shout as he stabbed, aiming for its belly, but the strike glanced off its body. The skin seemed too thick to penetrate.

Joshua regained his balance and scrambled after Jinny. But the second giant was already on top of her. Using a stump as leverage, she launched at the creature, half scrambling up it in the same manner she had climbed the tree. She reached its shoulders as it waved its arms wildly and drove her dagger deep into the side of its neck. It thundered as it reared back, blood spurting from the wound. It pulled Jinny forward and sank its teeth into her shoulder. She screamed, the sound echoing over the expanse. It tossed her onto her back. The neck wound didn't slow the giant down. It launched onto her.

But Joshua lowered his shoulder and barreled into it. It was like slamming into a wall, but it was enough to interrupt its attack. It charged Joshua.

Aim for its armpit.

He feinted right just as the giant reached him and rammed the sword under its arm. It howled and swung wildly. Then it shuddered and crumpled to the ground.

The second giant had slowed, as though assessing Joshua's skill.

Joshua sheathed his sword and grabbed Jinny under her uninjured arm. She squeezed her eyes shut and groaned. The bite had broken through her tunic and gouged her collarbone to her shoulder. Blood leaked onto the rocks beneath her. If it had bitten just a little further up, she would be lying next to the beast Joshua had just killed.

He helped her stand just as another growl came from the trees, then another. An entire pack ran at of giants broke out and ran at them, emboldening the one next to them.

"C'mon!" Joshua pulled Jinny's arm over his shoulder, half carrying her to the cave. Her left arm swung uselessly.

The cave had to be too small for the giants. If not . . .

He dove inside, the opening larger than it had looked from thirty feet away. Not good.

But it was deep, with a second opening tucked away in the back. Joshua pushed Jinny toward it, and she disappeared into the darkness. He dropped to his stomach and wriggled in after her. A giant grabbed his ankle. Joshua kicked, and Jinny pulled at his arms. The creature let go and Joshua pulled his legs in.

The smell hit him before his eyes could adjust. Stagnant water, dead birds, rotted wood, all within the area the size of Lily's bedroom with a four-foot ceiling.

The giants continued to growl and roar outside. Joshua scrambled further into the cave away from the grasping claws. Jinny was plastered against the opposite wall, staring at the opening where the frenetic shadows of the giants passed.

Even in the darkness, her shoulder looked a mess.

"Here," he whispered. "We gotta do something with that."

He helped her lie down while the giants roared and growled at the cave opening. "Can you wiggle your fingers?"

She nodded and tapped her thumb and middle finger together.

Joshua smiled and nodded. "Good deal. I'd like to get a better look. Think we can get your tunic off? "

Jinny shivered but pulled at her hem. Together, they worked her tunic over her head, leaving her arm for last. She sobbed silently as Joshua peeled the tunic from her shoulder, revealing her shredded undershirt. His back was sweating, but his fingers were cold and stiff.

The giants had quieted to an occasional huff. There seemed to be fewer, but those that remained hadn't completely lost interest.

Joshua ripped away the lower part of Jinny's cloak, surprised at how easily the suede material tore away. He dug his water out of his pack, popped the top off, and poured it over the wound. There would be no disinfecting it. Jinny gasped, and her eyes fluttered open. She looked at Joshua and her chin quivered.

"Be still. I need to get some pressure on it to stop the bleeding."

Jinny didn't acknowledge, but she didn't move. Joshua searched his pack and grabbed the towel wrapping the berries from Lima. He dumped them out and pressed it against the wound. Moving Jinny's delicate shoulder as little as possible, he wrapped the cloak fabric around her shoulder and pulled it tight over the towel, securing it as best he could with his numb fingers. As he finished the knot, Jinny took a deep, shuddering breath.

He tucked her cloak around her, then scooted around so he could lay her head in his lap. She continued to shiver as she opened her eyes and blinked at him.

"Guess Raelyn's choice doesn't seem so stupid now," he said, half hoping for a glass-is-half-full retort.

Jinny nodded and closed her eyes.

"We're safe for now," he whispered.

That they were. But they had a new problem.

They would be going nowhere.

CHAPTER FOURTEEN

A distant scream jolted Raelyn awake. She jumped to her feet, her heart pounding. Could it have been a bird? Something from her dream? She stood still, listening. But the wind, whipping her hair and billowing her cloak, didn't bring the sound again. The waves relentlessly pounded the cliff.

Lima stood on a narrow ledge just below the ridge they'd reached before the tide had come in. Their refuge barely cleared the exploding waves. They'd built a small fire and spent the remaining hours of the night and the morning resting and trying to keep warm. The sun rose in a cloudless sky, but the exposed cliff offered little protection from the cold wind blustering off the sea.

It was day four. One more day and they were supposed to be at the catacombs. It didn't seem like they were getting any closer.

"Lima!" Raelyn called down. "That was Jinny! I know it!"

Lima looked up with sad eyes, but with a lack of urgency that sparked a fire in Raelyn's heart. Even though the others hadn't followed Lima, she should at least care what happened to them. Isn't that what Guardians did?

"I fear they have encountered the giants of the forest," Lima said.

"No," Raelyn whispered. She craned her neck at the cliffside. It was impossible to pinpoint from where the scream might have come. She did a quick survey of the cliff. It didn't matter. She would climb to them. She shouldn't have left them. Her hands shook as she gathered her virtually empty satchel in which crumbs of bread and a few berries had collected at the bottom. She pulled the strap over her head and adjusted the Bokar. On turning, she nearly collided with Lima.

"Where might you be going?" she asked, her face placid and her voice calm. Raelyn glanced down at the ledge where the girl had just been standing.

"They're in danger." She tried to dart around Lima, but the girl stepped across her path.

"They were always in danger."

"I can't stay here!" Raelyn said and her hand went to the journal. It was an instinct she didn't totally understand. The Bokar gave her courage.

Lima's gaze lingered on the book, and she shook her head. "You cannot make the climb from here." She looked into Raelyn's eyes. "And you do not know where they are. *I* believe they are capable of overcoming whatever they face. Don't you?"

"Of course I do." Sweat beaded on Raelyn's forehead, turning icy cold as the wind blew across it. "Joshua's ten times the fighter I am. Jinny can see anything coming—" Raelyn ran a hand through her tangled hair and looked out over the sea. They were more capable. Had more of a right to be here. They were chosen. She was . . . *un*chosen. A trespasser. A fraud.

It was only one scream. They might have escaped. Or they might have been overtaken. Either way, how could she just keep going? Her chest tightened. She tried to breathe through the rising panic. It was no good. She yanked off her pack and threw it against the cliff, letting out a harsh scream that burned her throat. She kicked the still-smoldering wood, sending ash in a plume, then stalked back to Lima, her chest heaving and her face wet with hot tears.

"I can't just ignore what I heard." Raelyn's shoulders slumped, and she held out her palms, pleading for Lima to provide answers, comfort, a miracle. "I know you said they made a choice to go their own way. But they have to be close. Maybe close enough for us to find them."

"There are few locations that would allow us to climb. One is behind"—Lima gestured in the direction from which they had come—"the other is ahead. We cannot reach them from here, and we cannot delay our journey. The tide rises with every moment we stay. Unless you wish to spend another day on this ledge." Her eyes softened and she took Raelyn's hand. "Your hope must be in meeting them as you arranged."

Lima let go and skirted around Raelyn, picking up her bag and holding it out to her. Raelyn looked at it and then into Lima's dark eyes. The purple light swirled around the girl's head, shoulders, and arms. Raelyn heaved a sigh and took her pack.

Lima gave a curt nod and scurried down the side of the cliff, her head disappearing beneath the ledge where she had been standing. Raelyn took another tortured look above. Her chest felt as though it may burst, but rather than a scream, a harsh sob escaped her lips. But she followed Lima. She had no choice. Like the others, she had already made hers.

As they made the slow descent, the water slowly receded; each wave hitting the cliff with less fury. With the cold spray, every gust of wind stole Raelyn's breath. By the time they reached the beach, her fingers were numb and her tears frozen to her face. The waves still lapped close enough to dance around their toes before retreating. But the clouds had moved on and the golden sun, high and bright, glinted off the surface of the sea. It was the color of Kade's light, comforting and strong. She sniffed loudly and wiped her nose on the back of her sleeve. Self pity would accomplish nothing. She blinked her burning eyes and a pain shot into her temples. She blinked again. Between the salty spray and her tears, she hadn't noticed her vision had begun to blur. She could see Peter soon. But the excitement and solace she had always drawn from the anticipation now brought a new emotion. Shame.

She swallowed a rising knot.

"Is it far?" Raelyn called, glancing at the ocean. Though she had swum in a gentle lagoon, she had also lost Larken to the water dragon in those waters. A sea both calming and fierce, welcoming and foreboding.

Lima didn't answer.

"Lima?" Raelyn jogged up to walk next to her.

"We must reach the Hydd Cove before the next tide." Lima kept her eyes trained ahead as she took long strides. "There, we will find a suitable place to climb and continue on to the catacombs."

Raelyn nodded. Maybe from there she could double back and find Joshua and Jinny. She didn't need to share the thought with Lima. If the opportunity arose, she'd go. With or without Lima.

"Tell me about your brother," Lima said with a quick glance at Raelyn.

Raelyn blanched. "Peter? Why?" Such a random question. Maybe Lima was trying to take her mind off Joshua and Jinny. She couldn't know how defeating her revelation was.

"Now that you know he was the one called to enter Alnok," Lima continued, "it might be worth knowing who he was. How he might have approached the quest differently."

Peter. Strong, capable Peter. Pragmatic, charismatic, creative Peter.

A gull cried out as it soared above the waters.

"Well . . ." Raelyn swallowed and folded her arms in tight against the wind. "He's older . . ."

"You are close to him." It was a statement.

"Yeah, not always, though. Not growing up. But after . . ."

"After your mother and youngest brother were killed," Lima finished for her.

Raelyn nodded. The comment stung, but as though ripping off a Band-Aid. Better to put it out there than dance around the subject. Describing Peter would include some elements of her whole family. And Lima's vague description was a gentle way of putting it. She might have said, "When you drove the car carrying the two of them off an embankment after you'd been drinking . . ."

Raelyn swallowed again.

"He's an artist," she began. "But not just creative. He's highly logical. And strong . . . or at least he was strong. The illness, it did a number on him." She looked at Lima. "Kade said Cosyn caused Peter's illness. Was that to keep him from coming?"

Lima nodded. "Yes. But if the roles were reversed, would he have come? If he had not been ill?"

"I think so," Raelyn said. Peter had never been one to shirk a challenge. And he certainly would storm the gates of hell to rescue any member of their family.

"He was my dad's favorite," Raelyn continued. She'd never confessed this to anyone. "Dad loved—still loves—that Peter can paint a perfect cityscape and still do his own taxes." Raelyn chuckled, but it was filled with resentment. "I couldn't balance my checkbook . . . or draw a stick figure."

But her father had sailed out across the ocean to find her. He'd risked his life to close the plye. He obviously valued her more than she had ever imagined.

"Peter's strength, his connection to Alnok, grows."

"What do you know about that? Is it because he's supposed to be here? Not me?" Raelyn choked on the last word. So much could have gone differently if he had been leading the quest rather than her.

"I have no doubt your brother's part in the prophecy could not be stopped by a simple illness. Especially an affliction caused by one so inept."

"Cosyn? He seemed to do a pretty good job."

Lima scoffed. "With powers limited to triggering the flu?"

"Well—"

"And thwarted by a group of temporals able to close two of his plyes?" Lima glared ahead and increased her pace.

"Not everyone was thrilled about us being here." Raelyn jogged through the soggy sand to keep up.

Lima barked a bitter laugh. "Without a doubt. Most believed Kade's grief drove him to imagine a way for them to return."

"But we did. Return. Even if I wasn't the one meant to be here."

"You have accomplished as much as Peter might have."

"He just might have done it better." Raelyn's heart skipped. Peter entered Alnok at the bottom of the bay. If he hadn't been there, she never could have destroyed the portal. "Do you think he could help me close the plye at the catacombs?" The question burst from Raelyn before she had entirely formed the thought.

Lima looked at her. She seemed much older than twelve. Older than Raelyn. Even older than Kade. Raelyn's heart thumped as a shudder of fear ran down her back. Then Lima smiled and she offered an encouraging nod. She was the young girl again.

"Perhaps."

Like Kade, Lima was trying to help. Just in her own way. Raelyn couldn't mistrust the girl's intentions. The cold, the stress of the journey, avoiding the encroaching ocean, the guilt of leaving her friends. It was all wearing on her. Making her question everything. If the girl was a spy from Endyle, she would have held them there. If she was one of Cosyn's followers, why lead Raelyn to the catacombs? No, she would have done away with her before now.

But that didn't stop her from questioning herself. Soon enough, she would talk to Peter. Whoever had written those names in their family Bible did so on purpose. A clue to what she had suspected even then.

"So, Peter is smart and can paint," Lima said. "This is the extent of his skills?"

Raelyn frowned. "Well, no. He's a natural leader. Confident. He was always the president of some club or heading up a community outreach. Everyone likes him. He's not afraid of anything."

Lima smirked and gave Raelyn a sidelong glance. "Nothing?"

"I'm sure something . . ."

"Heights? The dark? Spiders?" Lima's tone became harsh.

"I—well, yes, he's afraid of tight spaces. Dad took us spelunking one time. Just the two of us. Harlan was still too young . . . anyway, we ended up in this small cavern and he just froze solid. Couldn't move. When Dad finally got us out, Peter spent the rest of the trip in the truck—"

Raelyn's vision blurred and she stumbled. She squeezed her eyes tight and then opened them. Her sight cleared, but the headache came on so suddenly, it was as though her head would burst. Her stomach rolled.

"You should take some of the tea," Lima said, strolling toward the cliff and pulling open her satchel. Raelyn followed, but the girl went out of focus.

"I thought maybe—" Raelyn snapped her mouth shut to keep from vomiting. She tried to focus on Lima, but she seemed to blend into the grays of the cliff wall.

With the next wave of nausea, the Durinial hummed against her neck. Raelyn gripped it and placed a steadying hand on the wall.

"Lima, something . . ." A warning. Danger. "Lima?" she called, but her voice sounded small.

"Here." Lima's voice seemed to echo all around her, even out into the water. But then she was right in front of her.

"The seripyn is in your pack," she said.

Raelyn nodded. "I'll drink it. But we may be in danger. The Durinial—"

"Danger, you say?" Lima didn't sound fearful. She sounded . . . eager. "Then we should hurry."

She pulled at Raelyn's arm and helped her continue walking along the firm, wet sand. The worst of the fading passed, but it wouldn't be long before she would have to make a choice. Drink the tea or fade and see Peter. Right now, she wanted to do neither. Discussing the revelation with the very person whom the prophecy had referenced would crystallize the truth. They might even trade places then and there. Maybe that was a good thing.

They didn't stop to retrieve the seripyn, but Raelyn's headache eased and her stomach settled. It was smart to drink it only when she needed to. They still had to get to the plye, and then back somehow. She listened for any further cries from the top of the cliff. The scream was only slightly more terrifying than the silence that followed. Her initial panic shifted to a steady drumbeat of dread.

They nibbled on the last of the dried fruit as they walked. Lima seemed focused on getting them to their next waypoint and didn't engage in any further conversation. This helped them cover a good amount of ground throughout the day. The waves, still at a distance, crashed violently onto shore, closer and closer, sending spray into the air.

Raelyn glanced over her shoulder and razor-like pain sliced across her temples. The fruit soured in her stomach. She stumbled as bile hit the back of her throat. The Durinial hummed again. Lima continued ahead until she was out of focus.

"Lima—" It was no use. Raelyn stopped, put her hands on her knees and vomited into the wet sand. She heard Lima's squelching footsteps approach, but she closed her eyes, willing the nausea to pass. She would fade soon. The thick pounding in her temples eased, her stomach settled, and she risked standing up straight. Lima stood five feet from her, in focus and smiling serenely. Another figure, a dark blur, stood ten feet behind her.

Oh God, no.

"Lima!" She lurched forward. *Lima didn't see him. She had to pull her away. Get between the girl and the figure.*

But she stumbled and landed on her hands and knees.

A chuckle. Taunting. Hateful.

Cosyn.

CHAPTER FIFTEEN

In the dark forest, the ground shuddered beneath Kade's feet. He halted. Avery froze, his breath coming out in short puffs of vapor. Flanking them, Othana and Emaline, pressed in close. Even Altizara and Tilman, who maintained their watch ahead and behind, stopped and waited.

The quake was undeniable, but from which direction? Impossible to tell, except that it came from deep underground. It could only be one thing. But if the dragon was stalking them, what did that mean for Gabe?

Kade shook his head. He could not turn his thoughts to what he could not control.

A shout from behind propelled them forward.

"Quickly now," he whispered, resuming his course down the mountain. He used the staff for balance and support. It may serve no further purpose, but it might also prove invaluable.

He ignored the prickly shrubs snagging his cloak. Shaldon was just ahead. But Ryla was not far behind. And the dragon was close.

"A little further," Kade whispered. It was the only encouragement he could offer.

"Kade, wor that the bloody dragon?" Avery whispered.

Kade nodded, but he saved his words. It was all he could do to maintain the pace. The pain was kept at bay with Emaline's dressing, but the wound drained his energy. Avery may not recognize it, but the others surely saw it.

His light was little more than a flicker. A battle with Ryla would require every bit of his remaining strength. If they were forced to fight the dragon, he would be of no use.

The thinning trees revealed a pale morning sky. A stone shed slumped in the distance. Unlike many of the temporal kingdoms, the people of Shaldon used the mountain rocks for their buildings. The outpost, though crumbling, stood in defiance of time.

The rumbling grew as they passed the single-store outpost, nothing more than a shell with a single window revealing a sad darkness within. A foreshadowing of what Shaldon had become. Scattered rocks suggested other buildings disintegrated or destroyed. The gold signot and blue lapis used in their construction lay among the deteriorating gray granite. Discards of a once proud kingdom.

Longing wrenched Kade's heart. The days when he would enter Shaldon to meet with their council were a distant memory. But what a welcome he had received. Thamsyn, Hinson, Nahor, all escaped. But so many did not. Kade sighed and made his way through the ruins.

"This is Shaldon?" Avery whispered.

"The outskirts, yes. But we must make for the southernmost point of the kingdom."

A shout came from the trees not far behind. Kade gritted his teeth; Ryla's soldiers were closer than he had guessed.

They reached a shallow valley, over which a bridge long worn away had once crossed. They skidded down the side, kicking up dust and sending rocks cascading down the hill. At the base of the valley, they would be exposed. They had to cross and reach the trees on the other side before Ryla closed the distance.

Unless she had already sent forces ahead. She had surely guessed by now where they were going. Kade scanned the bluff ahead. It was empty but for a few birds of prey circling above, too small to be hyram. Thank the Creator for small miracles.

They started up the embankment, clambering over rocks and boulders. Tilman steadied Emaline when she slid a few feet on loose gravel, but they reached the crest without incident. Altizara climbed ahead and hauled each of them up one by one.

They darted into the tree line and Kade took a deep breath of relief, wincing at the sharp pain in his chest. Othana put a hand on his arm, but Kade shook his head without looking at her.

He could hear the river's roar as it rushed from the great lake in the north. It was just ahead.

They dashed from the tree line. The tower keep rose in the distance. Kade imagined Thamsyn waving from the upper turret. Below, the leaning citadel did not fare as well. A hole gaped at the center of the fortifying wall. The gate, hanging from a single hinge, evidence of Shaldon's defeat. They would not enter the city, but they had to cross the river. If the bridge over the valley suffered the same fate as the city gate . . .

They came to the frothing river, pounding against the banks that skirted the western boundary of Shaldon. What had been the mill house on the opposite side was missing its wheel but was otherwise mostly intact.

"Is this the only place to cross?" Othana asked, gesturing to a dangling rope bridge sagging across the river, its center not more than five feet above the water. Two posts, driven into the ground, held a mesh platform of metal, not unlike chain mail, flanked by handholds of rope, frayed and revealing a similar metal reinforcement.

"The river was one of their greatest protections," Kade said. "There was once a narrow bridge"—he nodded to a pile of rubble a few feet away—"but the river has eroded the central arch and taken the stones back into the earth. This was the original crossing before they built the main bridge."

A foot-bridge was not ideal, but it was intact. Perhaps their ultimate escape route would be as well.

"I will go first," Tilman offered.

"No"—Emaline reached out a hand to stop him—"I will put the least strain on the rope. I will test it." Without waiting for a response, she gingerly stepped onto the woven metal decking and gripped the ropes on either side. Her hair swirled around her as air lifted under her with the force of the river.

Othana edged out to look at the water. "How is it a stone bridge was destroyed, but ropes did not rot away?"

"The bridge destruction was likely purposeful. A way to hem in the townspeople," Kade said, watching Emaline reach the halfway point, the bridge bowing in the middle as it bounced with her every step. "These are no ordinary ropes." He rubbed at the roughly woven hand hold, pushing aside the hemp to reveal the metal beneath. "The Shaldonians were marvels at engineering and construction."

"Even so," Tilman said, his hands clenched, "it has not been crossed since the temporals lived here. He watched Emaline with an intensity that suggested he would dive into the waters if she were to slip from the ropes.

But she did not. She skipped the last few steps to the other side, turned and waved them on.

"Avery, you next," Kade said.

"Wha—" He looked back at Altizara who was pacing, looking into the trees. Tilman stared at him with a furrowed brow, but Othana waved him over, offering a hand to help him onto the structure.

Avery squared his shoulders and tugged at his shield, assuring it was firmly attached to his pack. He took a deep breath and grasped Othana's hand. With an unsteady step out, he balanced himself, then took another. As Emaline had done, he held tight to the side ropes, easing across.

"Kade, you should go ahead," Othana said as Avery scurried up the last of the ropes and joined Emaline. "Avery may need you. And you may need Emaline." She gave him a compassionate smile.

"'Tis true, but I would feel better with a second soldier on the other side, should they need reinforcements—"

"Kade." Tilman looked over his shoulder at the trees where Altizara stood sentry. "Ryla is pursuing."

"You believe she has sent a troop ahead?" Othana's eyes were wide; she cut a glance at the two across the river.

Kade nodded. "She gained faster than I expected, given the hidden trailhead. I suspect her strategy includes a contingent stationed ahead to intercept us."

"I will go," Tilman offered.

Othana stepped aside.

Tilman took a wide step onto the bridge and crossed with a determined stride. The bridge bowed dangerously close to the river as he came to the center. He passed just above the furious flow. The ropes creaked in protest and one of the posts bent inward. But Tilman made it to the other side.

"Emaline was prudent to go first," Othana said, pushing at the post, testing its durability. "We may not all make it across."

"Kade!" Altizara ran up, skidding to a stop, breathing hard. "They are almost upon us!"

Kade nodded. "Go." He nudged Othana onto the bridge.

"Kade—"

He shook his head. "Altizara, when Othana reaches the midway point, you cross. Tilman weighs what both of you do together."

Altizara eyed the bridge with skepticism. "I can cover you as you cross."

"I will not risk adding my weight to Othana's."

Altizara pursed her lips, but prepared to step onto the bridge, waiting until Othana was halfway before hurrying onto the deck.

Shouts cut across the roar of the river. Kade glanced back. Shadows were exiting the tree line.

Kade leaped onto the bridge just as Altizara climbed up the opposite side. With no heed to the swaying, the creaking, and the bowing, Kade rushed across. Midway, the river drowned out all other noise. He did not risk a look back, instead keeping a tight hold with one hand, the other gripping the staff as he braced himself from tumbling over the other side.

The bridge gave a violent bounce.

They were following.

Kade glanced back. No; they were chopping at the ropes, tugging on the posts.

The bridge swayed and jolted. Kade was ascending the other side, but the bridge was swaying like a pendulum. Then it shook wildly as though a great hand were jerking it to and fro. Kade's right hand slipped. He went to his knees, gripping the staff with both hands. The bridge had dipped below the river's surface and was being battered by the current.

"Kade!" Othana screamed.

Kade pushed himself up and clambered a few more yards. He was almost there. Tilman stretched out his arm, anchored by Altizara and Avery.

A few more feet. He reached out for Tilman's hand—

The bridge gave way. He thrust the staff over his head. A temporary weightlessness was followed by a sharp jerk on the staff. His wound tore open and he gave a raw bellow as pain erupted across his ribs. He dangled, breathing hard, forcing his hands to clamp down on the staff as his feet tossed in the torrent. He peered up. Tilman's red face hovered above him. Behind him, Avery strained, his arm linked with Tilman's. They lifted Kade and dragged him onto the bank. Altizara, Othana, and Emaline completed the chain and fell backward in a heap.

Kade gripped his chest, pressing against the fresh flow of blood and struggled to his feet. He glanced across the river. A group of four or five soldiers stood at the edge, watching impassively.

"Follow me," he said as he limped away from the river, hastening south of the citadel wall.

"Kade, they can't cross now," Avery argued.

"They would not risk destroying their one way to cross unless—"

"There were already soldiers here," Altizara finished.

They followed what had once been the path into the city and hurried around a low building surrounded by tall evergreens. Someone let out a sharp whistle.

"They're waiting inside the walls," Othana whispered.

Kade peeked around the building and locked eyes with Ryla, surrounded by her guard, fifty yards away, galloping along the path. It had not been she who followed, but a few henchmen. She had guessed their destination and found a route around.

"This way," he whispered, and raced through the trees to a small but perfectly intact building made of massive, carefully cut limestone.

"Here we are," Kade said and ushered them past a splintered, rotting door. The horse's pounding hooves drew near as Ryla bore down on them.

"Kade!" Ryla shouted. Kade ignored the warning and climbed through a narrow doorway, yanking the door closed.

The light from Kade's fellow Guardians lit a small, empty room. They looked at Kade expectantly. He nudged Avery to one side and dropped to his knees, feeling along the stone floor until he found a small divot. He fished out a handle, felt alongside it, and located the second.

"Tilman, help me pull." Kade stood and gripped the first handle. Tilman took hold of the other and they strained. Warm blood leaked into Kade's dressing and pain sliced across the wound, displacing the low throb. Kade gritted his teeth and continued to pull until the stone grate lifted, revealing a hole in the floor and the first few steps of a spiral staircase. Tilman looked from the opening to Kade, his eyes wide.

"No time to explain," Kade said, gesturing for Othana to enter. Avery started to follow, but Kade put out an arm to stop him. "Wait." Kade dug into his satchel, retrieving the flask of seripyn, and handed it to Emaline. "As soon as Avery is on the stairs."

She nodded and disappeared after Tilman. Altizara went next.

"Othana, help Avery."

"Kade, I dunnit need a blasted babysit—"

Othana yanked him down the stairs after her.

The soldiers could only be a few paces away. Kade crossed to an opposite door and bashed it open with the staff as Tilman dropped through the opening. Kade returned and sat on the first step. He yanked on the grate, only managing to slide it halfway over the hole. Tilman tugged at Kade, moving him out of the way so he could finish pulling it closed. Kade grabbed a dangling chain with a pin and slipped it through a metal eye. He could already hear the hollow echo of the river below.

He circled down, following Tilman's steel-gray light to a long, narrow chamber. Avery and the three women were huddled on the final step. Where a wooden dock once stood, a wide but swift river gurgled and echoed through the tunnel, disappearing south into darkness. Dread creeped into Kade's gut. Surely he had not just trapped them here.

"Kade!" Avery called above the noisy river, his face slack and ashen. "I woren't there long, but I popped into t'house. Penny's not there. Sirens blaring. Out the window, fire everywhere . . ."

"We are close, Avery. Hold firm."

Avery blinked and nodded. "We're in—"

Kade nodded. "Velare."

"Kade," Tilman said. "I do not need to point out the obvious, but . . ." He shrugged and gestured to the water flowing at their feet.

"Aye," Kade mumbled and climbed back up a few steps, scanning the far side of the tunnel. Shaldonians, masters of engineering and a brilliant mason who crafted these stairs, could not stop wooden canoes from rotting away. But . . .

He spied them, two boats chained to the wall, glinting and dancing in the waters, nearly invisible in the darkness. He smiled. Hinson, however a brilliant stonemason, was not the only genius. Wilmot, always overlooked because of his simple nature, had possessed skills beyond masonry.

Two boats he had forged of tanom, light, strong and buoyant, had been stowed behind Wilmot's home. A knot formed in Kade's throat. The man had likely meant it to be a surprise for Hinson, but he never got the chance to show him.

Kade circled back down and pointed. "There. We need to reach those canoes."

Avery scoffed. "Who decided that wor the best place to store 'em? Couldn't dock 'em over 'ere?"

"And if the steps give way to the river?" Altizara snapped.

Kade put a hand on her shoulder. "Patience, my friend."

Altizara glanced up at him. Her face softened, and she nodded.

"As I grieved their loss, I brought the boats here." He gave a contrite smile. "Grief spurs strange but necessary reactions."

Othana cocked her head. "Anyone have a spoon?"

"What?" Avery said.

"Just trust me."

Emaline opened her bag and held it out to Othana. "I do, at the bottom."

Othana dug into the girl's pack and withdrew a heavy metal spoon. She tried to bend it, then shook her head and handed it to Tilman. "Make a hook."

Kade sat above them and watched them work. With each shallow breath, pain sliced through his tight chest.

Tilman bent the metal into shape as Othana pulled her own pack off her back and tucked it between her legs. She rummaged through it and withdrew a slender rope. She gazed at it with a sad smile.

"Complements of Gabe," she murmured. Then she took a sharp breath as though to clear the sorrow and pulled an arrow from her quiver. She lashed the spoon, now curved into a makeshift hook, to the tip of the arrow. She handed the opposite end of the rope to Tilman.

"The length will barely clear the river," she said as she pulled her bow from her pack and nocked the arrow.

Tilman nodded his understanding and eased into the water, using the stairs as protection from the current until the water was high on his chest. He held the rope above his head. Altizara gripped Tilman's arm, bracing herself on the lowest step.

"Ready?" Othana said and took aim. She let the arrow fly. It clattered into the first boat and Tilman lurched forward, straining to keep hold of the rope. Altizara yanked on his shoulder and he pulled at the rope. The spoon scraped against the bottom of the boat and then caught the edge, hooking onto the lip.

"That is the easy part," Othana said when Tilman had clambered back onto the steps, holding the rope as though fearful of losing a fish showing interest in a line.

"Someone will need to enter the boat to unchain it from the other side . . ."

"And not go floating down the river," Avery finished.

"Pull the boat as close as you can, Tilman," Emaline said. "I can jump."

"Ha!" Avery said. "And go floating down the river without a boat when you miss?"

"I won't miss." She was already climbing the steps toward Kade. She stopped and frowned at him. "You need more healing herbs."

Kade managed a tired smile. "There will be time."

She gave him a hesitant nod and turned to the boat. Tilman had already pulled it perpendicular to the river. It bucked and threatened to yank the rope from his grasp.

Emaline took a deep breath, leaned back, took two steps, and launched herself from the staircase, landing with a thump in the center of the boat. She turned and smiled.

"Well done," Kade said, but she seemed not to hear as she climbed to the bow.

She released the hook and attached it to the second boat before unchaining it from the wall. Tilman carefully towed it to the stairs. Once Altizara and Avery had a firm grip on the second boat, Othana retrieved the arrow with the hook and tossed it to Emaline. Though the river thrashed at her boat, she managed to secure the hook and unlatched the boat from the wall. Tilman strained to pull the boat, heavier with Emaline on board, across the river. But soon they had both boats, each with an oar made from the same material, and were tossing their packs into them. Emaline, Kade, and Avery loaded into one boat as Tilman held it steady. He released it and the boat swept down the river with Avery carefully steering them to the center of the river. Soon, Othana, Altizara, and Tilman floated next to them.

The tunnel widened and the river slowed. Only then did Kade take a deep breath and let it out slowly. Emaline turned and prepared to redress his wound. Kade dozed as she worked.

"Won't Ryla follow us?" Avery asked.

Kade opened one eye. "I did what I could to throw her off our trail."

"The door you broke down," Tilman commented.

"The hidden entrance," Othana added.

"Yes." Kade nodded and closed his eyes again. "And we passed through Velare."

"How's that?" Avery asked, easing his oar back and forth in the water at a slow paddle.

"We finished constructing this escape for the Shaldonians just before the dragons attacked. We had no time to relay the strategy to Malvok before Shaldon was destroyed. By the time the siege was over, the information was of little use and forgotten."

"But she was right on top of us," Avery argued.

"If she discovers our escape route, we will be far ahead by then."

"This was your plan all along?" Avery chuckled.

"Aye, but I did not know if the passage would be clear. In fact"—Kade frowned and lifted himself up—"I do not know if it is blocked ahead."

"The way Ditimer blocked the tunnel as we escaped Malvok." Avery's voice was filled with bitterness.

"But he did that on Lady Ryla's orders, not Cosyn's," Emaline offered.

Avery huffed and went quiet.

Kade lay back. He would need this time to gather his strength. Ditimer may have paid the price when he intercepted Ryla. But was his sacrifice necessary? If Kade had forgiven sooner, trusted faster, they might have escaped Ryla more easily. Ditimer had begged to be welcomed back. They had refused his plea. Kade shook his head and forced the melancholy to the outer reaches of his mind. Alternate choices would always seem better upon reflection.

"Where does the river go?" Avery asked.

"The river empties at the Bastek Fjord in the shadow of the Black Cliffs," Kade said. "From there, we will travel to the Schade Catacombs."

CHAPTER SIXTEEN

"I'm afraid you got what you asked for." Cosyn's deep voice dripped with sarcasm, mocking Raelyn with overstated reason.

She looked up at him through wet, tangled hair, her hands and knees sinking into the wet sand. Lima stood next to her. The Guardian seemed powerless to battle Cosyn.

His smooth pale face held a wide "I-told-you-so" smile of snow-white teeth. His furrowed brow might have been evidence of concern, but for the glee in his dark eyes. Tendrils of black smoke rose from his head. The sickly smell of rotten fruit and decaying leaves draped over Raelyn.

"Lima," she croaked, sitting back on her heels.

Lima glanced at her without a trace of fear. If she wasn't afraid, maybe she had a plan. She had to know these shores. She knew what Cosyn was capable of.

Lima stepped around Raelyn. "As did you, fool."

Cosyn's face shifted in an instant. Not fear. Not anger. Comradery.

"Lima," he chuckled. "Who is the fool? The one actively destroying Earth Apparent, or the one waiting like a spider in her web."

Raelyn's lungs stopped working. She hiccuped and managed a shallow breath. She struggled to stand, but her legs were lead, refusing to move. Lima had tricked her. Flashes from the last four days ran across her mind. In the cabin, basking in Lima's encouragement . . . saying goodbye to Joshua and Jinny . . .

Raelyn choked out another sob.

. . . Traveling through the forest . . . resting in the cave . . . climbing down the cliff . . .

Lima had counseled her. Consoled her.

And told her it was Peter who should have been here. She'd lied about everything. *Had she lied about that?*

Lima strode to Cosyn, her lilac light turning dark purple and then black, void of light.

"No . . ." Raelyn emitted a strangled gasp. Neither Lima nor Cosyn paid her any attention.

Lima tossed her black hair. "You are pitiful." But her words were coy, not angry. "So much effort to thwart Arkonai, when with a single pluck of my silk"—she crooked her finger—"I draw in the temporals and drain them dry. You could not even control one of your own."

Cosyn scoffed and strolled past her to stand over Raelyn. "Ditimer? He was Ryla's pet, and *she* remains loyal."

"But he certainly thwarted your plans to send the Cord back—"

"Do not use that term," Cosyn hissed. "They are a company of fools. Deluded. Doomed. Ditimer chose Kade's way. Arkonai's way. He will suffer the temporals' fate."

Raelyn's head spun. Lady Ryla had betrayed them. Betrayed Kade. And Ditimer, just as Jinny had discerned. But he had chosen good over evil in the end.

A dark fog nibbled at the edge of Raelyn's vision. She clenched her hands, digging her fingernails into her palms. She couldn't fade now, with no hope of returning. No one to administer the seripyn. Completely vulnerable to two enemies. She groped for her water-logged bag, fumbling with the opening.

"You are confident of Ryla's loyalty?" Lima continued, narrowing her jet-black eyes. "You struggle to determine your true followers." Her silky voice held a careful tension, like a taut violin string. Or a spider's web.

Raelyn reached into her bag and located the canteen with the crucial tea, pulling it out with shaking hands.

Cosyn strolled to her and reached down, stroking her head. She shrunk out of his reach, and he smirked, brushing his hands together as if to remove something dirty. He yanked the canteen away.

"I do not doubt Ryla's allegiance," he said, opening the container and sniffing the contents, "but her uses are almost at an end."

Lima gave him a cool look and folded her arms. "Then finish it"—she nodded to Raelyn—"here."

"So shortsighted," he sighed. "I made that mistake before. I will not do it again."

"She is dangerous, Cosyn—"

"Sending her on to the final realm would only strengthen her. I made martyrs of the Alnokian temporals—"

"That was only when you failed. You allowed the two to escape to Earth Apparent."

Cosyn bolted to her, like a cobra striking, towering over her. "I allowed *nothing*," he hissed. "Kade *hid* the prescail." He turned to Raelyn. "Kade will never see this coming," he said quietly, considering Raelyn for a moment before returning his attention back to Lima.

"I have spun a web of my own. In fact"—a satisfied grin rose on his lips—"every temporal and many Alnokians are in route to the very center."

Lima raised her eyebrows, finally appearing interested. "The Schade Catacombs? Why would any of the others enter the cavern?"

"I have one of their own. Young Gabe."

Lima rolled her eyes and gestured to Raelyn. "Only this one matters. Her brother has established a connection to Alnok through her. Alone, she has already destroyed two of your plyes. If they are united in the catacombs, even Velare is threatened. How does this accomplish your domination of Earth Apparent?"

Cosyn shrugged. "Why lure one when you can have them all? And"—his grin transformed to a leer—"there is a particular Alnokian leading them."

She gave him a quizzical frown. "Kade?"

"The one and only." Cosyn drew himself up, clearly pleased with his clever plan.

"I thought you cut him down. The dragon . . ."

"Has weakened him," Cosyn snapped, seemingly annoyed at Lima's lack of admiration.

"I will leave Kade to you." Lima gave a dismissive wave.

Raelyn groaned and tried to stand. The noise brought Lima's attention back to her.

"This one remains the priority," she said, looking down at Raelyn.

"Indeed, which is why you will hold her—all of the temporals—captive in Velare."

"What?" Lima's eyes narrowed with an irritated confusion.

Cosyn sighed again, shaking his head in exasperation. "We remove the obstacle"—he gestured to Raelyn—"we assure they never return, personally or by offspring, and . . ."

His wide smile returned.

"And?" Lima asked, her patience clearly running out.

"We torment Kade for eternity."

She was silent, seeming to work out his plan. Then she smirked. "Perhaps . . ."

"Ha! You could contrive no better!"

Raelyn glared at Lima and again attempted to stand. She got one foot under her.

"You . . ." Raelyn took a deep breath, but Cosyn's stench clogged her senses and she gagged.

"Aye." Lima widened her eyes and looked past Cosyn, nodding. She mimicked the innocent child. Then her eyes became slits. "Temporals. Always so easily deceived by a child. But you and your brother have proved able adversaries, even in your frailty. I commend you." She bowed her head. "But you understand, I never meant for you to reach the last plye. The giants may have been enough. But"—she gave Cosyn a disdainful glance—"we have seen how effective your creatures are."

"They have thwarted the girl and the soldier," Cosyn said forcefully, but his tone, one of an arguing child, overtook the strength of his words.

Lima maintained her focus on Raelyn. "So, this is where your adventure ends." She gave a wicked grin. "One you were never meant to take. You are close to fading. When you reconnect with Peter, I will bring you under my dominion."

Peter's name broke through the shadows gathering in Raelyn's mind. She snapped back to a sharp clarity. The cold water swirled around her knees; her wet cloak tight around her neck. The Durinial pulsed in time, slow, steady.

Lima seemed to notice the change in Raelyn. She lurched forward with a growl. The dark mist around her spread, blocking out Cosyn, then seemed to solidify, like a pool of tar suspended around her shoulders, and in each outstretched hand. The substance dripped into the water and sizzled away.

Raelyn staggered to her feet, unbuckling the Bokar as she scrambled backward out of Lima's reach. She yanked the book out of the holster. Lima stopped her advance, eyes wide. But she recovered, narrowing them to slits.

"That nonsense may work on Cosyn," she snarled. "But do not take me for a common demon. I have watched you, Raelyn." Her voice rose, echoing, drowning out the sound of the waves. She grew taller as her face melted away. Her dark hair dripped from her skull. Her black eyes rolled back until only the whites peered out.

"So intent on your own destruction." Lima's lips disappeared and her mouth barely moved. "But it was not your own life you destroyed."

Cosyn chuckled as he strolled through the tar mist, his face also transforming as though the substance peeled it away. Pasty, mottled, sunken cheeks, red eyes, black hair hanging in clumps. He rejoined Lima, and both focused on Raelyn.

"I've heard that before," Raelyn whispered. Her parched mouth and dry throat sapped the words of strength. Cosyn had attacked her worth at every encounter. Had used her own self-condemnation to beat her down.

She brandished the book and swallowed. "I've made peace with my past." Her voice was louder, stronger.

Lima cackled, her mouth peeling back in a maniacal grin. "What peace?"

"I'm forgiven," Raelyn rasped.

"By whom?" Lima roared. "You? Kade? Arkonai? What forgiveness can you hope for if you continue to make the same mistakes? First your mother . . ."

Raelyn's stomach soured despite her confident proclamation.

"Then Harlan," Cosyn added with equal venom.

The bottom fell out of Raelyn's stomach, and her knees buckled. She splashed into the shallow water, the waves swirling around her. Lima and Cosyn's attack, accusations, taunts, leeched her resolve, though neither made a move forward.

Raelyn's fingers went numb, and she slackened their grip on the journal.

"Now, Joshua"—Lima spoke his name with relish—"Jinny. All gone."

A hoarse sob broke from Raelyn's throat. The shadows billowed back into her mind.

"All because of you," Lima snarled and lunged forward, Cosyn right behind her.

Raelyn cried out as she hauled the book up, gripping it with both hands, and threw it open. A flare of white light poured from the pages.

All of them.

She squeezed her eyes shut. Lima let out a wounded screech. Cosyn howled.

Raelyn forced her eyes open. It might blind her, but she couldn't just stand there holding the book. She had learned. Even great, impenetrable power requires willing participation. She ignored the burning pain in her eyes and focused on the first page. Gold markings swirled across the surface. The marks came together. Warm relief surged from her chest. She understood these words.

"I am girded with strength for battle," Raelyn barely whispered, but another voice overlaid hers; deep, strong, calming.

"You are not strong," Lima said, but her voice lacked conviction. "Look at you. On your knees."

Raelyn looked at the water rushing over her thighs, filling up the beach, then pulling back, tugging at her. It didn't feel like kneeling. Not in submission, anyway. Not to Lima. Or to Cosyn.

But it was surrender, of a sort.

Nothing else existed. Just Raelyn, the Bokar, the voice.

"You have subdued under me those who rise against me." Raelyn mouthed the words, but the voice took over.

"Pitiful, weak," Cosyn launched the words as arrows.

"Cherished, strong," Raelyn lobbed back.

"Broken . . ." His voice faded.

"Beloved," Raelyn sighed. The title was a balm as much as a shield.

She finally looked up from the book. Everything was gone. Not just Lima and Cosyn. The waves continued to surge over her legs, but there was nothing but light rising to a blue sky.

Then, out of the light, a figure approached. Just a shimmering silhouette strolling toward her as though taking a leisurely walk along the shore.

A grin broke across her face.

Arkonai.

She found the strength to stand, the book still open in her hands.

Another figure walked beside Arkonai. Their forms took shape as they drew closer.

"Well done." Arkonai's voice, quiet and gentle, shook the cliffs and penetrated Raelyn's heart. Raelyn shifted her focus to the second figure.

Peter.

Arkonai faded; the light dwindled. The beach dissolved. In the distance a seagull cried, then another, and another, overlapping . . .

A siren.

The fading took over.

CHAPTER SEVENTEEN

The tunnel's onyx walls glittered with light. One side, Emaline's sage green. The other, bright yellow, deep orange, and steel blue. Altizara, Othana, and Tilman. Two boats, floating side by side, carried by a gentle but steady current. But for the hollow gurgle as the water lapped up the tunnel walls, all was silent.

Avery kept them under steady power, rowing and keeping pace with Tilman. Whatever reservations Othana, and even the others, had of the temporal, the man had proven himself capable. Not only by holding his own. They would not have escaped Ryla without him.

Kade settled back, taking perhaps the last opportunity to recover any strength he had left. Night would be upon them by the time they exited the tunnel. It might give them an advantage. Unless they had something waiting for them at the end.

"How is it the dragons did not destroy this tunnel?" Othana asked.

Kade considered the question. Shaldon had been destroyed by at least one dragon. Those who escaped, Thamsyn included, told tales of the attack. But since then, he and King Ellioner had hidden the tunnel entrance to Velare. Their junctions to that realm—Kulum, the Shalhalan waypoint, and the Shalhalan library—had never been discovered. Even by Cosyn. The connections had always been a risk. Velare held evil of its own.

"They could not have discovered it," he said. "Even if they were aware, they looked to destroy the people. They would not target an escape route hidden in a realm they do not understand, or of which they are unaware."

"Cosyn is aware."

"Aye. Thankfully, he is relegated to only a single place and time. Olyaund, Endyle, the catacombs . . . his attention has been divided enough. What benefit would it serve him to search Shaldon after he had driven out the temporals?"

"He may see a reason now," Altizara said.

"We will be well away from Shaldon, and out of the tunnel before he has time to regroup," Tilman reasoned.

"How did you create this tunnel?" Avery asked.

Kade offered a tired smile. "I was not involved. The tunnel was a series of caves beneath the kingdom. The Shaldonians mined material for building. And gems for their artisans. They crafted beautiful jewelry."

"The goblets in Malvok were a gift from Shaldon," Emaline added.

"Yes," Kade said. "Each temporal city had their own distinct talents. At the direction of Mistress Thamsyn, who commissioned a skilled mason, the people of Shaldon connected the caves and redirected the river to flow through."

"It was always meant as a way of escape?"

"Aye. When Cosyn began his attacks, first in Boiland, we sought a way to save the temporals in all the cities."

"Did it work? The tunnel?"

"It did for some. Including Nahor."

"Blimey," Avery whispered. "How far does it go?"

Emaline turned, eyebrows raised. Even Othana and Altizara were attentive. Of course, they would all be eager to prepare for the next leg of their journey.

"The tunnel continues beneath the mountains. If the current remains constant and we are not encumbered, it will take us the rest of the day."

"What of the troops sent from Herlov?" Altizara asked.

"We would have encountered them if we had stayed on our original course," Othana said.

Altizara scowled and shook her head. "Ryla may have had troops intercept them as well."

"Or they may be all gathered at the mouth of the catacombs," Tilman growled and gave a swift stroke, surging ahead of Avery.

Kade reflected on the betrayal they had all experienced. Tilman, Altizara, and Emaline by Ryla. Othana by Olyaund. He by Cosyn and Avery by his father. With trust in short supply, or offered too easily as he had with Ditimer, it was miraculous they had accomplished so much and come so far.

"Coming out at night should help," Avery offered.

Kade nodded. "Indeed. We will take the river as far as the fjord, if possible. Then continue on foot to the catacombs. Gabe . . ." An image of the dragon taking flight with Gabe in its claws stole his next words. The beast would take the boy to the deepest parts of the tombs.

"Have you been inside?" Avery asked softly.

"Once," Kade said and shifted to a more comfortable position, rocking the boat gently. He glanced over the edge into the dark waters. Tiny points of light darted in the depths.

"Two unruly youngsters snuck away from Shaldon. They fancied an adventure to the catacombs."

"Daft bairns," Avery breathed.

"Alnok was not always like it is now. The temporals enjoyed peace and contentment for a time. They knew it was forbidden but did not understand the danger."

"Even Guardians did not see the danger until it was too late," Emaline added.

Avery snorted. "Arkonai didn't think to give you a heads up?"

"I believe he did," Kade said. "But we chose not to see it. We often focus on what suits our own story. Guidance, direction, warnings can be easily ignored if such prudence does not fit our narrative. Even if the Author himself has provided the instruction."

"Did you find them?" Avery asked. "The kids?"

Kade sighed. "I did. But only to return their bodies to their families."

"We began to see Cosyn's treachery," Altizara said. "By then . . ."

"It was too late," Othana finished. "We finally understood what happened to my brother." She gave Avery a quick glance. "Olyaund."

"And we discovered the plyes," Tilman said.

Again, they fell silent and allowed the current to carry them. Apprehension stalked Kade's mind, trying to steal his determination. What was waiting for them at the end of the tunnel? Gabe's fate, Cosyn's plan of attack? His own destiny?

I need hope.

The boat tipped as Avery leaned over, staring into the water. Kade followed his gaze.

The small bright-green lights flitted along the river bottom. These tiny creatures had once filled the cave pools with a viridian glow, so bright, their light would have filled the tunnel and lit their way. Even the simplest creature had been diminished by Cosyn's growing power. Not an insect, tree, or stone had been unaffected. His brother's poison oozed into every crevice.

But here, at the bottom of a river in the outer boundary of Alnok, some resisted. Seeming in defiance of Cosyn's attacks, swimming in the river current, they gave off light despite the corruption. As if unaware of the realm crumbling around them, even with a shadow hovering over the land, they danced and darted in the water.

If basic life forms such as this could celebrate their existence, thus, fulfill their purpose by thriving within their fundamental design, could not he?

So intent on protecting the temporals, fulfilling the prophecy, battling Cosyn, fleeing Ryla, Kade had forgotten the unvarnished act of praise. In his zeal to obey his Creator, he had neglected simple worship.

"Brilliant," Avery murmured. He looked at Kade. "What's that in the water?"

Kade looked up and smiled. "Griten."

Avery cocked his head.

"It means green," Tilman said.

Kade let out a long, slow breath. It was time to surrender what he could not control. To rest in this moment. He let go of his anxious thoughts, one by one, as though setting them adrift on the river.

Their fate in the catacombs . . .

Raelyn's location and condition . . .

Ditimer's betrayal . . .

The current carried each away, the water dispersing them until they were diluted and powerless.

A heat kindled in Kade's chest. A stirring beneath the wound, deep in his heart, something in his bones. The heat flowed down his arms and to his hands. A light flickered in his palms. Pale, unnoticeable to anyone but him.

A golden light mingled with the sage along the wall.

Emaline turned, frowning.

"Kade?" Her eyes widened.

The tunnel filled with golden light.

Kade smiled. "Your restorative skill seems to be working."

Emaline did not look convinced. And rightly so. The herbs reduced the pain, but the wound had not healed. His energy had been draining. His light, fading.

This surge of power did not come from anything within. This was Arkonai, shining through him only after Kade had made room.

"Remember this moment," Kade said, as much to himself as to Avery. "The darkness we will encounter will be like nothing you have experienced. Cosyn will do everything to protect the remaining plye. The catacombs are not only guarded, they contain every vile form of Cosyn's twisted imagination. But this"—Kade gestured around the boat, allowing his light to spill from his palms—"escapes what he believes to be even his best-laid plans. The light, in many forms, is accessible to all." He gave Avery a pointed look and was satisfied to see resolution and courage reflected back.

"Do you know where the dragon will have taken Gabe?" Avery asked.

"I have no doubt we will find our path to him."

"That so?"

"Do you not know?" Tilman asked, his voice rough.

Avery sniffed and shrugged. "Know what?" But his troubled expression suggested he had some idea.

"You suppose it is coincidental Gabe was taken to the place where Cosyn protects his plye?"

"He's luring us there," Avery said dully.

Tilman nodded and dug his oar into the water, surging ahead as the tunnel narrowed and the current quickened. Eventually they could touch the cave walls and the ceiling bore down until all but Emaline were forced to duck.

"I think I see something ahead," Altizara called, straining to see.

Kade sat up, ignoring the pinch in his chest. Already his light had dimmed. "We should be coming to the end."

A dark archway appeared, outlining a darker night. The boats scraped the rock as they passed through the opening into the bitter cold. A sliver of moon hung low in the sky, peering behind filmy clouds. A heavy mist obscured the east side of the river, just beyond a thick tree line. It drifted into the river, clinging to the boats' hulls. Their wake sent it swirling, closing in behind. Towering cliffs rose to their left, disappearing into darkness.

"Now what, Kade?" Avery whispered.

"We should reach the Bastek Fjord by morning," Kade said. "Another day on foot to the catacomb entrance, if we hurry and are not intercepted."

"Not bloody likely." Avery cast a wary glance to a cluster of trees gathered on the riverbank as though monitoring their progress. "What's that?" he said, pointing past the trees.

Tilman growled and gave the river another aggressive push with his paddle.

The mist curled and danced around the trunks, drawing nearer.

"'Tis only a cloud," Tilman said.

But on the fringe of the cloud, a shadow seemed to move.

Kade kept his eye on it. "What it may conceal is something we best not find out."

CHAPTER EIGHTEEN

"Raelyn!" Peter's sharp voice brought Raelyn to full attention.

She snapped her eyes open. Standing over her in a small concrete room, her brother. His face was lined with worry, but his blue eyes shone. He took hold of her arms and pulled her up into a hug.

Of course, he could touch her.

Then he ducked his head and glanced around before steering her into a corner.

A few utilitarian tables along one wall held scattered papers and books. People, none of whom she recognized, stood in protective groups or sat at the tables looking through magazines or eating from plastic bowls. A woman sat in a chair with small children encircling her as she read a book to them. But every one of them seemed to be experiencing a low-level shock.

"Where are you?" Raelyn whispered.

Peter let out a breath and turned away from the room.

"The National Guard was called in. They ordered a curfew when the police couldn't control the riots." He swallowed. "Yesterday Dallas was bombed."

"What?" Raelyn whispered. "Who? Why?"

Peter shrugged. "Chinese? Russians? Canadians—"

"Canada?"

"I'm telling you, it's beyond crazy here. I came with most of the neighborhood to this church down the road. They have a basement where we go when the sirens start. Hey! Dad's here . . ."

He looked over his shoulder. "Somewhere . . ."

"Peter, look, there's something I need to tell you." Raelyn's throat threatened to close.

". . . he told me to find him if you showed up . . ."

"Peter, listen, you need to know this."

He started to turn around and Raelyn grabbed his shoulder.

"Peter! Forget about Dad for a second!"

"What're you talking about?" He turned back, frowning.

"I mean . . ." Raelyn took a deep breath. She couldn't waste time. The water was rising. "I found out why your name was written in our Bible. Why you can enter Alnok. Why"—she grasped his hand, exposing his palm—"you have this mark and not me."

Peter tried to pull his hand away. "Look, whatever it is, we have bigger fish to fry."

Raelyn shook her head, gripping his hand harder, tears leaking onto her cheeks.

"Rae, it's okay." Peter relaxed and gave her his full attention. "What? What do I need to know?"

Fear, despair, exhaustion rose in Raelyn's chest, as if the incoming tide was in her heart, not just washing over her feet. It built up in her throat and burst into a series of hitching sobs.

"It's you who's supposed to be here! Not me! That's why Cosyn attacked you. Made you sick. I was never supposed to be here! It's why I've made a mess of things! Why the world is falling apart!"

"Peter?" Her father's deep voice cut through the torrent of words. She gasped and looked past Peter.

Her dad, thin, haggard, gray, stood with his arms slack and his shoulders slumped as other people hustled past, oblivious to the family reunion. His eyes, Peter's exact shade, misted with tears.

"Is that . . . are you talking to Raelyn?" A hesitant smile played at the corners of his mouth.

Raelyn wiped her burning face. He couldn't see her. Couldn't have heard what she just said. Or he wouldn't be smiling.

He ambled up next to Peter, scanning the corner as though hoping to catch some glimpse of his daughter. Then he looked at Peter.

"She can hear me?"

Peter nodded and took a step back. Raelyn finally released his hand, eyeing her father.

Fulton's smile grew. He looked in Raelyn's direction, shaking his head. "Peter said . . . but I never imagined . . . couldn't have thought possible . . ."

He gave Peter a double take; his smile evaporated. "What's wrong? Is she okay?"

"Yeah, yeah, she's okay." He ran a hand through his hair. "At least I think so. She um . . ."

Raelyn shook her head violently. It was bad enough for Peter to know. He couldn't tell her dad.

"She seems to think I should be there instead of her."

Raelyn's mouth dropped open. "How could you . . ."

Fulton raised his eyebrows and turned back. "What makes you think you're not supposed to be there?"

Raelyn glared at Peter. "It's a firstborn thing."

"Only firstborns are supposed to go to Alnok?"

"No, I mean, I don't know. The prophecy only mentioned a child of Micah, our ancestor."

Peter shook his head. "But that would mean you too—"

"What's she saying?" Fulton asked.

"The prophecy, it somehow referred to me."

Raelyn shook her head. "No, not exactly. You don't understand—"

"She says we don't understand."

Fulton took a step into the corner where he guessed his daughter was, based on the direction of Peter's gaze.

"I understand more than you think. You suppose Mom didn't share her family history with me?" He dug into his front pocket and pulled out the amulet, nearly identical to the one around Raelyn's neck. "I know her family has always been under some curse. One tragedy after another. It wasn't until Peter told me he saw you in . . . Alnok that it all came together."

"Then you know it should have been Peter—"

"Raelyn," Peter interjected. "Why are you saying it 'should have been' me?"

Fulton frowned. "Should have been? There's a lot of 'should-have-beens' in our lives. 'Should have been' is never as important as what *is*. Raelyn, listen to me. No matter how all of this was predicted to happen, the fact is, you're there. Not Peter."

Fresh tears streaked down Raelyn's face. This man, who had spent so much time focused on her brothers, was looking at her as though she was the only person in the world who mattered. And he couldn't even see her.

"You closed the first two portals," he continued. "Not Peter. You saved your brother's life. All our lives."

"But I keep making the same mistakes! I was so stupid. I've tried to be a good leader. I thought I knew better than anyone. And Lima made me feel like I had all the answers. I just took off from the others. It makes sense now. Why I struggle so much. Peter should have led them."

"She's made mistakes," Peter relayed. "Listened to someone called Lima . . . Rae, you're not making any sense. You think I wouldn't struggle if I was there instead of you?"

Fulton shook his head. "You're not listening. You can't judge your strength by how you think someone else might have performed in your shoes."

Raelyn looked at Peter. Surely, he believed he could have done better.

"Rae, even if I was the one called, you were the one who answered. That's what matters."

"You should know something else," her father added. "I said I didn't realize everything that was going on until the day Peter told me he saw you. But if there was a prophecy about your mom's family going to Alnok, it would have been her."

Raelyn sucked in a breath. Could this have all started before Peter got sick? She'd never asked about the family lines of the others. Hadn't even thought about her mom's connection.

Fulton glanced at Peter and then back to the corner. "I think there was something else going on when you drove your mom and brother home."

Raelyn stood stock-still. Cosyn had tried to stop Peter, but would he have tried to thwart her mom first?

"Think back," her dad continued. "You thought you'd had too much to drink. But you weren't even over the legal limit. Could there have been something else?"

Raelyn couldn't breathe. All this time, could it have been Cosyn who caused the accident? She looked at the green tiled floor and focused on that day. The day she had spent a year trying to forget.

Something in the road . . . a shadow. Squirrel? Rabbit? She had jerked the wheel to avoid running it over. She'd tried to correct, but the steering wheel wouldn't move, kept turning to the left . . . like something had caught the tire . . . or controlled the wheel . . .

She looked back at her father, trying to get a breath. "Do you really think . . ."

Peter was looking back and forth from Raelyn to their dad. "Do you really think so?"

Fulton shrugged. "We may never know. But I think it's a likely explanation."

Raelyn's shoulders fell. "It doesn't matter now. Lima's gone. Cosyn's gone. I'm alone on the beach with no way to get back and the tide's coming in."

Peter stepped back and looked at Raelyn's feet, as though expecting to see water rising. "There's no one to get Raelyn back," he said to Fulton.

"Can you . . . are you able to . . ."

Peter shook his head. "I don't think so. Not with Raelyn here."

A siren warbled at a distance and the Durinial jolted like a shock. Those who had been wandering aimlessly began to scatter.

Fulton looked around the room and then at Peter. "Get to the inner room."

Peter frowned. "What about you?"

Fulton glanced at the amulet in his hand. "I can't say this thing will lead me to it, but I found one of the portals before."

The siren continued, rising and falling, the Durinial humming in time.

"Dad, I don't know what you can do—"

Fulton gave Peter a grim smile and then looked back into the corner, his blue eyes hard as steel. "I'll do whatever I can."

"But it could be anywhere," Peter argued. "There could be more than one."

Fulton's jaw was set. "Let me worry about that."

"Rae." Peter grabbed her hand. "Stay with me. I don't know what's happening in Alnok, but maybe together we can get you back there."

"I don't think so, Peter." Raelyn unbuckled the Bokar. "But with your connection, maybe *you* can." She held the book out to him.

He pushed her hand away, shaking his head. "No way, sis. Unless"—he looked down at the book—"I can get there and bring you back?"

"Cosyn took my seripyn away. It's the only way for me to remain in Alnok. But maybe not for you . . ."

She was grasping for anything. Some way to get to the plye. Some way to close it.

"Peter, the shelter," Fulton barked and then looked at Raelyn. "I'm coming, sweetie." He bolted from the room and disappeared into the chaos of people.

Peter shifted on his feet, his brow furrowed, looking from Raelyn to the Bokar.

"Take it, Peter!"

He pressed his lips together, so hard they turned white, and nodded. He reached for the book, and his hand went through it.

"Wha—" He tried again then looked at Raelyn. "I can't."

Raelyn's heart pounded; her stomach clenched. "No!" She tried to shove the book at Peter, but it passed through his chest.

Tears again filled her eyes. She looked at Peter as he blurred. But not from the tears. He was disappearing. Liquid trickled down her throat. The room faded.

"Peter?"

Water surged over her calves, and cold air hit her face as the beach came into focus.

"Rae!" Peter shouted.

"Raelyn!"

Another voice. A form taking shape, kneeling in front of her, shadowed with the setting sun kissing the horizon behind it.

Raelyn blinked, her eyes adjusting . . . the shadow moved in front of the sun—

"Larken?"

The Shalhalan, drowned at sea, was standing in front of her, his boyish face shining with a pale-blue light.

She shook her head. "I must be dead . . ." she whispered.

"Raelyn!" he shouted with joy and wrapped his arms around her, lifting her up with him, squeezing her until she couldn't breathe.

"What . . ." Raelyn could manage no more in his tight grasp.

He released her and looked over her face, as though to make sure she was still there. A wave surged up to her knees.

"I will explain later. First"—he pointed at the Bokar, still in her hands—"secure that."

Raelyn nodded and buckled the book back into its holster. Larken grabbed her hand and pulled her, sloshing through the next wave. The water receded and pulled at Raelyn's legs as though insisting she join it. She pushed her legs through. If she floated out to sea, she'd be right back where she started, in the Kaidilas with Nahesakai the water dragon.

The sand sucked at her boots, each step a battle of its own.

"We must get to the cove. It will take us inland and to higher ground. But it is miles ahead." He glanced at the sea as another wave pounded against them, rising to Raelyn's thighs.

But she couldn't take her eyes off Larken.

"I thought you were dead," she said as she let him lead her along the cliff wall.

"Nay." He shook his head. "Detained." He pulled her harder as another wave nearly took her off her feet. It drew away as Larken glanced at her.

"I am glad you are a strong swimmer."

CHAPTER NINETEEN

Raelyn gasped for breath as the next wave knocked her off her feet and shoved her against the cliff wall. The rocks sliced her hands as she tried to push away. Larken pulled hard, griping her hand, nearly pulling her arm from its socket. Her shoulder and back injuries came alive, aching reminders of the series of mistakes she'd made.

But Dad said the wreck might have been—

It didn't matter what he said. He wasn't here.

"Do not slow down, Raelyn!" Larken shouted as the wave receded.

She stumbled, righting herself, but another wave pounded her. Larken wrapped his arms around her and lifted her above the water. As the wave pulled back, her satchel, now completely water-logged, threw her off balance and she stumbled.

The next wave roared in.

"Dive beneath!" Larken shouted, running at the wave.

"Larken!"

He clasped his hands and ducked his head between his arms, diving beneath the foam. Raelyn yanked the satchel over her head, dropping it in the sand as she ran after him then mimicked his moves, sucking in a deep breath. The wave rolled over her and she rose to the surface. She had dodged the wave, but the sea had claimed the last of her supplies. Larken bobbed nearby.

"What about the dragon?" she called.

"Follow me! Stay near the cliff!" he shouted and waved her closer.

She swam with him as a swell lifted her and threatened to force her into the rocks. Larken pushed her off, swimming furiously away from the cliff. Then, as the water receded, they both swam toward the cliff to keep from being drawn out to sea. They followed the pattern, over and over as the sun disappeared, turning the water the color of hyram feathers. Raelyn kept Larken's light in her sight. It was the only way she knew which direction to swim. But her arms were on fire and her legs refused to kick.

"Come on, Raelyn!" Larken called.

His pale blue-light, shining like a beacon in the black sea, drifted away. A wave rose between them, and Raelyn stopped as the light disappeared.

"Larken!" she screamed.

Blind panic threatened to seize her muscles. Somewhere beneath her was the water dragon. Probably stalking her right now.

The wave rolled on and Larken's light winked in and out in the distance.

Raelyn grunted as she forced one arm, then the next, over her head, through the water, propelling her forward.

His light grew brighter. She was closing the distance.

She barely registered their change in direction as they rounded a corner and began swimming inland. Rather than fight the waves, she allowed them to thrust her forward. Finally, her feet dragged across the sandy bottom. Ahead, Larken was scrambling onto shore.

Foam swirled around her as she struggled to stand and waded after him, her arms hanging uselessly. Another wave battered her legs. She staggered, but Larken was there, his strong arm steadying her, heaving her onto shore. They both dropped onto the sand and sprawled out just beyond the tide, spluttering and gasping.

Raelyn turned to him. "Larken, how?" she managed, before coughing up more water.

"Come," he said, hefting himself to his feet and holding out his hand. "Let us get clear of the tide. It will continue to rise."

Raelyn complied, dragging her feet through the soft sand until they reached the back of a cove carved by the ever-crashing sea. They shimmied onto a ledge behind an overhang that blocked some of the bitter wind. When Larken seemed satisfied they were safely above the waterline, he eased Raelyn onto a rock and began collecting branches washed up by the sea.

She huddled, shivering, as she watched him, too tired to ask questions. It could all still be an illusion . . .

"Here," he said, tossing the sticks into a pile in front of her. He crouched and passed his hand over them. A blue fire burst from the center.

"We'll need more wood," he said, holding his hands out to the thin flames as they faded to yellow.

Raelyn nodded, staring at him, her mind blank with exhaustion.

Staring into the firelight, he seemed to be contemplating what to say next, so Raelyn waited. The waves roared just beneath them in the dark. Stars sputtered to life, high and cold, but the moon stayed away. Larken's blue aura, so familiar and comforting, chased away days of anxiety. But the memory of Jinny's scream rammed the fear back into place.

"What happened?" she finally asked.

Larken took a deep breath. "When the ship went down, I was dragged away," he began, the firelight dancing in his blue eyes.

"By Nahesakai?"

Larken shook his head. "Kaimir. Water sprites." Raelyn pictured tiny fairies with tails. Larken must have seen the look of skepticism on her face.

"As big as a man. And stronger." He grimaced. "And ugly."

"So, you were what, held captive?"

"Exactly. An island not far from the wreck." Larken suddenly looked serious. "I implored Arkonai for your protection and success in Endyle."

Raelyn nodded and swallowed.

"He heard my plea. I knew you had closed the plye because the kaimir retreated, or were called away. I swam to shore and have been tracking you ever since."

"Joshua and Jinny." Raelyn's heart pounded, hope and fear mingled with each beat. "Do you know where they are? I heard Jinny scream, but that was hours ago."

Larken shook his head. "I entered the Boiland ruin, but you had gone. When I picked up your trail, it had diverged. I chose your path."

Raelyn scowled. "Why?"

Larken blinked. "I did not know whose path I followed. I could only trust there was a good reason to split up, but to travel south . . ." He gave her a questioning frown.

"Was a stupid choice."

Larken shrugged. "I sensed something malevolent followed."

Raelyn drew her knees to her chest. She wanted to bury her hands in her face, hide from his questioning gaze. Instead, she looked into the fire.

"I was the one who followed. I left Joshua and Jinny. Just like Avery left us in Kulum." She held back her tears and forced herself to look at Larken.

He clenched his jaw but nodded in understanding. "Poor decisions can seem wise when they are manipulated. Deception comes in many forms. We presume to be incorruptible, but Cosyn finds new ways to snake into our choices. Making one look appealing, blinding you to the danger."

Raelyn shook her head. "It wasn't Cosyn."

Larken's frown deepened. "I sensed his presence."

"He did appear on the shore. But it was Lima."

Larken gave no indication of recognition. "One of his horde? I am unfamiliar with this creature."

"A girl. Or who I thought to be a girl. She saved us from the Endylites. Promised to take us to the Schade Catacombs. But then Cosyn appeared and they . . ."

She let go of her knees and turned to him. "Larken, she told me something. I—I don't know if she lied."

"As a cohort of Cosyn, it would be safe to say she lied."

"I don't know." The tears finally fell. "I think she actually told the truth. Some version of it, anyway."

"What did she tell you?"

"That I was never meant to be here."

Larken scoffed. "Raelyn, have you learned nothing from Kade—"

"Listen. I'm the only one who sees only one person. My brother. And he's the only one who's seen Alnok."

"Seen? You are sure?"

Raelyn gave a bitter chuckle. "Oh, I'm sure. Lima said every member of the Cord is a firstborn . . . but me."

Larken frowned and looked at the ground between them. "Yes, I believe this is true."

"The Bokar"—she unbuckled the book with trembling fingers—"it was never mine." She held it out for Larken. He needed to take it from her. Get it to its rightful owner. Anyone but her. But he only looked at it.

"I'm not the one who was called." She waited until he met her eyes. "It's Peter," she whispered.

"If that were so, he would be here." The simplicity of his statement jarred Raelyn's next retort: Peter would have been the true leader, he wouldn't have allowed Lydia to be killed, Avery to abandon them, Kade to leave, and he certainly wouldn't have followed Lima.

"But . . . the prophecy . . ." she said weakly.

"Said nothing of firstborns."

"Everyone else is. Cosyn attacked Peter to keep him from getting here. My dad said he attacked my mom—"

"Your dad said?"

"It's . . . it's a long story. The fact is, I never belonged here."

Larken leaned forward. "When Kade found the prophecy, no one believed him." He shook his head and gave her a bitter smile. "Some of us came around. But only he trusted the words completely."

"Okay, sure. Kade always encouraged me—"

Larken held out a hand to stop her. "Those who either believed the prophecy, or at least trusted Kade, began preparing for the temporals' return. Kade gathered skilled craftspeople from Shalhala to create the weapons you now wield. A shield, crown, torch, sword, and . . . staff."

Raelyn frowned, then shook her head. "I don't understand . . ."

"Kade went away to pray. He was gone for many seasons. When he returned, he called for a new item to be crafted. A book, powerful enough to house the pages of Shalhala. A book designed with one person in mind." He smiled softly. "A storyteller. A wielder of words."

"Me," Raelyn breathed.

"Only you."

"What happened to the staff?" She continued in a whisper, as though she may break a sacred spell. One in which her redemption hung.

Larken patted her arm. "That is a mystery for another time. You should also know, Altizara helped in the Bokar's creation."

Raelyn shook her head and looked back into the fire. All the talk of prophecies and callings, it never occurred to her the plan might have changed. Or contingencies could be made, their course altered. Not only was she supposed to be here, Kade and Altizara had prepared for her arrival.

As Larken searched for more kindling and tended the fire, Raelyn unbuckled the Bokar. She placed it in her lap and wiped a tear from her cheek. She traced the vine-and-leaf pattern pressed into the cover. The leather still showed no signs of wear. She opened the book and turned each page, a moment ago blinding her with light, now dark and quiet. But as she touched them, she could feel a current, not unlike the vibrations from the Durinial, beneath her fingers. She had always thought of it as a book. Text written long ago in need of a translator. But it was more of a journal, really. The writing and the reading, equally important. The words had always been exactly what she needed them to be, at exactly the right time. Nothing more, nothing less.

The Bokar was more than a weapon created in a hidden dimension. It was a book, a weapon created for *her*.

Larken stood and looked up. "I thought we may wait for morning . . ."

Raelyn jumped to her feet, a new energy flowing from her heart to her toes and fingertips. "Jinny."

Larken looked her up and down. "You are recovered enough for the climb?"

Raelyn nodded as she buckled the Bokar into its holster. "I could climb to the moon."

Larken chuckled. "Let us hope they are only at the top of the cliff."

CHAPTER TWENTY

On the horizon, a reluctant sun peered through a quickly collecting fog. The boats carrying Kade's company glided down the river toward the Bastek Fjord. But the struggling daylight could not chase away the mist or the darkness. The griten remained in the tunnel, as though barricaded in. The tunnel was the remnant of the temporals. This fjord belonged wholly to Cosyn. Without the creatures' cheerful green light, the river turned black. Even the lights of Tilman, Altizara, Othana, and Emaline's dimmed, as though suppressed beneath the shadows of Cosyn's lair.

"Are we close?" Avery whispered as he rowed, maintaining a consistent distance behind Tilman.

"Very close," Kade said, keeping a wary eye on the wall of mist, ten feet off the eastern shore.

Fog was not uncommon in Alnok. But this mist seemed to have purpose. It pressed in, building and growing, a wall of whirling white. It hindered any escape east, forcing them to the eastern shore. Or it concealed something within. Kade turned his attention to the river. The dark surface reflected his light, but something swirled beneath, independent of the current, a multitude of tiny whirlpools. This was not griten.

"I thought we might meet some friendly faces," Avery said, staring up at the towering obsidian cliffs. "How is it the soldiers from Herlov haven't made it here? We didn't have much of a head start. And we took the long way around."

His words were light, but his face was drawn and heavy with worry.

"We do not know what path they took," Kade said, struggling to sit up. His energy continued to flow, his light a steady glow, but the dragon's blight festered across his chest. It seemed he was correct. It would not heal as long as the dragon lived. "With or without additional troops, we will enter the catacombs and find Gabe."

"Right, of course," Avery said, giving the water another push with his paddle.

"Bring us just around this bend, Tilman," Kade said. "We will leave the river before we reach the fjord. Continue on foot."

Tilman nodded. As the river widened and banked right, he gave a few forceful strokes, then inserted his oar into the water, using a pry stroke to guide them toward the western shore. The metal boat grated onto a gravel beach.

Avery followed suit, then eased his oar into the boat, as he peered into the shallow waters. "Kade." Even in what could not be more than a few inches of water, the bottom remained obscured, ss though the river were made of ink.

"I think I see something . . ." Avery continued. "Yes! Right here!" He pointed, leaning over the water.

Kade grabbed his arm.

"Do not touch the water."

"All right, all right," Avery said, shrugging from Kade's grip.

"Not the griten, is it?" He shot a glance at Kade, his face grim.

"No. Do not touch the water," Kade repeated.

Avery nodded but remained mesmerized by the strange phenomenon.

Altizara, Othana, and Tilman clambered to shore. Tilman helped Emaline disembark. Once she was on shore, he held his hand out to Kade, who used the staff to steady himself.

"Avery, wait," Tilman said as he supported Kade until he was out of the boat.

Avery stood, continuing to look into the water, first one side, then the other. He clambered over his pack in the center of the boat. The canoe teetered right. He pinwheeled his arms and took one step out of the boat, splashing into ankle-deep water. Yelping, he scrambled back into the boat and onto shore. He nearly knocked Tilman over, as he tried to get away from the water, before crumpling to the ground, moaning and gripping his ankle.

Kade knelt beside him. Avery continued to writhe as Kade pried his hands off his ankle and raised his pant leg.

"What is that?"Avery sat up on his elbows, wincing. "Like a leech?"

He reached for the small oblong globular creature attached to his boot. It raised both sides of its body like engorged, slimy wings. A stinger was buried deep in Avery's ankle. Kade grabbed Avery's hand before he could touch the creature.

"Emaline," Kade said, nodding to Avery.

Emaline knelt at Avery's shoulders, her face stitched with concern. She took his hand from Kade and held him still.

Kade passed his hand over the vermin, illuminating it with golden light. It twisted and Avery screamed. Kade continued to pass beams of light over the creature until, with a shudder, it fell onto the gravel and was still.

Kade pulled off Avery's boot. From a perfectly round puncture, a green substance oozed.

"The wound will fester," Kade said.

"It's poisoned?" Avery groaned.

"Yes. We cannot travel until we treat it. Emaline, prepare the herbs."

Clattering sounded across the river. The rolling cloud moved closer.

"Kade, the mist . . ." Altizara said.

"Emaline." Kade gestured to Avery's ankle.

She moved from Avery's head to his feet, pulling a leather packet from her bag. Othana took up Emaline's previous position, holding Avery's shoulders.

Into her palm, Emaline shook out the healing blend. She spat into it, not wasting time with oils or pastes, and pressed it onto Avery's ankle.

Avery stiffened and squeezed his eyes shut, panting, his breath puffs of vapor.

Kade rummaged in his satchel for the seripyn. The canteen was notably lighter. He popped off the top and lifted Avery's head.

"We must go," Kade murmured as he tipped the contents into Avery's mouth. "Can you walk?"

Avery swallowed, then continued to pant, but nodded.

Emaline tied a frayed strip of cloth around Avery's ankle and, with Othana's help, tugged his boot back on.

Avery gripped Kade's arm as he was lifted to his feet. Othana was there, taking Avery's weight onto her own shoulder.

"Tilman." Kade waved him to the lead as they made their way to the cliff. "Scout ahead, we must get away from whatever gathers in the mist. Hopefully, we will encounter nothing ahead."

Tilman jogged past them all and Kade dropped back to walk next to Othana. She and Emaline flanked Avery, helping him limp along. Altizara, with Avery's pack and shield slung over one shoulder and an arrow drawn, walked backward as she watched the growing mist, now upon the river.

Steady sloshing joined the dull clanking, as though the fog stirred the waters as it passed.

"Kade," Altizara whispered. "There is something in the mist."

Othana glanced back. "The 'something' is following."

"How can it be so painful and numb at the same time?" Avery groaned, squeezing his eyes shut, oblivious to the pursuing fog.

"The pain will pass," Kade said, keeping his voice low. "The numbness may linger. But we cannot let the mist reach us."

He increased their pace, but they could not seem to pull ahead. A sly whisper, a hundred hissed secrets, drifted from the mist.

The sun, trapped behind thick clouds, brought no warmth. Rather than disperse the mist, the light gave it an ethereal glow as it continued to bite at their heels. White tendrils crept forward like feelers, reaching out, searching for their prey.

"Do you know what's in there?" Avery asked.

"Whatever it is," Emaline said, "we will do best to get as far away as possible."

Othana adjusted Avery's arm to get a firmer grip. "We will be trapped when we reach the cliffs."

They had created some distance, but only by pushing Avery's limits. It would not be long before Kade reached his own. Using his light to remove the leech had depleted precious reserves.

"Where do we go? How do we get away?" Avery asked.

"South," Kade said. "The entrance to the catacombs lies south. We will find no escape, but, perhaps, a source of protection?" Kade glanced at Avery, catching his eye. "You might hold the mist back until we reach our destination?"

Avery pressed his lips together and stared ahead with a furrowed brow. Then his expression cleared, and he nodded. He straightened his shoulders, which threw the women aiding him off balance, but Kade could not have been prouder.

"When the time comes," Avery said, forcing more weight onto his injured leg, "I'll keep us safe."

Tears of pride pricked Kade's eyes. The temporals's transformation from fearful businessman to fearless warrior was astonishing, though not surprising. Avery's determination seemed to motivate them all. They moved faster, catching up with Tilman. Even Kade found his breathing easier, his footsteps firmer.

Although they stayed ahead of the mist, a consistent clatter arose. As mid-day passed, a single shout pierced the veil.

Ahead, the cliffs rose. They hurried to the base, black and glistening as though slick with mucus. While they stopped long enough for Emaline to apply another poultice to Avery's ankle, Altizara handed him his shield and pack. She joined Tilman as they stationed themselves as sentinels.

The whisper grew, now only fifty feet away, moving as a slow wave about to overtake them.

Avery stood, tested his leg, and found he was stable. He grabbed the Cieskild and limped past Tilman and Altizara, who exchanged a glance that was part admiration, part apprehension.

More clanging. Another shout.

The mist swirled and shadows passed back and forth in a frenzy.

Othana moved to Kade's right, her bow raised and pointing into the cloud wall. Emaline appeared on his left; her stance ready to take on whatever was coming.

The mist broke away at the center and a shadow filled the space, growing in definition and size as it stepped out.

"Hello, Kade." Lady Ryla flashed a cruel smile.

CHAPTER TWENTY-ONE

As daylight rose, Raelyn gripped the cliff face with numb fingers, straining for the next handhold. The howling wind whipped at her back. Within the craggy rock, pin-like stickers pricked her fingers until they were raw and bleeding.

Even without a backpack full of supplies, she and Larken had made little progress through the night. She shouldn't have assured Larken she could handle a more direct route than the meandering switchbacks. Her snail's pace required Larken to pause and wait over and over. And she still couldn't see the top of the cliff.

She welcomed the pain. And the cold. At least she felt something.

The joy and relief of Larken's revelation was wearing away. The Bokar made for her? It was a good story. But was it true? Yet another instance of Kade withholding information.

He would say: "*I reveal only as much as you can handle.*"

Maybe so, but knowing the Bokar had been made especially for me might have gone a long way to confirming my calling here.

"*You knew the Bokar was created for you.*"

Yeah, but it just meant it was made for Micah's heir. That's Peter too.

"*If you had known Peter was first pick, would it have helped?*"

Okay, maybe Kade wouldn't put it that way. But he always seemed to have his reasons for how he prepared the Cord. What he told them and when.

And what about the Bokar? Her connection to the book was irrefutable. Peter couldn't have fared better.

Given the closure of two plyes, it certainly seemed she was meant to be here. But it didn't change the fact that she was the runner-up.

The mental ping-pong went on all morning until her head hurt. She forced her thoughts to turn to Joshua and Jinny, ignoring her aching hands and weary limbs.

"Are we close?" she called up.

"Yes," Larken whispered back.

What would cause him to keep quiet? She tried to listen past her panting and pounding pulse. Rustling trees? A grunt? Nothing discernable. But she stayed silent.

The sun trundled its way up a hazy sky, and by midday, Raelyn could see the top of the cliff and the trees beyond. As they crested the bluff, there was no mistaking the shuffling and growling somewhere within the trees.

Larken remained crouched as he moved away from the edge and Raelyn mimicked his stance. He ducked behind a mound of boulders and waited.

Jinny's scream had sounded so close. But that was over twenty-four hours ago.

"Larken?" Raelyn whispered.

He raised a silencing hand as he strained to see through the forest.

The trees creaked and parted. Raelyn had mental flashes of the varga, the hellhounds that had chased them from Durnoth. Then the goblin-like lushor in the forest of Endyle. But what lumbered from the trunks, twenty feet tall and covered in dark hair, was worse. Raelyn's heart pounded. This was what had caused Jinny to scream.

The creature caught sight of them, roared, and charged.

Larken leaped to his feet and dashed back toward the cliff. The giant hesitated for only a second before giving chase. Larken, his heels on the edge of the cliff, leaned forward, his eyes locked on the giant. One push and Larken would go careening off the side. A great crash sounded from the trees. Raelyn spun as a black mass, as tall as a house, loped after its partner. It caught sight of Raelyn and skidded to a stop, adjusting its trajectory.

"Larken!"

Larken yanked a dagger from his belt but spun and darted out of the way as the first giant closed the distance. It reached out for him but stumbled over the edge.

Raelyn ran toward the cliff. Maybe she could use the same strategy as Larken.

"Catch!" Larken tossed her the dagger and ran past.

She caught it by the hilt as Larken sprinted toward a third giant exiting the trees.

"Aim under its arms!" he shouted back.

Raelyn nodded. She tried to recall her hand-to-hand combat training. Nothing surfaced.

The giant was on her in seconds. She ducked as it swiped at her, hooked claws passing just over her head.

Though clearly strong enough to take off her head, its slow reaction allowed her to rise, spin, and lurch for its side, aiming for the armpit. But she missed and stumbled, splaying onto the gravel.

She barely got her weary legs under her before it was on her again. She sprung into its raised arms, its rotten breath filling her nostrils, shifted so she could get both hands on the dagger, planted the blade high on the creature's side, and jerked toward her. It slid into the soft flesh.

It roared and swung its long arms, batting at the dagger's hilt. Raelyn glimpsed Larken, standing over the third creature now on the ground, blue light surrounding them both.

Raelyn backed away from the giant. It had knocked the dagger from its flesh, but heaved for breath as thick, crimson blood flowed from the wound. It took an unsteady step toward her, then stumbled and fell forward.

Crunching footsteps rushed toward her.

"Come," Larken said, grabbing her hand. "There will be others."

Raelyn scooped up the dagger as they raced past the slayed giant. They hurried around a stone wall blocking the view of the sea. She blanched at the acrid odor of urine and the sickly smell of rotting meat.

"How will we find them?" she whispered.

"They must be—"

Larken was thrown sideways as a giant powered around a rock formation. It glared down at him, then looked at Raelyn.

Raelyn gripped the dagger in both hands, ready to attempt the same strategy as with the previous giant. But this one seemed brighter than the first. It shifted its gaze from the dagger to Larken, who was on his hands and knees, shaking his head.

Raelyn took a step forward, drawing its attention from the vulnerable Shalhalan. The plan worked. It strode forward, glaring, growling.

Rather than swiping at Raelyn, it rammed its arm forward and grabbed her hair, pulling her off her feet. Raelyn beat at it with the dagger, but it was like stabbing thick rubber.

It dragged her around the outcrop. She kicked, wrenched, and pulled, ignoring the pain in her scalp.

Finally, as though more annoyed than hurt, it let go and turned, roaring at her. She cowered as it advanced.

"Raelyn!" Larken shouted, but he was too far. The giant was over her. Raelyn closed her eyes and curled up, still gripping the dagger.

It roared again. In pain.

She watched as it spun. Behind it, Joshua back away a few steps, the Ruah glinting.

"Under its arm!" she shouted, staggering to her feet.

He gave a curt nod, advancing on the giant.

Larken dashed past her to Joshua's side and held his hands out, his blue light shining. Joshua stared at him, his mouth hanging open, but jolted from his shock when the giant, waving its arms as though to beat away the light, bellowed again.

Joshua darted to its side while it was blinded. He rammed the Ruah into the tender flesh under its arm. It wrenched away, howling, blood spurting in all directions. As it fell to its knees, its angry eyes held Raelyn for a moment before it slumped over.

"Joshua!" Raelyn ran at him and threw her arms around his neck.

He held her with one arm, the other still holding the dripping sword, and buried his face in her hair.

Raelyn jerked back. "Where's Jinny?"

Joshua let her go and waved her and Larken to follow.

"She's hurt," he panted. "Two of the giants attacked." He followed the stone wall around a corner. "I got one, but the other . . ."

He passed through a gap in the wall. "This way." He knelt a few paces away. "Jinny, I found them."

"Them?" Jinny called from inside the hole.

Tears filled Raelyn's eyes as soon as Jinny's head poked out. Dirt smudged her pale cheeks, and her dark hair was matted, but she smiled before disappearing back inside. She shoved a pack out and then another before sliding out, grimacing and favoring her left arm.

Larken and Raelyn helped her up as Joshua gathered the packs. She hugged Raelyn but didn't take her eyes off Larken.

"We must hurry," Larken said. "Can you travel?" he asked Jinny.

She winced as she nodded, her eyes still wide with shock.

"I am sure there will be more," Larken said, glancing over his shoulder. He paused and gave Jinny and then Joshua a quick grin. "It will take more than Nahesakai to defeat the great Larken," he said and chuckled.

"But—" Jinny protested.

"I will explain, but we must reach the Bastek Fjord before dawn." They raced from the cave back to the cliff side,

Jinny clutching her arm to her side. Once they were well clear of the trees, with their backs to an icy wind, they slowed just enough for Larken to pull Jinny's tunic to one side and look at her shredded shoulder. Raelyn blanched, swallowed, and forced her face to remain neutral.

Larken took a deep breath. "There are herbs in Alnok to heal this, but I have none."

"I'll be fine," Jinny said, pulling from Larken's grasp. "As long as I keep it still."

"We drank the rest of the seripyn," Joshua said. "Thought it might help her heal, and I couldn't risk fading while she was hurt."

Larken nodded. "That was wise, and likely why she is on her feet. Very good." He waved them on.

They finished the remaining food from Joshua and Jinny's packs as they walked. Larken began his tale of the kaimir, his escape and finding Raelyn.

"What about Lima?" Joshua asked.

Raelyn shook her head. The words caught in her throat. *I was wrong. I never should have left.*

"I—I'm so sorry. You were right. She's in league with Cosyn."

Keeping to facts, avoiding both of their gazes, she embarked on her own tale. She spared no detail, with Jinny stopping her from time to time with a question. Joshua remained silent.

"You swam all the way to the cove?" Jinny asked.

Raelyn nodded. "That's nothing compared to staying ahead of giants."

Jinny snorted. "And sleeping in a tree."

"What?"

Jinny nodded and filled them in on their own trek. She held her arm against her stomach, but her stride was fast and strong, matching her voice. Raelyn raised her eyebrows and looked at Joshua. He grinned and shrugged.

"After Joshua treated the wound, we could only wait. But when the giants left . . . we knew it was our only chance."

"And you know nothing of this Lima," Joshua asked Larken.

Larken shook his head. "Nay. Which means we should be on our utmost guard."

Raelyn shook her head and shivered. Weren't they always?

***

Once out of the forest, they traveled across a scrubby plain, away from the sea and west to the catacombs. When night fell, they pitched a hasty camp next to a sparse bush. Though still a few miles from the fjord, Larken was loath to get any closer without a plan. He lit a small fire, and for the first time since they parted ways at Lima's dwelling outside Boiland, Raelyn was face-to-face with Jinny and Joshua. The fire did little to chase away the chill, but the heat in her cheeks burned with shame.

"I never should have left you," she breathed, forcing the words as she stared into the flames. She looked at Jinny. Meeting Joshua's gaze, the light flickering in his blue eyes, was much harder. "I really thought I was doing the right thing."

"Who's to say you weren't?" Joshua asked.

Raelyn blinked and looked at him. "What'd you . . ."

She tried to say "mean," but her mouth went dry.

Jinny leaned forward. "He *means*, things might have turned out differently if you hadn't left. We do not know if Lima might have stopped us from leaving at all. She might have even kept Larken from finding us."

"The point is," Joshua continued, "we're all together again. Larken found you and got you to safety. You both got to Jinny and me in time."

"But I was so blinded by Lima's . . . lies," Raelyn choked. "She made it seem like I was the only one who could finish the quest."

"Well," Joshua drawled. "That's kinda true." He gestured to the Bokar.

Raelyn shook her head. "That's not how we ended up closing the one in Endyle. And besides . . ." She glanced at Larken, who offered a small smile. She had to tell them. They had to know.

"It was my brother who was meant to be here." Before either Joshua or Jinny could argue, Raelyn relayed all Lima had told her, followed by what Larken had revealed about the Bokar.

They spent a few moments in silence, the fire dancing and crackling in the steady wind. Raelyn let the two of them work through everything she'd said.

Joshua shrugged. "It goes back to what I said before. You goin' with Lima ended up working out. You comin' to Alnok did too. I'm sure your brother woulda been capable. But . . ." He cleared his throat. "I'm glad it was you."

Raelyn's heart swelled. Simple statements. But he couldn't have said anything more encouraging than if he had handed her the Nobel Peace Prize. Whatever Raelyn was about to face, reconciling with Joshua and Jinny filled her with fresh determination.

Larken smiled. "Each of you has contributed to the success of the quest. But you have yet to face your biggest challenge. You discovered your skills in Malvok and tested them on your journey to Shalhala. You learned to gird your mind in Endyle. All of this has shaped and trained you for what you are about to come up against."

"What is that?" Jinny asked. She leaned forward, her left arm still hugging her body, but her right resting on her knee. Gone was the fidgeting, the tense shoulders. Eager, but not fearful. She looked determined. Strong.

Larken sighed. "I only know of what Kade told me long ago. Entering the caverns was forbidden. It is land completely lost to Cosyn. But Kade loved his brother so. He always believed Cosyn could somehow be redeemed. Reconciled."

Raelyn tried to imagine the monster she had encountered ever wanting to be reunited with his brother. Impossible. He not only chose to defy his Creator, he reveled in the destruction he caused.

"Kade's been in the Schade Catacombs?" she asked.

Larken nodded. "To my knowledge, once."

"Kade mentioned them but never gave us details," Joshua said.

Larken blew out a heavy breath. "I wish I could give you a description. A weakness. A strategy. But what you will face will be different for each of you. Cosyn will find the chink in your armor and target it with the fiercest of his horde. This is the last remaining plye in Alnok. His last access to Earth Apparent. He will defend it with every weapon, both sword and vile creature. He will hew against your mind with temptation and bore into your spirit with despair."

Raelyn shivered and pulled the Bokar close. She may have been second pick, but she held the book crafted for a storyteller. Created for her.

They were quiet for a moment, each lost in thought as they watched the fire dwindle. A fine mist crept close to their camp.

"What do you suppose your chink is?" Jinny finally asked, looking at Joshua and posing the question as though asking about his favorite milkshake.

Joshua leaned back and gave her a cockeyed grin. "I dunno—"

"Fear," Jinny answered for him.

Joshua raised one eyebrow. "Oh?" He maintained a bemused expression. "The Seon tell you that?" He nodded to the circlet on her head.

"You are strong. And smart. And have much knowledge of war and battle. But you lack the control you think you should have. And that scares you."

Raelyn stole a glance at Joshua, sure an angry remark was coming. But he shrugged.

"You may be right," he said softly, squinting past the fire into the mist.

"What about you, Jinny?" Raelyn asked.

Jinny studied the ground. "Doubt," she said softly. "My parents were always the center of my universe. My father especially. I never considered a life outside what he dictated. But it was all coming apart when my mother became ill. Then I came here . . ."

"And now?" Joshua asked.

"I must acknowledge a path beyond my father's direction and outside my own understanding."

"If Kade were here, he'd say you overcome doubt with trust," Raelyn said.

"What do I trust?"

Raelyn picked at a stray thread on her pants. A good question that deserved an honest answer. What did *she* trust?

"Larken, for one," she offered.

Larken bowed his head to Raelyn.

"Me," Joshua added and winked.

"And me," Raelyn said, and grabbed Jinny's hand.

Jinny gave her hand a squeeze.

Raelyn would prove she could be trusted.

As the night wore on, Larken launched into tale after tale of Kade's continual protection of the temporals in Alnok when they ruled the royal cities. How he battled Cosyn when he waged war against them. His absolute belief in the prophecy.

"He is tireless in his defense of you." Larken looked at each of them. Jinny wiped at her eyes and nodded. Joshua stared into the flames, as though reliving some of those conflicts.

"I tell you this," Larken continued, "so you understand Kade confronted the full force of Cosyn's power in the Schade Catacombs. Kade's faith, like that of all Guardians, is unshakable. His devotion to Arkonai does not deviate. But what Kade encountered nearly destroyed him. Not his body. Not even his mind. He nearly lost hope. And without hope, he would have been defeated."

The mist continued to encroach. A layer of cold moisture draped Raelyn's hands as they dangled over her folded knees. The fire sputtered. Much like the fog through which Raelyn, Joshua, and Gabe traveled to rescue Jinny from Olyaund, it signaled both hope and fear. They could stay hidden, but so could any of Cosyn's horde.

A swift shuffle, quiet but consistent, began within the thick fog to the north. It was impossible to tell the proximity or the source of the noise. Jinny and Raelyn huddled closer on Jinny's blanket.

"We should get on to the fjord," Joshua said, glancing over his shoulder into the darkness.

Larken nodded, poking at the fire. "We will. Soon. Take some rest. We must get across without coming into contact with the water."

Joshua cocked his head. "Why?"

"Something Kade mentioned. The water belongs to Cosyn. Just as we avoided Theurham, we must avoid the fjord"

"All right," Joshua nodded slowly. "We'll need a boat?"

Larken shook his head. "I do not know. Boat, bridge, tightrope. There must be a way."

CHAPTER TWENTYTWO

Avery launched at Ryla. "You back-stabbing bi—"

"Avery!" Kade shouted.

Tilman grabbed his arm and yanked him back.

Avery jerked his shoulder out of Tilman's grasp, taking two hobbling steps away from him.

Ryla gazed at Avery, her eyes flitting to his ankle, as though bored. Then she looked at Kade with raised eyebrows as though to question his choice in champions. Ruby-red light seeped from her shoulders, her auburn hair which was pulled back in a tight bun, and from her hands, making them seemed stained with blood. A sneering smile curled her lips. The mist danced behind her, swirling with shadows. It rolled back to reveal two rows of soldiers. Kade recognized a couple of them from the mountains. A dozen more stood at attention, surrounding Ryla.

"You never give up, do you?" she said.

"No," Kade said. "But it seems you have. You gave up on your people and your Creator."

Ryla rolled her eyes and rested her hand on the hilt of her sword, belted to her waist. "So single-minded. Your love for the temporals"—she jutted her chin to Avery—"blinds you to anything else."

"I believe I see clearly." Kade maintained a conversational tone. The longer she spoke, the more time he had to recover what energy he could.

Ryla shrugged. "You see what you wish to see. You read what you wanted to read in that prophecy." She cocked her head and opened her eyes wide, mocking. "Everyone knew it was your infatuation with these weak, insignificant beings that conjured those words. No one believed them."

"Oh? Lord Talmond as well?"

Something flickered in Ryla's eyes for a moment. Uncertainty . . . regret? But then it was gone; the pious nonchalance firmly back in place.

"The lord of Malvok bowed under your persistence that the temporals would return to defeat Cosyn. But he never believed."

Kade looked past Ryla to the soldiers. "He is here?"

Ryla's smile froze. "No."

"So, he believed, after all."

"He showed weakness."

"You sent him on?"

Emaline gasped.

Ryla's smile grew.

"Perhaps I should have. I may yet. But I have faith he will see clearly."

"Lady," Kade said as he took a step forward, his hands raised in appeal. "You once placed your faith in Arkonai. Not prophecies, not me, but your Creator. Could it not be again?"

Ryla gripped the hilt. "Do not speak to me of Arkonai. Where is the strength in one who requires the aid of temporals?"

"A far greater strength is revealed when those weaker are mobilized to battle. Success born out of the unlikely is that much greater."

Ryla threw back her head and laughed. "Success, you say? This is success?" She opened her hand to them.

The mist rolled back, exposing row after row of soldiers, all the way to the banks of the river, where it lingered. Some soldiers were Malvokian. But not all. It seemed Ryla had recruited from Shalhala and Keala as well. Even the bulging eyes of Olyaunders peered from the ranks. Radan was gone, but they had found a new leader. Though they had once been Shalhalans, it was clear they would never go back. They would never embrace their true nature.

"You are a fool," Ryla purred.

The crowd of renegades gripped their weapons: swords, daggers, bows, and spears. Most of their light—feeble flickers of blue or green, and faded shades of the palest yellow and orange—died away into the fog that still obscured the fjord. The closest soldiers looked on impassively. But it was impossible to tell how many Ryla had in her ranks.

Kade's heart broke. Surely, they missed their connection to their Creator. So many. The rebellion against Arkonai was unfathomable. Corrupted or coerced, he could not save them. They had made their choice.

"When Cosyn approached me," Ryla continued, apparently so sure of their impending demise, that she saw no need for urgency, "I will admit, I resisted. I was under the same delusion." Her eyes darted from Kade to Altizara, Tilman, and Emaline. "Then Cosyn said something that changed everything."

She allowed a dramatic pause.

"Why you?"

Another pause.

"Why you, Kade? What makes you so superior, insightful, powerful, to be the one to direct all of Alnok around your obsession with these temporals."

Kade's anger disintegrated like packed earth beneath a rainstorm. Cosyn had tapped and twisted a deep struggle Ryla perhaps already had. Pride.

"Ryla," he murmured, taking another step. "I have no higher purpose than you, or Tilman, or Altizara"—he gestured to the two on either side of him—"or Ditimer. There is one purpose, to which we all take equal part."

"Such admirable humility," she mocked. "I do not recognize your purpose. And Ditimer did not either."

A weight fell on Kade's shoulders. "It is not my—"

"Enough!" she shouted.

Kade leveled his gaze at her, the anger reforming. She was not blind. She was willfully deceived.

Tilman and Altizara took two firm steps forward, planting themselves just ahead of Kade, with squared shoulders and lifted chins, but drawing no weapons. Avery limped around Kade and stood directly in front of him. He secured the shield on his arm, bracing it against his left shoulder.

Kade clenched his teeth against the growing pain in his chest. He moved in line with the two Malvokians as Othana appeared next to Altizara, and Emaline moved next to Tilman. Kade opened his heart, grief and hope, anger and compassion filling him as his golden light grew.

Arkonai, in our weakness, may you show your strength.

Rising and mingling, bright-yellow light from Altizara and deep orange from Othana joined Kade's light. Tilman and Emaline's blue light grew, his hard steel, hers pale and delicate.

Ryla flinched and narrowed her eyes. She raised a hand and paused, then brought it down hard. With a roar, the first row of soldiers surged.

Avery hunched his shoulders, went to one knee, and gave a shout. Kade braced, warm blood soaking his tunic. The Alnokian light, together with Avery's shield wall, fused into a shimmering rampart. It spread until the soldiers on the other side were nothing more than a rippling blur. Kade felt a slight push as the soldiers reached the barrier. Avery gasped as they burst into glittering light, evaporating as they floated toward the heavens.

But the wall thinned with the assault. The troops beyond came into clearer focus.

Ryla's smirk melted, as though a mask of wax, reforming into wide-eyed shock. She staggered backward and the soldiers closest to her drew away. She recovered with a hardened glare.

"Reform the line!" she barked, then took a deep breath.

"Enough games," she hissed. "Go!"

The next soldiers were not as bold. They marched forward but stood just out of reach of the wall.

"Go!" Ryla screamed.

The soldiers drew their swords, lips pursed and eyes dull in hopeless resolve. They struck. And disintegrated.

But the light wall was nearly gone.

Tilman unsheathed his sword and Avery leaped to his feet, still favoring his right ankle. The two braced for an assault. Othana and Altizara dropped back, arrows nocked. Kade maintained his light but, like the mist, which continued to expose soldier after soldier, it was fading. Even if his light had been full, powerful, and focused, eventually, they would wear it away. There were too many. Then, depleted, Avery and the Guardians would be entirely vulnerable to Ryla and her army.

"Altizara," Kade whispered, "swords and arrows will not be enough."

She glanced at him but kept her bow pulled taut.

"I'll hold them, Kade!" Avery called over his shoulder. "You go on to the cave!"

Ryla seemed unsure. Her gaze darted from Avery to Tilman, then Altizara, then Othana.

She did not know he was injured. She still feared their power.

"Is this what you wish?" Kade shouted, striding up between Avery and Tilman. "To see your soldiers destroyed?" He forced a pulse of light into his hands.

"You cannot withstand all of us!" Ryla called. "You may take some, but we will annihilate you all!"

"You see our power. Our unity is our strength."

Avery gave Kade a furtive glance. Kade gripped his and Tilman's shoulders.

"How many, Ryla?" Kade bellowed. The gash across his chest strained as though it might break open. Warm blood flowed. "How many can you spare?"

"Brantel! Graden!" Tilman shouted, seeming to recognize some of the soldiers with whom he had trained. "Do you not know whom you fight against?"

These men had once been allied in their protection of the temporals. Had served Lord Talmond. Had followed Arkonai.

"They know who they fight *for*!" Ryla taunted.

This could not go on. Ryla would gain confidence. She would attack. They would not convince thousands of Guardians who had marched from all corners of Alnok to abandon their orders. Or give up what they had been promised. The deception went too deep.

A murmur rose from the distance. Shadowed movement in the mist. Kade's shoulders fell. If they had had any hope of escaping Ryla's soldiers, whether by sword or wit, it was gone. Ryla had not yet revealed the full force of her army.

Ryla looked at her soldiers on her right and left. They glanced behind.

A great splash and then a thunder of hundreds of footsteps was rushing toward them.

A shout. A scream.

Ryla spun as her troop broke ranks, shoving and pushing. They scattered in all directions but seemed to forget Kade and the rest of their quarry.

Swords clashed at a distance. A voice rose out of the roiling fog.

"For the valor of Arkonai!"

The mist parted as a crowd of soldiers rushed into the middle of Ryla's quailing troop.

"Soldiers from Herlov!" Othana cried with a wide, triumphant smile.

Tilman and Avery launched at the closest soldiers, who turned and ran. But others engaged. A tall Olyaunder thrust his spear at Tilman, who deflected it and slashed at the enemy soldier's neck.

Othana and Altizara dropped back, firing arrows to cover the men. Kade lost sight of Ryla in the skirmish.

A hand grasped Kade's. He looked down. Emaline.

"Gabe."

"Aye," Kade said. "Let us go to him."

CHAPTER TWENTY-THREE

A shout echoed through the fog. Raelyn jolted awake, scanning the camp for Larken. Joshua was already on his feet, edging past the dying coals, staring into the darkness. Jinny sat up and narrowed her eyes, straining to see through the mist.

"What is it?" Raelyn whispered. Clicks and knocks followed the cry. A splash.

A hesitant smile lifted the corners of Jinny's mouth. "Rescue."

"For us?"

Her smile faltered. "No . . ."

"For who?"

Jinny shook her head. "I don't know."

"Where's Larken?" Joshua asked.

A dim blue light grew from within the swirling mist before Larken burst through, striding to the camp.

"Whoever it is," he said, kicking out the coals, "and whoever they are here to rescue, it does not matter. We must go."

Raelyn's hands shook as she helped shove blankets into Joshua and Jinny's packs. She squeezed her eyes closed against an oncoming headache. A battle had just exploded somewhere to the north and they were about to head toward it with no knowledge of who or why.

Malvok and Keala were both so far away. Who needed rescuing?

The fjord was closer than Raelyn had guessed. Their footsteps crunched scrubby grass covered in a fine frost as they approached the shoreline. The water lapped at the bank, quiet and gentle. A few trees, tall but bare, clustered along the water's edge. Daylight lit the mist; a glowing white, blinding them to the opposite shore. It was as though they stood within a loading computer program, a blinking cursor on a blank screen. What would appear when it cleared? What game would launch?

The tumult continued in the distance. A louder, deeper boom shook the ground. Raelyn jolted, but Larken didn't react. Neither did Joshua or Jinny except to look at her questioningly.

"What's wrong?" Joshua asked.

Raelyn pushed damp, stray hairs from her face and checked the buckle on her holster.

"I dunno," she mumbled. "I thought I felt . . ."

Larken looked at her, eyebrows raised. "Felt what?"

Raelyn shook her head. "Like a bomb went off. If you didn't feel it, maybe it was my imagination." The headache, fear, and anticipation all fed a growing irritation.

Larken frowned, but nodded. "Perhaps." He began rummaging through his bag. "You should have some seripyn."

"Later," Raelyn said, touching his arm. "It's almost gone. We might need it. I'll hold out a little longer."

Larken held the flask and looked at her. Then he nodded. "Tell me if it happens again." He watched her a moment more before he went back to searching the bank.

"Okay." She knelt and peered into the lake. "Any plan how to get across?"

The murky water might have been two feet deep, or two hundred. But on the dark surface, hundreds of tiny whirlpools stirred, creating iridescent colors swirling in an aquatic ballet. Their spinning and twirling was quite peaceful.

"Raelyn!" Jinny pulled at her shoulder. "Don't touch the water."

to Keala. Now he seemed older than Kade. Ancient and tired.

He crept forward, inching to the middle of the trunk, the center bowing dangerously into the water. But he hurried to the other side, where he traversed the few bare branches and jumped onto shore.

"Easy peasy," Joshua said, but his grim expression belied his words. "Jinny? You wanna go next?"

Jinny took a deep breath and scanned the waters. Heights. Not her forte. She had refused to climb down from their Shalhalan room to escape the attacking Olyaunders. It was only the rope Raelyn had tied around each of their waists, promising to keep Jinny safe, that had coaxed the girl out onto the wall. They'd made it, but only after falling the last ten or fifteen feet.

But this wasn't height. This was balance.

"Jinny," Raelyn said, grabbing her hand. "You were rock steady on the boat. This is no different."

"Easier," Joshua added. "It's not moving and there's no sea mon—"

Raelyn jabbed him. Why mention anything that could be in the water?

"We'll be right here," she said and urged Jinny to the tree.

Jinny nodded and pressed the Seon firmly on her head. She scrambled over the roots and crouched with her hands on the trunk. She eased to a standing position and shuffled one foot forward, then brought the other to meet it, holding her arms out for balance. Step by step, she made her way to the other side. As she approached, her foot slipped. She pinwheeled her arms, leaning back dangerously before gaining her balance. Larken reached out his hand through the branches and helped her down.

Raelyn let out a breath.

The mist was nearly gone. Several hundred yards north, three arched gaps appeared on the cliff side. The catacomb entrance. But further north, the mist continued to linger, blocking the view of the clamor. Dark, frantic movements behind the fog hinted at the fervor of the battle. But it wasn't just the mist that obscured Raelyn's vision.

She should have taken some of Larken's seripyn. Even if it was almost gone.

"If Jinny can do it . . ." Joshua tore his eyes from the opposite shore and gave Raelyn an encouraging nod. He swept his arm toward the makeshift bridge, indicating she should follow. Everything around him rippled. She had to get control.

She shook her head. "You go."

Joshua frowned. "Why?"

"Yeah, I, uh, just need a minute." She swallowed back an urge to vomit and squeezed her eyes shut.

"You sure?" He took a step toward her.

She opened her eyes and forced his face into focus. "Yep. I'll be right behind you."

Joshua nodded, drawing even closer. "All right." He brushed her cheek with his thumb and searched her eyes. "I'll be waiting on the other side."

He bounded around the roots and hopped onto the trunk as though to prove there was nothing to it. He rushed across, using speed rather than balance. His strategy proved successful as he hopped from the last branch to the shore.

The battle, or rescue, in the north, was coming into full view. Hundreds of soldiers, still too far to see from which kingdom, were locked in a frantic battle. They hadn't blocked the space between the fjord and the arched cliff opening. Though the way seemed clear, they had to make it without being spotted. Unless the soldiers were friendly. Maybe they would have help after all . . .

She was stalling.

Raelyn scrambled around the roots and squatted as Jinny had done. She peered at the water on either side. A wave of nausea joined her headache. She cleared her throat and shook her head. She couldn't fade. Not yet.

"Rae! I'm right here!" Joshua called. But he was miles away. An ocean stood between them.

Just thirty steps, give or take. One at a time.

She looked at Larken. Then Jinny. Finally Joshua. She took a deep breath and stood.

Just take the first step.

One . . . two . . . three . . .

She crossed the dark water.

Seven . . . eight . . .

The battle noise swelled as she reached the halfway point. The water swirled with tiny whirlpools beneath her feet, as though the fjord was a pot of boiling soup.

Seventeen . . . eighteen . . .

Nearly there.

Twenty . . . twenty-one . . . twenty-two . . .

She should have checked on her dad and Peter. They were in the middle of an air raid the last time she'd seen them. Did Cosyn know they were right outside the catacombs?

Raelyn looked up at the cliffs and her foot skidded. She gasped, held out her arms, regaining her balance. Her heart pounded against her ribs.

She shook her head. Focus on getting across. Then worry about home.

Twenty-five . . . twenty-six . . .

Her vision went black. Shouting, right next to her. She jerked back.

"Who—"

"Raelyn!"

Peter!

She reached out. Fingers intertwined with her own. Slipping away. Falling . . .

CHAPTER TWENTY-FOUR

As Kade pulled his dagger from his boot, his knees buckled. Emaline caught his arm, keeping him from collapsing, and tugged him away from the fiercest fighting. They made their way along the base of the cliff, the battle deafening.

So many had rebelled. Almost as many as now defended Alnok and the temporals. In the declining mist and the rising light, swords flashed, and soldiers shouted in triumph or fear. Alnokian fighting Alnokian. From every kingdom. Cosyn had won. His vision of a realm torn apart, one in which he could rise victorious, was closer than ever. If he could deceive the Guardians of this realm, how much more could he dominate the temporals of Earth Apparent?

Kade stumbled. He should have persisted in persuading Lord Talmond, King Ellioner . . . Othana, others, of the legitimacy of the prophecy. He had settled for acquiescence, not conviction. Compliance, not belief.

Pandemonium surrounded him and Emaline as they scurried past the battle. Had he been wrong? By insisting the Guardians inculcate rather than observe the temporals? By engaging, not only protecting, had he set the two realms in opposition? It hadn't been enough to fulfill their role as Arkonai had ordained, Kade had wanted more. He desired the role of father, comforter, guide, and mentor. But having immersed himself so deeply, had he influenced their lives? He had established himself as their leader. Was he that much different from Cosyn?

No. I do not wish their destruction. Only their well-being.

Even so, he had set himself above them. And expected the same of the other Guardians.

But the prophecy, *that* called the temporals back to Alnok. To battle Cosyn.

If Kade had simply co-existed with the survivors of the Great Plague so long ago, rather than inserting himself in their day-to-day lives, Cosyn might not have been so tempted to rule them. The prophecy might not have even been necessary.

A sick realization hit Kade. He had sparked Cosyn's jealousy of the frail outsiders. The desire to not just lead, but to overpower them.

He had created Cosyn.

This war was his doing. How could he abandon his own? Watch them tear each other apart?

He brandished his dagger and tried to pull away from Emaline. She gripped his hand. He yanked away from her and started out into the midst of the battle. Searching faces, weaving between soldiers, he strode toward the fjord.

If he could reach Ryla, he would make her see. She was not too far gone. He could save her. Save them all.

"Kade!" Emaline gasped as she caught him.

"This is my doing. I must put a stop to this destruction."

"What?" She tugged at his cloak.

Two soldiers, locked hand in hand, backed into Kade. Kade grasped the sword hand of the one nearest. It was impossible to tell if he was of Herlov or one of Ryla's men.

"Brothers! We must stop this!"

The soldier tore away from him, glaring in fury. He turned on Kade.

Emaline, her shoulder lowered, rammed into him, throwing him back.

"Kade! We must reach Gabe!"

Kade blinked. Tears filled his eyes. Entreat for peace among his people or save a temporal from the very leader of this rebellion. An impossible choice.

Othana appeared, jogging backward with her bow drawn. She bumped into Emaline as she shot her final arrow. She spun, pulling a short sword from her belt, then gasped.

Mouth opened in surprise, she looked from Emaline to Kade before her expression turned hard. She gave a curt nod of understanding.

"Go! We will hold them here."

Kade shook his head. "Othana—"

"We came for a reason." She bolted into the swarm of soldiers. "Do not let him win!" she called and was gone.

Kade cradled the staff in the crook of his arm and wiped his face as he backed away. The battle was reaching a frantic pitch. Ryla's soldiers seemed to have recovered from the surprise attack. One after another, soldiers, friend and foe, disappeared in flashes of light. Alnokians would enter the next realm. Temporals—Avery, Gabe—would as well. But Gabe's father, Avery's wife; would they ever know of the men's sacrifice?

The fighting spanned the land from the shores of the fjord to the cliffs. Kade could not offer aid. Not now. He must abandon them. Gabe could wait no longer. And he had nothing to spare.

They waded back through the combat. Leaning on the staff, Kade stumbled forward. They snaked their way back to the cliff, then traversed south, darting around soldier after soldier. An Olyaunder, distorted beyond any recognizable Shalhalan, swiped its spear at a young Herlovian, who ducked beneath. Kade could only look on as he hurried past.

He skidded to a stop as a Kealan soldier stepped in front of him and drew his sword. A maniacal grin spread across the soldier's face. Emaline darted past Kade and ducked, sweeping her leg under his feet. He tottered but reacted too late and went down. Before he could scramble to his feet, Kade and Emaline raced away.

"You cannot save me from every soldier," Kade gasped and gave Emaline a quick smile.

Her eyes sparkled. "You may engage the next one."

As they drew nearer the catacomb entrance, a new dilemma made its way to the forefront. If they made it past the battle and into the catacombs, he would face the dragon alone. Or worse, Cosyn. His remaining energy would have to be enough to rescue Gabe. Perhaps he would not need to engage the enemy at all . . .

A Herlovian stumbled backward into Kade as a Malvokian bore down on her with a sword over his head. Kade thrust the staff at the oncoming soldier, who ran full force into it. He gasped, looking at Kade, eyes wide with shock, before stumbling back. The Herlovian took advantage of this diversion and advanced, her sword held high. Kade and Emaline traveled on before witnessing what happened next.

Kade shuffled on. No words of comfort. No opportunity for repentance or reconciliation. He looked at his hand, the soldier's blood now mingled with his own.

Arkonai, open their eyes. Gather them to you.

No answer, no assurance. As they wove through the embattled soldiers further and further south, the fighting thinned. A chill made its way up Kade's back to the base of his neck. The noise faded, but the ensuing silence was as a bated breath, awaiting the next strike. The smell of charred wood filled the air.

"Kade?" Emaline whispered.

"The entrance is just ahead."

"I know. I can feel it. I know we have no choice but to try, but can we really find Gabe and escape the dragon? The egg, Cosyn . . . the plye."

Kade frowned without slowing his pace. "We must trust Raelyn and the others will reach the portal and destroy it. Gabe is our priority."

"And the dragon?"

"I have little energy left. But that could be to our advantage. When I enter the catacombs, the dragon—even Cosyn—would likely not sense my presence. If I could reach Gabe undetected . . ."

"That is possible?"

Kade sighed. "It must be. I cannot fight."

"And me?"

Kade slowed as they came to a towering arched entrance, the first of three. Dark, crumbling gates hung from the opening. An icy breeze blew from the belly of the caves, freezing the sweat on Kade's brow. He stopped and leaned against the dusty cliff, looking down at the girl.

"If I have any hope of secrecy, you cannot come."

Emaline looked into the dark entrance, seeming to search for some argument.

"Perhaps not," she finally said. "But I could provide a distraction for you. I would give you a better chance of concealment."

"Enter the caves with me?" Kade asked.

She looked at him. "We must reach Gabe at all costs. It is only you and me. I offer nothing by remaining here."

"He will need healing—"

"I will meet you back here, after you have the temporal."

Kade shook his head. "Emaline, the risk, the chance you might become trapped . . ."

"Is as great as if I am attacked here." She gestured to the continuing battle that was drawing nearer.

Kade looked from the fighting soldiers to Emaline, to the first entrance of the catacombs. The plan increased the likelihood he could retrieve Gabe and get out. But the chances of Emaline escaping . . .

Kade continued to the central entrance. The sweeping arch was pitch black beyond the broken gate. The cavern gobbled up any light venturing past the entrance.

Kade pressed his hand to his chest. It came away wet.

"I must treat your wound before we go further," Emaline said as she dug through her bag.

Kade put a hand on her shoulder. "I am past all methods of healing. And I cannot risk gaining any strength. I need to be depleted to remain hidden."

Emaline stopped and pressed her lips into a thin line.

"Remain just inside the entrance. You need only provide a distraction. Not engage in a fight."

"What might I encounter?" she asked. She hardened her voice, but her brow knit.

"The dragon will be deep within the catacombs. Cosyn's protectors will have no set form. They will use trickery and confusion. Remain vigilant and escape should their numbers grow."

Emaline nodded.

Kade sighed. "I had hoped others would join us in this quest."

"We are fortunate Othana, Altizara, Tilman, and Avery will keep the battle away, if it is within their power."

Kade leaned on the staff and gazed into the distance. The fighting showing no signs of abating in the fading light. The mist was gone. Thin daylight glinted across the black waters of the fjord. Kade scanned the land across the waters, gathering what strength he could before entering the darkness.

Movement in the south caught his eye. Someone on the opposite side of the fjord.

"Herlovian?" Emaline asked, following his gaze.

"So far from the battle?"

"Then who?"

Kade drifted closer to the stray group, scurrying up and down the shoreline. He counted four. One with a glittering blue light trailing their movements. They went still. The Alnokian with the blue light leaned against a nearby tree, which shivered and then crashed into the water. Kade quickened his steps toward them.

The Alnokian clambered across the newly created bridge. Then the second person, with long, dark hair.

The third person reached the shore. Planting the staff every few feet to keep from toppling over, Kade hurried to the fjord, ignoring his burning lungs, his aching chest. He was almost close enough to make out their features.

The fourth person started across. A . . . blue tunic. Dark hair . . .

"Kade," Emaline breathed, jogging next to him. "Is that—"

"Yes," Kade choked, tears filling his eyes. "Joshua . . . Jinny." He broke into a full run. "Raelyn."

CHAPTER TWENTY-FIVE

Ice-cold water filled Raelyn's mouth. She spluttered and flailed to the surface, treading freezing water. But she was on fire, as though she'd fallen headlong into a hornet's nest. Her arms, stomach, and legs were pricked by a thousand needles full of boiling poison. Peter's face flashed before her, then was gone.

Something flapped against her hand. Another sting. She tried to swim for shore, screaming and gasping. She couldn't keep her head above water. The pain was too much. Tiny flapping against her face and neck.

A shout. A splash. Then a hand locked onto her arm and yanked.

"Gotcha," Joshua grunted.

But the water, or the stinging things, held her. Joshua let out a guttural yell and pulled.

She tried to help. But the pain took over her strength.

Joshua pulled again, dragging her to the shallower waters. The flapping things were all over her, even as she scrambled out of the water. She fell onto the shore, Joshua's hand still clasped firmly to her elbow. Raelyn howled and beat at the creatures. Through a haze of pain, she saw them, gray leeches with bulbous wings attached to her through her tunic, pants, and boots. Whatever poison they were injecting sent white-hot liquid under her skin.

Raelyn's legs cramped. She shivered uncontrollably. Joshua groaned next to her but continued his grip on her elbow.

The stinging became a blistering burn. Her body was on fire. Her blood boiling. She clenched her fists and curled around the pain, biting back a scream. Surely, she would explode in flames.

Hurried footsteps drew near. Someone lifted her, warmth covered her body. Unlike the brands of fire, the sensation was more like easing into a soothing bath. The stinging quieted, the fire abated, though the aching remained. Someone pulled off her tunic, applied a salve across her belly. The relief was instant. The same applied to her arms, neck, face. She squinted her eyes open. Fresh tears burned her eyes.

It couldn't be. The poison was causing hallucinations. Cosyn was tricking her . . .

"Kade?" she croaked, tears continuing to pour down her cheeks.

He smiled and stroked her hair. "Shh, yes." He looked up at the girl applying the balm.

Raelyn followed his gaze.

"Emaline?" she asked.

Emaline nodded, but her expression was grim. "Kade . . . there are so many . . ."

Raelyn struggled to sit up. "Joshua—"

The hand on her elbow tightened. "I'm here," he said.

Raelyn forced her trembling body to relax. But waves of heat brought new tremors.

A siren wailed. She searched the skies.

Strong arms encircled her, squeezing. A golden light surrounded her. The siren grew louder.

The pain was gone.

And Peter was staring into her face.

***

"Rae?"

Raelyn scrambled to a sitting position. "Peter!"

"Shhh!" He pulled her up and steered her to a dark corner.

"You're still at the church?" she whispered, then shook her head. No one could hear her.

"For a solid week." Peter hunched his shoulders, keeping his eyes trained on her feet. "You okay?" he mumbled. His surreptitious behavior suggested others were nearby.

"No." Raelyn looked over his shoulder. The basement was dark except for a few oil lanterns. It was more like an Alnokian castle than a modern church. Clusters of people huddled on the low benches, crowded around tables. A steady murmur was punctuated by an agonizing sob here or there. Some from children. Some not. It smelled musty, stale. Something like a long-shut cellar whose contents had soured.

"What's happening?" Peter scratched his head and looked her up and down before casting a paranoid glance behind.

Raelyn looked at her arms and pulled up her undershirt. Tiny red marks covered her skin.

"I'll explain later. Are things worse?" she breathed. Her throat constricted. "Where's Dad?"

"Yes, and I don't know." He looked up and held her gaze. "Rae, I think it may be too late. The bombing that started two days ago hasn't stopped. All the major cities took a beating."

"What d'ya mean 'too late?'"

"Russia and China demanded a full surrender. But it's not just them. It's a lot of countries all over the world. Whoever agrees to the one world." He sighed. "We only have spotty radio signal down here, so I don't know the details. But the president, he just gave in." He rubbed his face, as though trying to wipe away the fatigue and defeat. "Those of us around here, well, we weren't ready to give up so easy."

"Dad?"

Peter nodded. "One of the first to join the NGI force."

"NGI?"

"Never Give In."

"Wow," Raelyn whispered. "They're fighting the Russians and the Chinese?"

"Some of the resistance fighters are. Dad's part of a sabotage contingent. They block streets, cause misdirection . . ."

Raelyn frowned. Peter wouldn't sit still if anyone else was fighting. "What about you?"

"Search and rescue."

"I need to you to stay safe. I told you, you're the chosen one for this quest. I can't afford for you to get hurt. I'm betting I'm going to need your help in the end. I'm so close. If we get this last portal closed . . ."

Peter shook his head with a scowl. "Then what? It's not the same as volcanos or illness. Just people fighting people."

Raelyn frowned. How was Cosyn using this last plye?

"You said the president didn't even try to defend—"

"Not just here. The UK, France, Germany, everyone just went along. Sent out these PSAs about how we could become a new world order. Seems everyone wants China at the helm."

Raelyn frowned. "New world order . . ." Everyone under one big umbrella. Afraid, confused. What better way to—

"That's it," Raelyn gasped. "Cosyn isn't using illness or natural disasters. Those things may have played a role, but right now, he's using deception."

"I don't get it." Peter's brow was creased with confusion, but he seemed more tired, defeated. Compliance was so much easier when the population was worn down. Even Peter seemed willing to give up. She had to get him to see.

"Think about it. This is the last portal, but I bet it's the oldest; the most protected. Maybe best hidden. This attack has been going on long before Cosyn reached out from the others. Been going on for centuries. I'm sure keeping us out of Alnok was important. And destroying the world with volcanoes would've suited him. But deception's his expertise. What if he's causing some kind of illusion?"

Peter shook his head. "I dunno Rae. People can be idiots without some otherworldly evil twisting their arms."

"True, but how'd it go so bad, so fast?"

"Natural disasters will do that."

"And we know who caused those."

"Okay, so say Cosyn's been whispering secret plans in everyone's ears; the damage is done. Closing a plye won't undo this."

She grabbed his hand and exposed his palm. "You're right. Destroying the plye won't immediately eliminate the damage, but it will thwart Cosyn's influence. People will realize they've been manipulated—"

"Not everyone."

"No, not everyone. There will be some who enjoy controlling others or are comfortable being controlled."

"What if it's already gone too far?"

"As long as there's one person resisting, it can't be too late. There would be no NGI. What's Dad fighting for if there's no hope?" She placed her hand over the red mark. "As long as you're there and I'm here, we won't stop until the portal's closed."

Peter took a deep breath and offered a tired smile. "You're right." He closed his hand around hers. "It's hard to imagine anything going back to normal."

Raelyn barked a laugh. "Who said anything about normal? I'm in the fifth dimension. Even if I make it back, nothing will be normal. At least what we thought was normal."

"You'll make it back."

"I know."

The floor shuddered, and Peter stumbled. Someone screamed. Bits of debris fell from the ceiling.

Peter looked up. "It's like contractions."

"Excuse me?"

"Explosions are getting more and more frequent. Between the bombings, they go door to door. Mostly to intimidate, but sometimes they take people."

Raelyn shuddered. In less than a year, everything had changed. But had it only been this year?

No, she had no doubt the last plye had been active for a very long time.

Footsteps pounded above them.

"Peter?"

The basement went completely silent. Those who'd been at the tables stood and looked at the far side of the room.

Peter nodded and leaned over to her ear. "It's okay," he whispered. He pulled his hand from hers. "NGI troops." He turned. "Maybe Dad—"

"Stop!" A command came from above.

Peter gasped and darted to the nearest couple, a woman carried a toddler on her hip. He ushered them to a hallway without looking back.

More shouting, closer.

The people in the room, oblivious to Raelyn, hurried in the direction Peter had gone. No one made a sound as they moved in a collective scramble.

Someone pounded on a door.

Liquid poured over Raelyn's lips.

A group of men and one woman in black uniforms marched into the room. Clustered between them was a group in camouflage. Bloodied and bruised. Several young men, two women, and . . . her dad.

Raelyn tried to run to him, but the room spun, blurring, going dark and . . .

Kade's face swam into view.

CHAPTER TWENTY-SIX

"Are you really here?" Raelyn rasped. She swallowed the rest of the seripyn. Afraid to move, her gaze darted from Kade, who cradled her in one arm to Emaline, standing over Kade's shoulder, watching as though assessing Raelyn's recovery.

Raelyn touched his shoulder and then gripped it as though he might be a mirage, gone at any moment. Another of Cosyn's tricks. Making her think she was safe. Or the water, those things, had poisoned her mind.

She didn't care.

The levy holding her emotions broke. She buried her face in his robe and sobbed. Grief flowed with every breath. The fear, the bitterness, the anger drained away. Even the pain subsided as she released her sorrow into Kade's shoulder. He pulled her close, his chest rumbling with words she couldn't make out. After what seemed hours, but could only have been seconds, she pulled away. She had to see him. Make sure . . .

He smiled, the gentle smile she had longed to see. She laughed with a raw, relief-filled joy.

"Aye," Kade said softly, stroking Raelyn's hair. "I am here."

She glanced at the fjord and then back at Kade. "My dad, Peter; the soldiers found them—"

Kade patted her hand. "We have a plan for that. I have every confidence your father and brother will hold the line until we can get to the plye."

"I fell. How did I—" She turned to find Joshua sitting a few feet from her, holding his arm, watching. He had saved her from the water. Again.

She pulled away from Kade. Though her arms and legs ached as though they'd been pummeled with a sledgehammer, she crawled to Joshua and wrapped her arms around his neck.

"Thank you . . ."

"Hey, hey. It's okay," he mumbled into her damp hair. He wrapped one arm around her waist and pulled her close.

It wasn't okay. Nothing was okay. A battle was raging only a few hundred feet away. Their families were in more danger than ever, and they were no nearer to closing the plye. But from the moment Joshua had driven up in his old pickup at the warehouse in Silo, he had been with her. Solid. Stable. Unwavering.

He had saved her from being washed down the river near Deshill, rescued her from drowning after the shipwreck, and now, pulled her from the fjord and the attacking leeches. What she had viewed as his inclination toward calculated caution, had been fierce protection. His cool logic was tender guidance. Every time she had encountered some new danger, he had been there to snatch her out of harm's way.

Gratitude mingled with a reckless and overwhelming affection.

Joshua gave her one last squeeze, then eased out of her grasp, his hand resting on her shoulder. Raelyn sat back on her heels, the puncture wounds once again pulsing with a white-hot pain. She studied his face, expecting to see stoic gray eyes, a set jaw. Instead, his eyes were filled with tears. A shy smile pulled at the corners of his mouth. He moved his hand to the back of her neck and drew her close.

She let go, leaning in. He kissed her full on the lips. The pain vanished. Only the electric spark between her mouth and his remained. Battles, rivers, caves, all distant, *faded*. The warmth of his lips drove it all from her mind. They parted, and Kade cleared his throat. Joshua released her and they turned to him in unison.

"Your steadfast unity will be critical in finding your way through the catacombs," Kade said. "We must go."

Joshua scrambled to his feet and helped Raelyn to stand. He took her hand and didn't let go.

Kade remained seated on the ground until Larken took his elbow and pulled him up. Kade held Larken's shoulder and used the staff to get to his feet. Larken stood near, as though Kade may fall over any second. The Kade Raelyn remembered was gone. His bronze skin was pasty, his cheeks hollow. His shining black hair was dull and lank.

"What happened?" Raelyn said, stepping forward. "What's wrong?" She glanced at the staff he was using as a sort of crutch. Her body tensed. It was the final confirmation that everything was true. As though cards had been laid on a table, one after another. Larken's account of the staff's creation, Joshua and Jinny's reassurance she was always meant to be in Alnok, her family's history, relayed by her dad, Peter's ability to enter Alnok, and now the staff, right here, bringing all the stories together. Making it all real. A full house.

Jinny stepped in front of Raelyn. "Where is Gabe? Is he with you?"

Kade nodded. "He is near," he said, drawing her into a hug. "But we must retrieve him."

"Retrieve—"

Othana bounded up, gasping and covered in dirt and sweat. Her orange light flashed and reflected in her sword as she sheathed it.

"Othana!" Raelyn cried. The last time she had seen the Shalhalan warrior was to watch her race away with Olmund to rescue Gabe from the Olyaund siege.

Othana rushed to her and kissed her cheek, then hugged Joshua and Jinny.

"Gabe is in the catacombs," Kade said to Jinny and held up a hand to stay her next question. "Othana, the others—"

"Others?" Joshua asked.

Kade glanced at the fighting soldiers in the distance. "Altizara, Tilman, and . . . Avery."

"You're all here?" Raelyn looked from Kade to Othana to Emaline. She took a step forward, but gripped Joshua's hand harder.

"We must hurry. My brother . . . he's in a church basement in Fort Worth. They're bombing them. But the soldiers found the bunker. They were there with my dad."

Joshua squeezed her hand. "My folks have my daughter in their cellar." He shook his head. "It's worse than the volcanoes."

Kade nodded. "The stakes could not be higher. You must reach the plye."

Raelyn blinked. "Us? What about you?"

Kade grimaced and turned toward Emaline as he pressed his hand to his chest. Raelyn looked at his soaked tunic and gasped.

"You're hurt."

"A dragon," Emaline said.

"It has taken Gabe captive," Othana added.

Jinny let out a strangled cry.

A dark-skinned, slender soldier broke away from the tangle of fighting and sped toward them.

"Raelyn!" she called.

"Altizara!"

She rushed up with a hug that nearly took Raelyn off her feet. Still gasping for breath, she glanced at Kade. "Tilman and Avery are right behind me."

Raelyn turned her attention back to Kade. "If you don't come with us, how will we know where to go? Larken said you're the only one who's been in there."

Tilman and Avery bounded into their midst. Avery halted, looking from Joshua to Raelyn to Jinny. A gash across his forehead was leaking blood into his right eye.

"Kade," Tilman said. "Ryla's soldiers will soon block the catacomb entrance."

Avery didn't move, and Raelyn couldn't take her eyes off him. He was almost unrecognizable with shaggy, salt-and-pepper hair and a scruffy beard. He held his shield in front of him, as though to block the accusing stares of the Cord he had abandoned.

Jinny stepped forward. "I'm glad you're safe."

Avery's expression softened, and a ghost of a smile touched his lips. He glanced at Raelyn and then Joshua, who gave him an affirming nod.

"I will lead you," Kade continued. "But it will be up to you to finish the quest." He knelt with a grimace. "There are three entrances." Kade drew three arches in the dirt, the central one larger than the others. He pointed at it.

"We will enter here. Bear right and then circle back to the left." He continued to draw out the cavern map. "At the first opportunity, take the tunnel on the right. This will take you to the central cave with four passageways leading out." He drew what looked like a spoked wheel. "You must take this one." He indicated the second exit on the left. "Then a quick right." He drew what looked like a zigzag and then sighed. "You will know you have arrived."

He stood with a grunt. "It has been a long time since I was in the catacombs, and even then, not for long."

"But this map"—Avery gestured to drawing in the dirt—"it's accurate, right?"

Kade shook his head. "It is the best I can offer. And we have no more time to plan." He looked at Othana. "When we reach the inner sanctum, you and Larken find the egg and immediately make for the Echelon Cavern. Do not wait for anyone. It must be returned."

Othana strode to Larken. "I will explain on the way," she said.

Larken nodded.

"Tilman," Kade said. "You and Joshua stay with me. We will draw the dragon away so Jinny, Avery, and Emaline can reach Gabe and get him to safety."

Tilman stepped next to Joshua, who let go of Raelyn long enough to shake Tilman's hand.

Kade looked at Altizara, standing to the left of Raelyn. "Stay with Raelyn until you find the plye."

"I will."

Kade swept his gaze over them and took a deep breath. "For the valor of Arkonai."

"For the valor of Arkonai," Raelyn repeated with the rest of them. Their voices were subdued, but they shared the same steely expression.

Kade strode past them and set out at a labored jog toward the cliffs, holding up his walking stick. He was careful to keep a distance from the battle. Three arches loomed ahead. Two smaller ones, each blocked by a mangled gate, flanked a center one at least fifty stories high. But utter darkness seeped from all three. The sun had slipped to the horizon behind them, bathing the obsidian cliffside in orange light. But even the sun couldn't banish shadows within the mouth of the cave.

The battle was so close now. The fighting soldiers seemed to be moving toward them as one globular creature.

Angry shouts, the clash of swords. A contingent of soldiers split from the battle. They made a beeline for the Cord and Guardians. In the lead, a woman with wild black hair and streaming red light. Lady Ryla. She held her sword high in one hand as she charged, screaming.

"It is over, Kade!" she shrieked. "You have gathered the temporals only to see them destroyed!"

She and half a dozen soldiers rushed in front of them, blocking their way into the catacombs.

Tilman, Larken, and Avery stopped, standing shoulder to shoulder behind Kade. But Emaline slipped up to stand next to him. Joshua pulled Raelyn close and took a wide step sideways, drawing them both closer to Jinny. He drew his sword. Othana and Altizara dropped back, covering their rear.

Lady Ryla pointed her sword at Kade. The soft-spoken woman who had stood at Lord Talmond's side looked like a lunatic with a wide grin, her eyes roving from Kade to each of them. Her crimson light, once regal, was garish and grotesque.

"Such a waste," she hissed. "The great and mighty Kade, destroyed with the very temporals he sought to save." She stepped forward. "I say again, you are a fool."

"Not so, m'lady," a voice said from behind Raelyn.

Raelyn, Joshua, and Jinny spun round. Othana and Altizara parted, allowing Ditimer and a dozen Malvokians to pass. Ditimer carried a quiver full of arrows in one hand, but where his left hand had been was a tattered, blood-stained cloth over a stump.

"Did I not destroy you once?" Ryla said with a smirk. She glanced at where his left hand once was, and her smile widened.

"I am persistent," Ditimer said softly. "Altizara!" he called and tossed her the quiver without taking his eyes off Ryla.

"Thank you, my friend," Altizara said.

"May each arrow represent my tears of regret and my pleas for forgiveness."

"You need ask no forgiveness, brother," Tilman said as he stepped to the side, letting Ditimer pass.

Ditimer stood next to Kade, who looked at him with a mixture of grief and fatherly love. "Forgiveness was always yours," Kade said softly.

Tears stung Raelyn's eyes.

With a shout, Ditimer drew his sword. His troop followed suit. Ryla's smug smile faltered as Ditimer charged. Ryla threw one last glance at Kade before raising her sword to defend against Ditimer's fierce attack. She and her troop backed away. Kade darted around them, rushing toward the arch.

The cold hit Raelyn's face first, followed by the stench of burnt trash and sewage. She gagged and covered her nose as she followed Kade into the catacombs, where they were plunged into darkness.

CHAPTER TWENTY-SEVEN

Raelyn's eyes slowly adjusted to the darkness. She turned in a wary circle. Emaline's green light pushed back some of the shadows. Larken, Altizara, Tilman, and Othana's lights flickered blue, yellow, and orange, but didn't illuminate more than a few feet around them. Kade had all but disappeared.

Even the light from outside the arch couldn't penetrate the threshold. In fact, the battle outside the cavern had faded. Though it was impossible to discern, the hollow echoes of their breathing suggested the cavern was massive.

Raelyn took a few more steps forward; the ground squelching beneath her feet, as though a layer of matted hair covered a floor of thick mud.

A block of ice sat at the bottom of her stomach as she reined in thoughts of the red-headed scientist from Texas. Could Gabe still be alive in a place like this? She wasn't more than a few feet inside and thick animosity, and evil hung heavy in the air.

An impulse to race ahead, find the plye, and end all this was only tempered by a lack of direction. She took a step toward the corridor on the right. But then what? Left? Then . . . right? Another left?

She'd never find the plye on her own.

Othana and Larken, orange and blue lights shimmering, stood on one side of Kade. Emaline, her pale-green light illuminating Avery and Jinny, stood on the other. Altizara drew close to Raelyn, her yellow light like pale sunshine. Kade's golden light, which should have filled the cavern, was nothing more than tarnished brass. The glow sticks Raelyn kept in her freezer as a kid to prolong the light had maintained a brighter glow.

Altizara yanked the arrows from the quiver Ditimer had tossed to her and handed half of them to Othana.

They moved as one to the right of the chamber, four members of the Cord and six Guardians.

The Durinial throbbed. A red glow reflected off the obsidian walls to their left.

Ryla?

Raelyn turned.

Cosyn.

He strolled from a tunnel opening in the opposite wall. Sleek black hair, pale skin, wicked smile. His sick chuckle filled the cavern.

Tilman and Larken started toward him, but Kade broke away, holding out a staying hand as he strode to his brother.

"Get to the plye!" he called over his shoulder. His golden light pulsed. Cosyn took a step back, perhaps in trepidation, but his smile never faltered. A darkness spread behind him. It overtook him as an embrace. Kade collided with the shadow with a flash, and both of them were gone.

"Let's go," Joshua said. He fumbled for Raelyn's hand and pulled her into the tunnel.

Altizara's light led the way. Avery and Jinny huddled next to Emaline.

Othana, Larken, and Tilman followed directly behind Raelyn.

The Durinial vibrated again.

"Raaaaelyn." A whispered voice, echoing around her.

"Joshua?"

"Here," he said, but let go of her hand. As he drew his sword, the high ring of metal cut through the whisper. She should have had her bow. It had been so long since she'd thought of it. Two of them, in fact. One splintered, the other lost to the sea.

Arrows won't close the plye. Stick to the plan. Get to the sanctum.

They rounded the corner. Overpowering dizziness hit Raelyn. She stumbled and reached for the wall, then recoiled and snatched her hand back, shivering. Rather than a hard, rough, stone surface, a smooth, warm membrane seemed to swell beneath her fingers, as though the tunnel had taken a breath. She wiped her hand on her pants and pressed her fingertips to the Durinial as it continued to pulse. The indiscernible voice murmured all around her.

"Do you hear that?" she asked, but she could barely force the words from her dry mouth.

"Tilman," Joshua called. "We need to go in ahead. Make sure it's clear."

Tilman nodded and the two of them rushed up the corridor, Tilman's light fading.

The whispering grew louder.

Altizara, her bow drawn, waved the rest of them to follow her. "This way!"

They turned right into a tunnel that narrowed so much, they were forced to continue single file. Raelyn hugged her waist to keep from touching the walls. She looked ahead, straining to see Tilman's steel light. But directly ahead of Altizara, the shadows strangled any light.

The tunnel opened suddenly onto a wide chamber. They stopped just inside.

"The wagon wheel," Raelyn said.

"What?" Avery asked.

Raelyn shook her head. "Nothing. Kade drew four passages leading out of here. He said we should take the second left."

"I can't see more than a few feet ahead," Jinny said, keeping her voice low, but the words bounced around the cavern, regardless.

Othana and Larken swept past them.

"The tunnel must be just ahead," Othana said and jogged past them, her and Larken's light—a blazing sunset and a cool mountain lake— lit up the chamber. Four dark, arched exits circled the room.

"We will retrieve the egg," Othana called, slowing just enough to look over her shoulder. "I pray we will see you again. Go with Arkonai."

Larken did a complete turn, then jogged backward while touching his forehead and gesturing to Raelyn. He nodded at Avery and Jinny before the two Guardians dashed through the opening on their left.

Altizara raced after them, followed closely by Emaline, Jinny, and Avery. Raelyn took a few steps but skidded to a stop when a shadow slid across the wall and entered the tunnel after them.

"Avery! Jinny!"

It was an illusion. Keep going.

She bolted into the tunnel, but Altizara and Emaline's lights were dwindling in the distance as they rushed ahead.

"Altizara?" she called, then turned around.

A thick darkness, as though the space were made of tar, surrounded Raelyn. The whispers rose, voices overlapping, louder and louder. The words, nearly discernable, seemed to murmur urgent instructions. Whatever they were telling her to do, the commands would only cause death and devastation.

Like a thousand hissing snakes drawing closer, the noise filled her ears and her mind. It pressed against her as though trying to penetrate her skin. She took a shuddering breath and put her hands over her ears. She couldn't see anything. She was blind.

"Kade!" she screamed. Her head was spinning. She stumbled backward and reached out to catch herself. Her hand pressed into the cool, fleshy surface of the wall. It twitched and she yanked her hand back. The Durinial was on fire.

She couldn't think past the voices. It was all she knew. What was she supposed to do? Why was she here? What was she looking for?

"Rae!" Altizara lit up the tunnel, sending wild shadows around her as she raced toward Raelyn. The voices retreated.

Raelyn ran toward Altizara, and they collided, Raelyn gripping the Guardian's shoulder as though to keep from drowning in the darkness.

"Jinny . . . Avery," Raelyn gasped.

"Just ahead. We're almost there."

A low growl somewhere deep within the caves, or from the walls themselves, rumbled low, thick, and lazy, almost a purr.

Raelyn froze.

"We must go." Altizara tugged on her arm.

The Durinial shook so hard, Raelyn thought in would wrench off her neck. She took hold of it and squeezed. The shadows continued to dance around them, darting in and out of Altizara's light.

Raelyn pulled away, frowning. "Where's your bow?"

Altizara's eyes darted back and forth as though searching for something in the passageway.

Something wasn't right.

Raelyn looked down at Altizara's hand. Usually warm and strong, it was cold and rough. She looked back at the warrior, her beloved trainer.

The Guardian's light faded from daisy yellow to the color of a murky water stain. Raelyn tried to yank her hand away. Altizara gripped harder. Her ebony face darkened, her features melting away. She was crushing Raelyn's hand.

Raelyn reached across and fumbled with the buckle to her holster. The Altizara shadow jerked her backward into the central chamber. She could make out the entire circular room. The walls stretched like diseased skin. The other exits, the spokes Kade had drawn, gaped like open mouths.

A strange purple light illuminated the cavern. A similar shade to . . .

A shadow slid from the closest wall. Then another. Raelyn yanked frantically to free herself from the Altizara-shadow. More and more shadows peeled themselves from the walls. Dark figures, at least a dozen of them, took stiff, jerking steps toward her. The purple light illuminated gaunt faces and hollow, black sockets. The figure closest to her opened its mouth, revealing sharp fangs.

Raelyn staggered backward, dropping the Bokar. She fell onto the soft, wet ground and the Altizara-shadow finally released her.

Raelyn felt along the sticky cave floor, unwilling to take her eyes off the oncoming creatures. She finally chanced a quick glance around her and spotted the book a few feet to her left. She reached for it. Icy fingers pressed into her shoulders, claws piercing her through her tunic and digging into her skin. The smell of rotten meat hit her. She gagged and pulled away, stretching her hand out. The tips of her fingers brushed the edge of the binding.

The fingers were tearing away the skin on her shoulder.

Screaming, she stretched farther, wrenching and struggling to break free of the grip.

The creatures continued to close in, their movements halting and unnatural. More shadows slid from the walls, joining the mass. The whispering grew in a language she didn't recognize. But her name rose above it all.

"Raaaaelyn . . . Raaaaaaelyn . . ."

She tried to reach for the Bokar. But more hands grabbed her wrists.

"Raaaaelyn . . ."

She pulled against her captors. "No! No!"

She gave one more lurching grasp, catching the cover with the tip of her finger and flipping the Bokar open.

Shining white light filled the chamber. The shadows let out a deafening screech as the hands released her shoulder and wrists. She scrambled to her book and pulled it close.

Its light was already diminished, but the shadows were pulling back, dissolving into the cave walls.

A final cry trailed off.

Raelyn was once again plunged into darkness. She staggered to her feet and gripped the Bokar to her chest. The stench of rotten meat and burning hair drifted through the chamber. She took two steps forward and sniffed. The charred smell was definitely stronger.

A distant shout—*Joshua?*—up ahead. Then a roar. It was impossible to tell how far. Raelyn tried to recall the turns they had made until now, but it was a blur. She could only follow the growing scent. The last turn they were to make was to the right. That's what she'd do.

Swallowing the impulse to gag, she reached out her right hand to the tunnel wall. The fleshy substance rose and fell, contracting in and out. She groaned and gritted her teeth, but maintained contact. Trailing her hand along the bumpy surface, she staggered forward in complete darkness.

More shouting. Tilman. Maybe.

The whispers threatened to fill her ears again, but Raelyn pressed the Bokar against her chest like a shield, and the noise subsided.

The tunnel curved right. Shadows moved ahead. Raelyn stopped, her heart pounding. It could be another trick. She held the Bokar so tightly her fingers ached.

The shouts grew louder. Definitely Joshua and Tilman. Another roar and a bright flare of light set the tunnel aglow. A blast of heat swept Raelyn's hair back. She stumbled forward.

"Emaline! Over here!" Jinny cried.

"Raelyn, this way!" Joshua yelled behind her.

Raelyn spun. A blanket of darkness. She backed away, then turned and ran, keeping her eyes on the flickering light bouncing off the wall ahead.

Finally, she came to an arched opening to a short corridor on her left from which a dry heat radiated. A frantic array of yellow, blue, and orange flashed within.

The opening swelled and drew away as though she were about to walk into the belly of a diseased monster.

"Joshua!" Raelyn stumbled forward, waving her hand wildly in front of her. After the complete darkness, the light stabbed her eyes, blinding her.

"Raelyn!" Altizara shouted from somewhere within the cavern.

Raelyn's eyes adjusted as she crossed the threshold into a massive temple. A crumbling stone floor was a stage of chaos. Disintegrated walls covered with tarnished gold paintings soared to an arched ceiling. No fleshy, diseased walls. No gelatinous ground. It looked to have been an opulent cathedral. One that had been the site of a fierce battle. Carved wooden pews, many broken and burned, flanked a central aisle. An altar, split and sagging at the center, seemed a mockery of the most solemn observance. But it was the blue light glowing from a circular opening at the back that drew Raelyn's eye.

The plye.

CHAPTER TWENTY-EIGHT

Kade marched toward Cosyn without looking back. He was leaving the others behind, but he could not allow Cosyn to attack. A heat rose in his chest, weak at first but growing. Whatever light he could muster, he would use it all to stop Cosyn's attacks. The others would have to fight the dragon, get the egg, and close the plye.

This is where he needed to be. Confronting his brother.

Cosyn cocked his head and gave Kade a lazy smile. But beneath his composed demeanor, uncertainty flickered. As Kade approached, Cosyn stepped back, sweeping his arm behind him. A gash appeared. An opening to a dark void. Would he try to escape?

Kade rushed forward.

Cosyn stepped back into the hole. Kade reached for him. Something jerked him forward, off his feet. They both tumbled into a separate chamber. As the opening sealed behind them, Kade turned in time to see Tilman's back as he ran in the opposite direction.

Then silence.

Kade got to his feet. The dark room was not as cold as the main chamber, though a chill penetrated his bones. The walls and floor were made of hewn stone, perfectly aligned, and washed in gray paint. Though smaller than the central cavern, the far corners were lost in darkness.

A wet, musty scent replaced the burnt odor. Though only he and Cosyn stood in the center of the chamber, Kade sensed many others.

He faced his brother, now standing only a few feet away. His smooth, pale skin, brilliant blue eyes and shining dark hair, only a mimic of his former magnificence. Beneath the mask was a tortured, broken, evil creature.

But his brother, nonetheless.

Kade raised his hands in a gesture of peace. "I had hoped to see you once again."

Cosyn opened his arms wide. "Here I am." He grinned. "It is a shame you will not see your precious temporals again."

"Perhaps. But not because you deem it so."

Whispering shadows, not cast by Kade's light, crept across the walls. They moved within the joints and cracks, almost taking shape before fading. Others appeared, shifting deeper into the chamber then disappearing again. Over and over in a strange pattern. A ritualistic procession. Though lacking substance, Kade sensed purpose.

He looked around the chamber. Familiar, but no longer Alnok.

"Velare?"

Cosyn shrugged. "A necessary alliance." His smile widened. "You thought yourself clever in your escape from Shaldon. Crossing into Velare did not keep you as hidden as you had hoped. Did you wonder how Ryla so easily intercepted you?"

Kade matched Cosyn's nonchalance. "I surmised she had been guided. I did not, however, imagine *you* would have needed assistance." He swept his arm at their surroundings.

Cosyn scowled, his aloof attitude slipping. Kade suppressed a satisfied grin. Provocation might not be the wisest course of action. But if Cosyn wanted games, he would play.

"It is understandable," Kade continued, meandering to the cave wall, ignoring the pain in his chest. "We were designed for collaboration. For community."

He ran his hand over the level surface. A shock ran up his arm and he yanked it back. He rubbed his palm as he turned back to Cosyn. They were not alone. Something else was here.

His chest throbbed. Something within the wound pounded to escape. As though the dragon thrashed inside him, filling him with its angry fire. He could almost hear the creature's roar.

Cosyn glanced at Kade's chest and smirked. "Dragon?"

Kade nodded. "Aye."

"I am surprised you have withstood the effects so long."

"I have a capable healer."

Cosyn snorted. "Perpetuating your agony. Nothing you do will change the inevitable."

"Inevitable?" The longer Kade could keep Cosyn's attention directed at him, the more time the others had to find the sanctum.

"What is it you think will happen?" Cosyn said. "Your troops are nearly defeated. Your temporals will soon be dead. Earth Apparent will be under my complete control."

"You presume much. But my troops have turned the tide on Ryla's soldiers. The Cord is reunited. Earth Apparent is not yet destroyed. It seems your alliance was not enough."

Cosyn's eyes flashed red. "I do not require an alliance. I *choose* with whom I conspire. *I* choose."

Kade's shoulders sagged. "Indeed. Choice is both a privilege and a curse."

Cosyn threw back his head and laughed. "You are coming to understand! The temporals were cursed from the beginning. I gave them the choice to live under my rule or die."

Kade sighed, weariness sinking deeper in his soul. The dragon continued to rage, draining his energy. His light was nearly extinguished.

Just a little longer. Give the others time . . .

"You offered options cloaked in deception," Kade continued. "You lie, manipulate the outcome. Whatever curse the temporals are under, you can be sure redemption is always near."

Cosyn shook his head and sighed. "And that, my brother, is the root of your weakness. Eternal hope in a perfect salvation."

"That is weakness?"

Cosyn leered and leaned in. "Not everyone wants to be saved," he hissed.

"Not everyone can be deceived."

"Wrong again. Everyone can be deceived, just not in the same way. You see, once I determine which temptation wields the most power—vanity, lust, greed—I tailor the deception accordingly. Even if a man could withstand me, he cannot turn away from himself. His true self. His own needs. His own desires."

"Yet, how many have?"

Cosyn narrowed his eyes. "Only those I destroyed."

"Ditimer resisted."

Cosyn laughed with genuine mirth. "So, it is in a Malvokian minion you put your hope?"

"In him, yes. And many like him. Redemption is not found in perfection. In fact, it is exactly the imperfection of Ditimer and Avery and Joshua and Raelyn that gives redemption, forgiveness, and salvation their power. In your desire to overcome the world, you missed one simple calculation."

"Oh?" Cosyn raised one eyebrow, seeming bored, but a twitch in his cheek showed the chink in his armor. He knew the answer. He knew Kade spoke truth.

"Love." The word seemed to dispel some of the shadows, though they immediately pressed back in.

"Love is the weight that tips all the scales," Kade continued.

"Enough!" Cosyn thrust his hand forward, blasting Kade with a thick, black smoke.

Kade threw up his arms, going down to one knee, sending out light to rebuff the smoke before it reached him. The wound blazed. It deepened, sinking past his flesh into his heart. It would split him in two. He staggered to his feet.

Cosyn nodded his head knowingly. "Not long now," he whispered.

CHAPTER TWENTY-NINE

Raelyn marched two steps into the sanctum, her eyes laser-focused on the plye. But a red-scaled, horned dragon, ten stories high, rose up, towering over Joshua and Tilman. It stood on its hind legs and spread tattered, translucent wings as it roared in anger. Its abdomen inflated like a balloon.

Joshua and Tilman ran to the far side of the cavern.

A yellow light charged from Raelyn's left, tackling her into an alcove as a fireball filled the room.

Raelyn flailed, gripping the Bokar to her body with one hand and pushing and punching at Altizara with the other.

"Rae!" Altizara tried to take hold of Raelyn's wrists. "Rae!" she shouted into Raelyn's face.

It looked like Altizara. Sounded like her. But so had the other one. How could she be sure? Raelyn stopped fighting long enough to squeeze one of Altizara's hands. Warm and soft. She pushed Altizara to one side, getting a look at her back. Her bow was secured there with her quiver, which held a single arrow.

"Zara?" Raelyn gasped.

"Yes!" Altizara said, jumping to her feet, but careful to stay tucked in the cleft. "Who did you think?" She held out her hand for Raelyn.

Raelyn shook her head and took the offered hand, allowing herself to be pulled her up.

"What's happening?" she whispered as she peered out, searching for Joshua and Tilman. The dragon had backed away, crouching, focused on the place Tilman had disappeared.

"Where's Jinny and Avery? Did they find Gabe?"

"Yes, everyone else is with him."

"He's okay?"

The dragon roared again as Tilman leaped from behind a pillar and charged it.

"I do not know," Altizara shouted, gesturing for Raelyn to follow. She darted to a fallen boulder and crouched behind it, pulling Raelyn down next to her.

Tilman stopped just out of the dragon's reach, as though waiting for it to charge. But it didn't give chase. Rather, it crouched low, eyeing Tilman as it huffed, snorting smoke from its nostrils.

"We found Gabe," Altizara whispered. "And the egg. In a nest at the furthest corner of the sanctum. When we realized you were not with us, we tried to go back for you. But the dragon awoke. Only I made it past. The others are trapped."

Tilman and the dragon seemed to be in a standoff.

"Tilman and Joshua have been trying to draw it away since. It will not leave its egg, nor its prey."

"That's not all the dragon's blocking." Raelyn nodded at the plye, little more than a flicker of blue light.

Altizara nodded. "We will continue with Kade's plan. Trust Larken and Othana with the egg. And Jinny, Avery, and Emaline to rescue Gabe. We must get to the plye."

A knot of panic rose in Raelyn's throat. The enemy had entered Peter's bunker. Her dad and the other NGI fighters couldn't hold them off for long, if at all.

It can't be too late.

"How?" Raelyn eyed the dragon, settled in front of the plye and blocking any path to the corner where Altizara said the others were. "Can we cause a distraction? Help Joshua and Tilman?"

Altizara heaved a sigh. "Perhaps, but it will not be enough."

"What d'ya mean?" Raelyn looked away from the dragon. Altizara met her gaze, her forehead knit and her brown eyes filled with worry.

"We must destroy it. Or we will lose Kade."

Raelyn frowned. "Kade—"

Tilman charged again. The dragon swiped at him with dagger-like claws. Tilman sliced at its leg, his light and blade connecting with a steely flash before retreating again. The dragon reared in a fury. It folded its wings back and ran at Tilman.

Altizara and Raelyn darted around the boulder, staying crouched, as they made for the outer wall of the chamber.

They skirted the wall, Raelyn keeping her eyes on the dragon's tail as the creature pursued Tilman.

"Look!" Altizara whispered, nodding to the far corner as they came around.

Emaline and Jinny huddled in front of a pile of rocks crouching over what looked like a bundle of dirty laundry. A short blast of fire from the dragon lit the chamber. A tuft of red hair stuck out from one end of the green fabric.

"Gabe," Raelyn whispered. Her heart pounded. He had to be alive.

Jinny glanced toward Raelyn and Altizara, then did a double take. She gestured wildly and Avery, Othana, and Larken rose from behind a crop of craggy rocks behind them.

Avery bolted around the rocks. As the dragon was still focused entirely on Tilman and Joshua, he scooped up Gabe and threw him over his shoulder. With Jinny and Emaline close behind, he ran toward Raelyn and Altizara's hiding place.

But their movement caught the dragon's attention. It twisted around with another mighty inhale.

Avery darted behind the boulder and dumped Gabe off his shoulder. Jinny dashed around in time to soften Gabe's landing. His frayed, charred backpack hung on one shoulder and the Leohfaet peeked out from the top.

In an instant, Avery yanked his shield from his back and stood over them. The dragon's fire exploded. The flame hit the shield and poured over them in an arc around the shield and Avery's expanded barrier where the stones had risen.

The blast ended as the dragon roared again. Raelyn peered over the boulder. Joshua had sunk the Ruah into the dragon's flank. The dragon spun, writhing, and jerked Joshua across the chamber.

Raelyn jumped up to run after him, but Altizara grabbed her wrist, yanking her back down.

"You cannot risk it!" she hissed.

Raelyn watched as Tilman shot a blast of light at the dragon's back, allowing Joshua to get to his feet. The dragon lurched one way, then the other, seemingly unsure which man to target.

Gabe groaned. His soot-covered face was thin and sunken. His hair, always sticking in every direction, was matted and singed.

"Jinny," he rasped.

"I'm here," Jinny whispered, taking his hand. "We're getting out." She looked up at Emaline, her eyes pleading.

"Will he be . . ." Raelyn began.

Emaline nodded and glanced toward the exit. "We must get him to a proper healer."

Avery, staying crouched, repositioned Gabe over his shoulder. Altizara nodded and peered over the boulder at Joshua and Tilman. They continued to engage the dragon, but the beast kept its body turned toward the cavern entrance. They couldn't risk drawing its attention.

"I can't carry him and use the shield," Avery said between heaving breaths.

The last time Raelyn had seen Avery at the Kulum outpost, he had been a frightened, angry coward. He had fled, forcing the rest to continue without the aid of his shield. Avery met Raelyn's gaze. His face, once clouded with fear, was hard and determined. The worried frown was now a blazing glower. Whatever had happened, Avery was a transformed man.

Altizara took one last look at the dragon, then ducked back down and grabbed Raelyn's hands.

"I said before, you are stronger than you know. Now close the plye. End Cosyn's reign on your world."

"Zara, what—"

Altizara jumped to her feet and sprinted toward Tilman. She grabbed her bow and the single arrow as her light grew, filling the chamber with rays of sunshine.

The dragon shook and turned toward Altizara, baring its fangs. It lowered its head, but hesitated. Altizara didn't slow as she nocked her arrow and pulled back.

The dragon bellowed, then drew a breath.

"For the valor of Arkonai!" Altizara cried and let the arrow fly.

It found its mark in the dragon's left eye.

It roared again, scraping at the arrow with its claws, breaking it in half. It scrambled backward, slashing its tail from side to side.

"Go!" Emaline shouted at Avery.

Gabe moaned as Avery rose.

Raelyn stopped him. "Avery, in the tunnel, there are—"

Emaline grabbed Raelyn's arm. "I will see them through."

Raelyn nodded. She tried to reach out to Jinny as she passed. Jinny had one hand on Gabe's back and took no notice.

As the dragon continued to writhe in pain, Raelyn watched them raced to the arched doorway and out into the catacombs.

Altizara, Tilman, and Joshua had the dragon's full attention. It charged one way and then another. Whether because of the pain or the inability to see, its attacks were erratic and confused.

But it was moving away from the corner where Gabe had been.

Raelyn holstered the Bokar and ran directly for the corner, taking a chance on the dragon's distraction. She ran onto the grouping of stones, behind which Larken and Othana had been hiding with Avery. There was no sign of the Shalhalans, just a nest made of splintered wood, crushed rocks and bones.

An empty nest.

"Raelyn!" Othana shouted from a crevice just past the nest. Larken stood next to her, both arms around a red-scaled egg the size of one of Aunt Betty's prized pumpkins.

Sudden tears blurred Raelyn's sight. She blinked them away and the cave was gone for a moment; the dark bunker flashing before her eyes.

Then Larken was running to her.

"I can stay! Othana can return the egg!"

"No! Kade said not to wait!"

Larken glanced at Othana. He looked down at the egg. The dragon continued to rage.

"It's okay! I've got this!"

Larken pursed his lips and shook his head with a deep frown. But he turned and ran after Othana, disappearing into the darkened cavern.

Raelyn edged to the plye. The same hazy blue light glowed from within. But something was different. Rather than a stone arch set upon a ritualistic dais, it was recessed into the cave wall and framed by an elaborate gold casing. But that wasn't it.

It was the light. The shadows just beyond the blue opening were there, but rather than swirling and undulating, they were stationary. The light itself, static.

It didn't matter. She was here. It was time to finish the job.

A darker shadow passed in front of the others.

Raelyn unbuckled the Bokar without taking her eyes off the shadow. Here, at the end of her quest, she would face Cosyn without Kade. Without Peter. Without anyone.

The shadow took shape.

Raelyn opened the book.

The shadow passed through the opening.

Raelyn looked at the page, searching for the words.
"Hello, Raelyn."
Raelyn jerked her head up.
Lima.

CHAPTER THIRTY

osyn strolled to Kade until he was inches from his face. "Enough of these games. We both know you cannot overcome me. Not now."

It was too soon. Kade had to hold Cosyn's attention a bit longer. He drew his shoulders back and forced his knees to straighten. Cosyn took a step back and rolled his eyes.

"Truly, you do not know when to give up."

Kade smiled. "Lady Ryla noticed that too." His smile sagged. "My persistence has many objectives. My joy would be full if you would only open your eyes. I will never give up the hope I have in your return to Arkonai."

"Why?" Cosyn's question seemed earnest.

"If you think it is too late—"

"It is, but not for the reasons you think."

Kade said nothing. Whatever Cosyn said could not be trusted. But he would let him speak.

Cosyn began pacing. "Since the Great Fracture, Arkonai has sought to unify the temporals. But he is wrong. If he truly loved them, he would value their choice. He would celebrate whatever choice they made. Why punish one temporal for starting a war and reward the other for negotiating peace? Why call one wrong and the other right?"

"All choice brings about a desired result?" Kade asked.

Cosyn shrugged. "Results are inconsequential. Freedom to choose is the greater measure. You believe there was a time in which I wished to please Arkonai. To be his dutiful

Guardian and hold vigil over his precious temporals." He drew up his shoulders and grinned, as though about to share a wonderful secret. "I never did. You only thought so. It is not too late because so much time has passed since my choice to turn from Arkonai. It is because I exercised my choice to forge a different path from the beginning."

"Then there truly is no hope."

Cosyn gave an impatient wave of his hand. "Again, hope for whom? You will always think like a Guardian. Pious or wicked. Right or wrong. Good or evil. You see only two alternatives. I see millions." He made an odd move to his right and glanced over his shoulder.

Kade gazed into the back of the chamber, where the shadows seemed to gather, and then looked back at his brother. "Where there are millions of alternatives considered equal in worth, there is heartache, fear, and death. All of which you have ushered into Earth Apparent."

He released a pulse of light through his left hand and gripped the staff in the other. Shadows sprang to life and lifted from the walls, murmuring. The air crackled.

Cosyn arched an eyebrow, his mouth a straight line. But his eyes darted around the chamber as though looking for a quick escape.

"There are powers you have *chosen* to disregard." Kade lifted his chin. "A strength beyond your varga"—his light grew—"your sibukyn"—brighter still—"your bloht, your lushor, your dragons, and your shadows."

Cosyn's eyes flashed red, and he took an uncertain step backward. "You—you are gathering what little strength you have left." He drew himself up, puffing out his chest. "Your destruction is near."

His words echoed. The shadows' whispers rose in a chant, joining Cosyn's voice. They climbed the walls and slithered across the ceiling. The stench of rotting meat filled the room.

Cosyn clenched his hands, then opened them wide. Black filaments rose from his palms, drifting and joining the shadows. His presence filled the cave. "Arkonai is not coming."

The ground trembled and the smooth stone floor fractured at Kade's feet. Dark, jagged rocks shot through the cracks like a charred, graveled lava flow. The shining black rock contained flecks of cobalt-blue lapis. The same compound making up the catacombs in Alnok oozed from the fissure. Before he could step away, the rocks spilled across one boot, then the other, hardening and sealing his feet in place.

Kade used the staff as leverage, trying to free his legs. But the rocks gripped tighter.

A chamber located in Velare, but rock leaking from Alnok. This went beyond Cosyn's trickery. Passing from one realm to the next, sowing descension, luring followers, did not seem to be enough. But this was more than a link between Alnok and Velare. The two realms, so closely layered, now intertwined.

Velare had always seemed a convenient escape. A temporary aid in protecting the temporals. But he hadn't been the only one to use it. Maybe his strategy had backfired. It seemed Cosyn had his own uses for the alternate realm. He had even produced an ally. If his aim was domination over Earth Apparent, what did Velare—

Cosyn raised his hands. The ceiling split. He brought his arms down, raining sharp black rocks on Kade. They pounded his shoulders and seemed to liquefy as they ran down his arms. The weight sent Kade to his knees, bending his feet to the point of breaking. He slumped forward to relieve the pressure, bracing himself on his palms. The stones rolled onto his hands and bonded them to the ground. The rocks on his shoulders solidified.

Cosyn paced in front of Kade. "You see it now, do you not? The joining of the realms."

Kade lifted his head as best he could to look at Cosyn.

"Yes." Cosyn smiled at Kade as he continued pacing. "I thought ruling the temporals was my highest calling. But then I met Lima, ruler of Velare. Together, we saw a greater destiny. A larger power." He stopped, his smile fading. "One realm. The way it once was." Cosyn's shoulders slumped. He seemed suddenly sad. "Before the fracture."

Kade strained against his granite bonds. "You cannot join the realms by destroying them. The coming of the single realm is not for you to decide. It is not within your power, or your purpose."

"We shall see . . ."

Kade's wound flared again, as though someone had stabbed him with a branding iron and twisted it in his chest. He groaned and let his head sag. Cosyn continued to speak, but Kade barely heard. A roar went off in his head. He panted, trying to conceal his distress as best he could as the pain consumed him.

Cosyn was right. It was over. What time Kade had bought for the Cord was hopefully enough. He had paid dearly for it. Now, he would pass on from Alnok, Velare . . .

He closed his eyes, waiting for his own fading.

But his energy did not drain away. An ember of light kindled beneath the pain; a warmth beyond the wound. Pressing through his agony, Kade directed his full focus on the spark. A bubble of peace within the torment. Perhaps one last moment of tranquility before the end. The burning of a flame before the final flicker is snuffed out. He could not hope to outlive the dragon.

Perhaps I will see Olmund . . . Lydia . . .

But the flicker did not wane. It grew. Brighter and hotter.

The whispering increased all around the chamber. The shadows danced just within Kade's view. All around, chanting, louder. It was a celebration. The jubilee of a slain enemy. Though who, or what, danced with glee, Kade could not fathom.

Still, Kade did not pass on.

A warbling hum, quiet and comforting, came from behind him. A vibration that Kade felt as much as heard. The shadows withdrew, skittering back into the corners of the chamber. The hum he knew well. One he had not heard in a very long time.

Kade craned his neck, looking back at Cosyn, who gasped and took a few stumbling steps back.

The dragon's roar filled the cavern, as though not just in the same realm, but in the same room. The sound was not just in Kade's mind. Its shriek came from directly behind him. And it seemed to be in great agony. A death cry. Then all was silent but for Cosyn's ragged breath.

"It cannot be," he whispered.

"Kade?" A sweet, familiar voice.

Kade smiled as a warmth spread across his chest. "You were correct, Cosyn. Arkonai is not coming. He was already here."

CHAPTER THIRTY-ONE

Raelyn stumbled backward, shaking her head. Though her thoughts spun and her chest tightened, a flame sparked in her gut.

Lima smiled as she stepped through the plye. "Surprised?" Her wide brown eyes glittered. The swirling light framed her glossy black hair spilling over her shoulders. She no longer wore the puritanical frock. A velvety cloak of blood red covered an elegant black dress. Relaxed, even curious, she leveled her gaze at Raelyn, ignoring the roaring dragon blasting fire at the embattled warriors.

Despite her formal attire, her smooth, pale features, delicate frame, and dainty movements, she still looked like the young girl who had saved them from the ruined village. But her shrewd gaze and knowing smile transformed the innocent child, the facade. Even this version of Lima only represented whom she thought Raelyn wanted to see.

Raelyn wasn't surprised to see her. She was angry. Stinging tears blurred her vision and she gritted her teeth. This girl was as evil as Cosyn. Probably more so. What Cosyn had tried to do, break Raelyn down so she stopped trying to save her brother, save the world, Lima had nearly accomplished. She had known the precise chink in Raelyn's armor. Not only was she a screw-up. Second-best. Replaceable. Lima had confirmed what Raelyn had always imagined. She had never been a consideration at all.

Invisible, irrelevant, unnecessary. Even after Larken had explained the truth. Even now.

But if Raelyn gave in to her lies, none of it would matter. She would be bowing to Lima's corruption. She would be handing over the Cord. She would be handing over her brother, her father, and the world.

Raelyn's chest tightened more, squeezing her next breath. The flame in in her core was spreading. Heat rose into her chest, neck, face. She let out a choked sob.

Lima's smile widened. She'd mistaken Raelyn's reaction for fear.

Like Cosyn, this brat had a weakness. She had shown a marked aversion to the Bokar. Raelyn placed a hand on the exposed page, narrowing her eyes at Lima.

"You know," Lima said, tilting her head slightly, "destroying this plye is quite pointless."

"Then why protect it?" Raelyn growled. She wouldn't be able to contain the heat. Her chest would explode. She gripped the book until her fingers ached.

"Is that what you think?" Lima swept to one side, holding her arm out wide. The dress and cloak swished around her feet as she invited Raelyn to step up. "Come, read your book. Say the words." Her smile hardened. "You will find silly incantations are powerless."

Raelyn wanted to rush the girl. Wanted to ram the book into her smug face. She wanted to scream. But her feet wouldn't move. Instead, she looked down at the open book. The page swirled with golden markings. She pressed her palm over them. They prickled her fingers, as though her hand had fallen asleep. The words that had always brought confidence and peace and filled her with a sense of power, continued to be elusive. Any minute, the words would appear. Not incantations. Truth. A truth she didn't always understand. But she would speak anyway. If the swirling marks would only create words.

"You have done nothing more than prolong the inevitable," Lima continued. "You will only cause more pain for those you love."

Raelyn kept her eyes glued to the page, her breath coming out in rough gasps. She couldn't make out a single mark. The tingling in her fingers traveled up her arm and mingled with the heat in her chest. Rather than peace, anxiety. Confidence became restlessness.

No. Urgency.

Come on. Show me the words.

Don't look up. Trust the Bokar. Trust the words to appear at exactly the perfect time. Trust the book that was made for you. The words meant for you.

Raelyn bent over the Bokar, scrutinizing the marks. Her tears dropped onto the page, blazed gold, then melded with the swirling marks.

"Peter would have known what to do with that ratty book," Lima chuckled.

Don't look at her. Keep your eyes on the Bokar.

The plye's blue light, just on the edge of her vision, shifted. The glow shrank away. Her gaze pulled from the book as though she had given up control of her eyes. Up, up, to the hem of Lima's dress . . . her child-like hands relaxed at her sides . . . her triumphant leer.

Behind her, the plye no longer pulsed with blue light. Lima stood next to what seemed to be a window or a doorway. On the other side, Raelyn's dad, in a wrinkled button-down shirt, sobbed over Peter's hospital bed. Raelyn shook her head. It was only a vision of the past.

But the insistent whoosh of the ventilator, forcing breath into Peter's lungs, the beep, beep counting down his days, were so real, so familiar.

Raelyn pulled the Bokar against her chest.

"Cosyn's already tried these tricks!"

Her throat ached. This should have no influence over her. She knew this ruse.

But the scene was so real. She could see every line around her dad's drawn mouth, every whisker on his sunken cheeks. They weren't in a different realm. They were in the next room. Her brother was still sick. Nothing had changed.

She took a step toward the plye. Her arms grew heavy with a sinking defeat. If she stepped through, she'd be with them.

She pried her eyes from the scene and surveyed the dark stone surrounding the plye. The flecks of gold from a long-faded gilding.

The dragon roared from a great distance.

Dragons . . . plyes . . . Guardians. What if none of it were real? What if Alnok was nothing more than a hallucination out of an overwrought sense of guilt?

Her knees buckled before she could take another step.

Everything she had experienced—Malvok, Shalhala, Endyle—was an illusion. Kade, the father from whom she had wanted forgiveness.

Tears poured down her cheeks.

Lydia as Harlan, the child she'd failed. Altizara, Othana, even Olvida, parts of the mother she couldn't save . . . Cosyn, the part of herself she despised. And now Lima: a glaring light on her ultimate failure. Raelyn closed her eyes. Her tears had dried up. She had nothing.

It was all a creation out of her own imagination. Alnok played out from the pages of a manuscript crammed away in the bottom desk drawer. The last six months, parts of her book taking shape in an unconscious mind. All of it, a way of coping with her failure.

She finally looked up into the plye/window. Her dad was looking at her. When she met his gaze, his face hardened.

Of course, he was angry. His favorite child was dying.

He turned and stalked to the door, yanking it open and . . .

He was dressed in a dark suit, his shoulders shaking as he stood over two caskets. One with a spray of pink roses. The other, smaller, with red, white, and blue carnations.

Peter wasn't sick. But Harlan and her mother were still dead . . .

What if she had never gained consciousness after the crash? She had only dreamed she'd cradled her little brother's body on the side of the road. No matter how real the sirens wailing in the background, the court hearings, Peter's illness, Kade . . .

Peter wasn't the one in the hospital.

She was.

Raelyn's stomach rolled. She rocked as she shook her head. The Bokar thumped to the ground.

"No," she moaned, looking at Lima. "You're doing this—"

"*You* did this," Lima snapped, her teeth bared, her dark eyes flashing.

The dragon's roar echoed. The cavern shook. Lima blinked, her expression clearing. Her lips turned up in a sympathetic smile.

"It's not too late," she said quietly, drifting closer.

The funeral dissolved. The plye again filled with blue light.

Raelyn stayed on her knees and gathered the Bokar into her arms.

"Make it right, Raelyn," Lima cooed, and knelt beside her. She put a gentle hand on her shoulder. "Go back and make it right."

Raelyn looked at her, blinking away tears. Lima gave her an encouraging smile. Raelyn nodded, but she didn't know why.

"That's right," Lima said, helping her to stand. She steered her close to the plye. Raelyn shuffled her feet. Shadows danced on the cave walls surrounding the plye.

"Raelyn!"

Raelyn jerked. Her head cleared for a moment.

Joshua?

"Close it!" he shouted.

She glanced over her shoulder.

Joshua, brandishing his sword with both hands, called to her. The dragon whipped its great head, staring down at him.

"The Bokar!" he cried before darting behind a pile of crumbled rock as the dragon's belly swelled.

The Durinial sent out a shock. Raelyn gasped and looked at Lima, who stood next to her with a wide grin.

"Too late." She gave Raelyn a shove into the plye as a scorching fireball exploded at her back.

CHAPTER THIRTY-TWO

Raelyn tumbled through the plye, splaying out on her belly onto a smooth stone floor. The Bokar jolted from her hands. Pain erupted in her temples. Her stomach rolled. She tried to get to her feet, but the room was spinning. She managed to get to her hands and knees.

At the center, a dark mound seemed to grow right out of the ground. Spilling from the top of the pile of black, craggy rock, was dark hair.

"Kade?"

He was bent over, buried in the rubble. Cosyn stood a few paces in front of him. Kade mumbled something about Arkonai being there.

But Cosyn ignored him and stared at Raelyn.

This was it. Her mind was broken. She had finally lost it.

"I see you are having fun," Lima said to Cosyn as she skirted around Raelyn and Kade.

"As you can see, I have completed my assignment," Cosyn growled. He looked like a disgruntled child.

"I am getting to mine."

"We agreed . . ."

They continued to argue as Raelyn crawled to Kade, a hostage within a prison of rocks. She focused on getting to her feet, grunting, as she reached out to the rocks holding Kade. The moment her hand touched them, her head cleared.

She stayed crouched but kept her hands firmly on the mound.

"What's happening?" she whispered, visually sweeping as much of the room without moving her head. Apart from the pile of rubble, the chamber looked nothing like Alnok. The cinder-block walls were painted cream as though to humanize an otherwise cold, utilitarian space. It seemed more like a . . .

Basement.

A church basement. The one where Peter had been ambushed—

No. She wasn't in any of those places. She was in a coma, dreaming all this up.

Heat filtered through her fingers, as though she had placed her hand on a sun-drenched sidewalk on a summer day. She looked down. Golden light peeked between the stone.

A shadow slunk along the wall, peeling away, coming near. Raelyn shrunk away, letting go of the rocks. Instantly, her head swam. She slammed her hand back onto the mound. Cosyn and Lima noticed nothing as they continued to bicker.

"Be still," Kade whispered.

A tear trickled down Raelyn's cheek. "None of this is real," she rasped. "I'm . . . I'm dreaming. It's all in my head."

The rocks grew hotter. But she didn't dare let go. Imagination or not, she didn't want the dizziness to take over.

"All experience is bound to interpretation," Kade said. "Everything happens in your head."

Raelyn wanted to laugh. Such a Kade thing to say. She wanted to cry. He agreed this was all in her mind. Did she continue to act out this illusion?

The rocks over Kade's shoulders shifted, some of them turning to dust and coating her hands in a black film.

"The Bokar," Kade said.

Raelyn nodded. She lifted one hand and then the other. The room tottered but didn't spin. She rubbed the dust between her index finger and thumb and the room steadied. Something about the rocks . . .

She edged around Kade, keeping her eyes glued to Lima and Cosyn, whose argument had escalated. Her foot kicked something. The Bokar. She bent to pick it up.

Lima stopped in mid-sentence; she and Cosyn looked at Raelyn.

"What do you hope to accomplish with that?" Lima spat the last word and jerked her chin toward the Bokar.

Raelyn slowly rose, the book in her hands. Neither Lima nor Cosyn reacted as though they cared.

One of the wall shadows lurched toward Raelyn. Raelyn gasped as it wrapped around her arms, binding them to her body. She couldn't lift the book. The shadow tightened its grip. She couldn't breathe. Wrenching, she tried to pull away, but she couldn't move. She was losing her hold on the book. With every ounce of will, she held tight. But she'd never be able to read from it.

The hair on Raelyn's neck stood up and a rhythmic hum began behind her. The plye. Or what she thought was the plye.

Golden light flashed around the room. The rocks holding Kade crumbled and flowed off him. His light rose as he stood, the remaining mound falling away. Beams of gold poured from his head, his shoulders, and arms. It filled the room. He stood tall, taller than Raelyn ever remembered him. His black hair, once again glossy, his face radiant and his jaw set. In his left hand, he held Peter's staff. He looked ready to part the Red Sea.

The shadow loosened its grip on Raelyn. She yanked free and held the book up as though to swat away the shadow should it close in again. The blue glow flashed behind her. Footsteps rushed up. She spun, ready to beat off whatever approached.

"Raelyn!"

"Joshua!"

Joshua gripped her shoulders and then pulled her close, squeezing the Bokar between them. They turned to see Lima watching them with a shrewd gaze. Cosyn glared at his brother. Darkness, like black soot, gathered around their feet.

Altizara and Tilman burst into the room from the false plye and gathered around Kade.

Lima's eyes flitted to the Bokar and then back to Raelyn. "It is over." Her tone was dull, without emotion, but several voices overlapped hers. "The book cannot help you. Kade cannot help you. It is over," she repeated.

Raelyn glanced back. It was true. The plye in the sanctum was a decoy. She couldn't hope to find the real plye now. The Bokar was useless.

Lima made a slow turn with her arm outstretched. All along the wall, as her hand passed by, the shadows peeled away, one after another. A whispered chant filled the chamber. Different from the voices Raelyn heard from the catacombs, but just as chilling. The stench of rotting meat made Raelyn gag.

Some of the shadows melted onto the floor and slithered along the ground. Others jerked and lurched toward Raelyn, Joshua, and the Guardians, huddled at the center of the room. Dozens of dark masses closed in.

Lima continued to conjure the shadows until it was hard to tell one from another. Darkness filled the space.

The Durinial pulsed.

The shadows continued to chant as they encircled the room. The black smoke coming from Lima and Cosyn, darker and thicker than the surrounding shadows, battled with Kade's golden radiance. Altizara's yellow light and Tilman's steel-blue aura rose, mingling with Kade's, creating an iridescent barrier to the shadows and the smoke.

A low moan rose beneath the chanting. It grew to a steady warble. A siren. An air-raid siren.

Raelyn took a step forward.

Joshua grabbed her arm and pulled her close, keeping her within the Guardians' light.

Something illuminated the back of the chamber, behind Lima and Cosyn. Another blue light, brighter than the plye from the catacombs, flickered to life. A shadow stepped out. Not a shadow. A person.

Peter.

His eyes widened when he saw Raelyn. Then his face hardened, as though comprehending some measure of what was happening. The siren continued.

Cosyn's gaze fell on Raelyn, but she was too late averting her eyes from the new plye. He spun around.

Peter jumped back, but Cosyn didn't react to his presence. He turned back with a satisfied smile, then a chuckle.

He stepped away from Lima, widening their linked shadow. Lima glanced over her shoulder, then shook her head and gave Kade a smile one might give to a hapless child.

"You believe you have us ensnared? About to deal the death blow?" She tutted. "No," she said softly, "this is exactly where you should be. In fact"—she strolled to the far wall—"the temporals will never leave. They will remain in Velare, without seripyn, without Kade, without hope." She flitted her eyes to the right. "I believe it is time for a reunion."

CHAPTER THIRTY-THREE

Lima raised both arms and swept them across the wall, as though to bring out more shadows. Instead, the wall crumbled. Raelyn flinched and Joshua blocked his eyes as daylight poured into the room through a cloud of dust.

The torrent of the battle, still ongoing outside the catacombs, was deafening, overtaking the shadow whispers.

As the dust cleared, dark forms scurried throughout the light. One came close to the new opening.

"Bloody hell!" Avery said, coughing and waving away the dust. He stopped short and swayed. He caught sight of Lima, then Cosyn, and tried to yank his shield from his back, but he stumbled. "A little help here!" he called over his shoulder.

Emaline appeared, placing a steadying hand under his elbow. She fumbled in her bag, pulled out a flask, and handed it to Avery. He took a quick swig and instantly steadied. Avery held it out to his left. As Jinny, supporting Gabe, limped out of the dust, she took the flask, swallowed a mouthful, then gave it to Gabe. A short man dressed in the simple brown uniform of the Shalhalans, dashed up next to Gabe as he drank and grasped his left arm.

"Lovid?" Raelyn whispered.

Lima giggled with delight. A smile spread across Cosyn's face.

"It is what you have always wanted," Lima breathed, and gestured to the plye leading back to the catacombs. "A way home."

Avery glanced past her, and his face dropped. He lowered his shield and shook his head. "Penny?" He stepped forward.

"Avery, no!" Raelyn shouted. "Whatever you see, it's not real!"

A minute ago, she was sure she was in a coma dreaming up all this stuff. But she was wrong. This was a battle of good and evil. A battle for those they loved. One they had to win for Earth's survival.

Shadows moved in and surrounded Avery, Jinny, Emaline, and Lovid.

Jinny stared at the false plye and clapped her hand over her mouth. Emaline tried to grab her arm, but Jinny batted her away as she joined Avery. Gabe strained to break Lovid's hold on him, but the older Shalhalan wrangled him to Kade.

Raelyn looked into the fake plye but saw nothing. Whatever the others were seeing, it was more of Cosyn's deception.

Altizara, Emaline, Tilman, and Lovid started after the temporals, but Cosyn raised a hand and stopped them in their tracks.

Raelyn searched for Peter. He had to still be there. Their connection was now complete. He was the link between Alnok, Velare, and Earth. If she couldn't close the plye, he had to. And do so without becoming trapped in Velare with the rest of them. He had to close the plye.

She looked back at the Bokar. Three words rose to the surface of the page. Raelyn blew out a long breath. Finally. She smiled. Again, words that were meaningless to her. But she trusted they were exactly what she needed to say.

"Frid Giefan Eow."

The shadows spun in a frenzy but seemed to draw away from the light. Jinny, Gabe, and Avery paused, though they still stared into the fake plye as though in a trance. Lima's smug smile evaporated.

Raelyn waited for more words to appear, but the marks faded. The pages went blank.

The shadows closest to Raelyn broke apart, seeming to melt, bubbling and crackling, to the floor. Some drifted back to the walls like blowing dust in a strong wind, reforming as writhing shapes in the corners.

Lima growled and rushed toward Raelyn, hands outreached, grasping for the Bokar. Raelyn raised the book over her shoulder and brought it around like a baseball bat just as Lima reached her. She gave the girl a satisfying whack. Lima stumbled back, her eyes wide and her mouth a perfect circle of shock.

She had no power.

Kade stretched out his arms and golden light enveloped Lima. She bowed and covered her face.

Jinny, Gabe, and Avery stirred and backed away from the fake plye, Cosyn's spell broken.

"Peter!" Raelyn screamed, desperately scanning the back of the chamber. The siren drowned out all other noise. A shadow still bubbling on the ground shot up and grabbed hold of Raelyn's calves. She screamed, trying to stomp on it.

Joshua drew his sword. Altizara gripped Raelyn's shoulders, pulling her from the shadow's grip as the Ruah connected with it in a flash of light. It slumped at her feet and faded into the ground.

The siren grew louder, but just beneath, shouts and calls outside the chamber, drew near. Altizara, Tilman, and Emaline ran to the opening, their lights merging in a single beam as they drew their weapons to defend against the encroaching battle. Lovid collected Gabe, Jinny, and Avery, guiding them away from the fake plye to Kade before he hobbled over to assist the other Guardians.

The diminished shadows continued to seethe at their feet, reaching, grasping. Gabe, his pale lips pressed in a determined grimace, brandished the Leohfaet, in which a flicker of white light kindled. It was enough. The dark spirits drew back, some disintegrating entirely. Jinny, the Seon firmly on her brow, stood at his side, alerting him to shadows creeping up from behind. Avery planted his feet, the Cieskild tight against his shoulder, buffeting the closest shadows. Joshua continued to strike those that rose with renewed power.

The blue light shone from the corner; from the settling dust, Peter reappeared, wearing the amulet. The siren was overpowering. Raelyn's ears ached. She looked down at the Bokar. The pages were alight but blank. She looked back at Peter.

Raelyn took a deep breath and snapped the book closed.

Lima lowered her hands as a flicker of hope crossed her face. She glanced at Cosyn who adjusted his defensive stance to one of triumph, both of them clearly under the impression Raelyn was giving up.

"You see," Cosyn wheezed. "She knows. She doesn't belong here."

Raelyn glanced at Kade. He smiled and nodded.

"Okay," she whispered. She dropped the Bokar. "Peter!" she shouted, taking the staff as Kade handed it to her. "Catch!"

She launched it, like a javelin, high over Cosyn and Lima's heads, to the blue light at the back of the chamber.

Peter jumped and caught it.

The shadows continued to bombard the Cord. Joshua, Avery, Gabe, and Jinny fought harder.

Raelyn retrieved the Bokar from the ground. Peter could close the plye. The Cord could handle the shadows. Kade would have to deal with his brother.

Raelyn met Lima's eye and smiled. She would take care of the girl.

She opened the book. The pages glittered with a frenzy of unintelligible marks.

Kade's light filled the room. Cosyn growled. But his eyes flickered with fear. Kade raised his hands and Cosyn cowered. His hair thinned and his skin began to bubble and blister.

Lima charged at Raelyn.

"The night is almost gone." Raelyn read the words that took shape, sharp and clear. Her voice echoed across the chamber, over the screeching siren. "The day is near."

Lima took another labored step forward. A shadow rose in front of Raelyn. Joshua ran across and slashed it away before continuing to the next one.

"Let us lay off the deeds of darkness," Raelyn continued. "And put on the armor of light."

Lima flinched; her face contorted with rage. She narrowed her eyes to slits, but made no move forward. The little girl was gone; the creature from the beach stood before Raelyn.

"Let the powers of the wicked be blown away as the chaff before the wind," Raelyn said. A sweet, cool wind, like the breeze before a summer rain, blew past Raelyn. Lima cried out and staggered back. Her skin faded, becoming gray and translucent. Finally, the shadows withdrew from Raelyn and gathered around Lima's feet, pulling her down and away.

"Let them melt away as unending, flowing waters."

Lima screeched and tried to stamp out the shadows. But she melded with them, fading into a formless mass, sliding along the ground and onto the wall where they disappeared.

Cosyn stood alone before Kade and the Cord. Reduced to a husk. Withered, impotent. A shadow of what he once was.

The siren continued to warble.

Raelyn opened the Bokar and scanned the first page. There had to be something. Some word to destroy the enemy of Earth Apparent, Alnok, and every temporal. The monster who cursed her brother with a disease that nearly killed him. Who set the world on fire and sent shadow demons into her world, stationing them at the four corners of Earth to bend the ear of leaders of families and nations. Who caused her mother and brother's death.

He needed to die.

The siren rose and fell. Her hand trembled as she flipped to the next page. Nothing.

What now?

Kade nudged her. She looked at him, and he nodded past Cosyn, to the back of the chamber.

"Peter!" Of course. What was she thinking?

"It's not over, Rae!" Peter shouted over the siren.

"Close it, Peter," Raelyn cried. "Close the last plye!"

He nodded and stepped through. He raised the staff high. "Come home, Raelyn!" he shouted and brought the staff down. Blue light flared. The chamber went silent and dark.

"Noo," Cosyn sobbed.

Raelyn looked up at Kade, streams of golden light coming from his head and arms. He looked at Cosyn with sad eyes.

She shook her head.

"Kade, you can't let him go!"

The ground trembled. A great chunk of the ceiling broke loose and fell with a dusty crash to the floor. Then another.

Cosyn loped to the fake plye. He glanced over his shoulder. Fear, anger, and misery contorted his already misshapen features. Then he was gone, the plye sealing behind him.

"Raelyn!" Altizara appeared in the cave opening, waving.

"We gotta go," Joshua said, grabbing Raelyn's hand and pulled her back to the entrance.

"C'mon!" he shouted to Avery, Jinny, and Gabe.

They stumbled after him and Kade followed not far behind.

The opening was filling up with rubble; the daylight growing smaller and smaller.

Another chunk of the cave fell directly over Raelyn. She ducked and covered her head, but it never touched her. She looked up. Avery was holding the shield over her.

"Go, go, go," Joshua said, tugging her through the diminishing exit.

Altizara and Tilman ushered them from the cave: Raelyn, Joshua, Avery, Gabe, Jinny, then Kade. The entrance crumbled closed behind them.

The dazed, dirt-covered Cord stood in a small circle as Kade joined Altizara, Emaline, Tilman, and Lovid. Distant skirmishes continued, but many Malvokian and Shalhalan soldiers were on their knees in surrender.

Raelyn's ears were still ringing; dust filled her nostrils. Gabe leaned on Jinny, his eyes closed and his head laying on the top of her head. Avery secured his shield to his back. Joshua, his dark beard almost white with the cave dust, took Raelyn's hand and kissed her palm, then pulled her close and kissed her forehead. He looked over her face, as though seeing her for the first time. Then he kissed her tenderly on the lips. He was smiling as they broke away.

"Well done!" Kade exclaimed as he strode up, the other Guardians following. "Your perseverance, your faith, your love, has seen the quest to the end. Cosyn's plyes are closed and a more sinister plot was thwarted. Well done!"

He glanced over the battlefield. A hint of sadness crossed his face before he smiled again. "Now, let us make for Herlov Kingdom."

CHAPTER THIRTY-FOUR

The Cord, Kade, Altizara, Tilman, Emaline, and Lovid trekked north along the cliffs back toward Shaldon. Their breath came in heavy puffs of vapor as winter seemed to have arrived in earnest while they were in the catacombs. Though every stop compounded the cold, causing Raelyn's nose and fingertips to go numb, Gabe required frequent breaks. His long, mutinous hair and full red beard made him look older than even Joshua. Thin, pale, and quiet, he gave little insight into his days in the catacombs. It wasn't only his physical wounds. Emaline applied the same balm she used on Kade to the deeper gouge on his shoulder and the scratches on his face and arms. Lovid crafted a healing draft that brought the color back to his cheeks. But the haunted look in his green eyes held the same shadows as those in the caves.

Jinny never left his side. Her quiet observations and perfect instincts guided her to know when to ask questions, if Gabe was ready to speak, and when to remain silent. When to hold his hand and when to give him space. The Seon truly was the perfect weapon for her. She already had a gift for discernment.

"At first, I had enough strength to keep the Leohfaet lit," Gabe said during one of their early stops as they chewed on jerky and took swigs of the last of their water. "The dragon wouldn't come near me. Then I looked for opportunities to sneak away. After a while, I didn't have the strength. As I became weaker, the dragon showed less and less interest."

Kade nodded. "Cosyn held you captive, but wanted you all together, alive."

Gabe nodded. "That's what I surmised. I might have been able to get past the dragon, but pretty soon I just got too weak."

Avery nodded knowingly. "That dragon scratch nearly done Kade in."

"Yeah," Gabe said, working his shoulder.

"It may take a little more time," Kade said. "You will heal."

Ryla's army had been subdued. The Cord and company of Guardians passed rows of soldiers marching traitorous Malvokians, Shalhalans, and Kealans toward Herlov. Low clouds joined heavy smoke from the battle.

"I do not believe you will require an escort back," Altizara said to Raelyn before turning to Kade. "Tilman and I will stay behind and help put the area back in proper order." She looked at Emaline. "If you feel Gabe is healed enough, we could use your gifts with the soldiers here."

"I can watch after him," Lovid offered.

Raelyn stepped in front of her friend and trainer. "But Altizara—"

"Not to worry," she said, patting Raelyn's arm. "We will see you in Herlov soon."

Emaline gave Kade the last of the herbs from her packet and hugged Jinny and Gabe. Tilman shook Joshua and Avery's hand, and the three Malvokian warriors jogged back toward the cliffs. Raelyn watched them until they had disappeared within the plumes of smoke.

At nightfall, Kade and the Cord rested on the banks of the fjord, the exact spot Avery had fallen in, he informed them. As they prepared to camp for the night, a group of soldiers marched by. At the helm, Ditimer, his pale-gold light flickering, escorting a bound Lady Ryla. She scowled but did not speak. Without pausing, Ditimer nodded at Kade.

"What will happen to them?" Joshua asked.

"Some may entreat forgiveness," Kade said, settling onto the ground in front of the fire. His golden light once again drifted around him. "For those, it will be granted. Though they will never again be Guardians. Others may continue to follow Cosyn's ways. In that case, banishment."

"What about Cosyn? Seems banishment's too good for him," Avery huffed, tossing a branch into the fire.

Kade raised an eyebrow. "I am grateful to not be called his judge."

"Tell me more about Endyle," Gabe said as he drew close to Jinny. Aside from a quick recap of how they had closed the second plye, they'd spared no time to recount the shipwreck and the bewitchment they fell under while they were looking for the plye.

"And the giants?" Avery asked. "They sound right chuffin' nasty."

Raelyn stifled a grin. Same old Avery. Fiery, bold, outspoken. But with a kindness, a humility, that softened his impertinence.

Joshua gave the highlights of his and Jinny's battle with the giants.

"You think Larken and Othana are okay?" Raelyn asked Kade.

Kade looked into the fire. "I believe so. We might soon find out."

"You said we circumvented another of Cosyn and Lima's objectives," Joshua said. "What exactly were they planning? Aside from holding us captive in Velare?"

"They wished to link Earth Apparent, Alnok, and Velare so they could rule all three. We all eager await the day every realm becomes one, but that day is not for any of us to decide. Even then, we serve but one ruler."

"Right, Arkonai," Avery said. "These realms, how many are we talkin' about?"

Kade shook his head and chuckled. "Eight of which I am aware."

"Blimey," Avery breathed.

They fell silent, each considering the implications of a multitude of dimensions.

"What about the dragons you lured to the forest?" Jinny asked.

They shared stories, one after another, until Gabe had fallen asleep and Raelyn couldn't keep her eyes open. Joshua sat, leaning against a tree, and opened his arm to her. Raelyn's face burned. She glanced at Kade, who lay on his side, propped on one elbow, gazing into the fire. The others had found places around the dancing flames, either asleep or close to it and, in Avery's case, snoring. She scooted close to Joshua and nestled against his chest.

For the first time, no one kept watch.

Before dawn, snow began to fall. They broke camp and continued north, making a wide berth around the fjord. Although Kade assured them Cosyn no longer held sway over the creatures of Alnok, no one had any interest in putting a toe in the water.

The temperature continued to drop. Raelyn had long given up keeping track of the days and months, but they were likely entering the holidays. An excited flutter set off in her stomach. She might be home in time for Christmas. Her excitement soured when she thought of her dad, leading the NGI army, and her brother looking after the wounded. Would they have come through unscathed?

"Kade," she said, letting go of Joshua's hand so she could walk next to her old mentor. "Peter's staff. You had it the whole time?"

"No. King Ellioner kept it in a vault in Herlov Castle. I retrieved it before we traveled on to Shaldon."

"How did you know you would need it?"

"I did not. But it seemed prudent, if only to get it to you, to pass on to Peter."

"I don't suppose we could've destroyed the plye without him."

Kade shook his head. "It took all of you. It was not just a plye connecting Alnok to Earth Apparent. They had formed a convergence of all three realms within that chamber in the catacombs. Alnok, Earth Apparent and Velare. Cosyn and Lima's ambitions lay well beyond ruling

Earth Apparent. They sought to forge a link between the three realms, maybe more, and dominate them all. You not only closed Cosyn's plye, you sent Lima back to Velare and cut off her influence here. The three realms are again as they should be. For now."

"For now?" Joshua asked.

"The realms were never intended to be fractured as they are. In time, Arkonai will heal the lands and bring them together."

"Let's hope he won't need help!" Avery said.

Kade chuckled. "Indeed."

By midday, they had no choice but to cross the river to make the trek west to Herlov.

When no one would enter the water, Kade stepped off the bank and splashed into the river, wading in up to his waist. He turned and lifted his arms as though to prove all was well.

Lovid mimicked Kade's example, except the water reached his chest. Avery reluctantly went in after. Gabe and Jinny, holding hands, crossed the stream together.

Raelyn took a breath and stepped into the water. Pins and needles pricked at her, and she jumped back with a gasp.

"What?" Joshua said, grabbing at her and frowning.

"It's cold!" Raelyn laughed.

Joshua rolled his eyes and waded in, pulling her in after him.

It took them three days to cross the Rift to the border of Herlov. The mountains, rivers, every tree, seemed different. They weren't, but Raelyn was looking at them with fresh eyes, free of burden and uncertainty. Plus, they were on their way home.

Halfway through their second day of travel, a dust cloud rose in the south. The old nibble of fear gnawed at Raelyn's gut. She glanced at Kade when he stopped.

Avery cupped his hand over his eyes. "Kade, you don't suppose that could be—"

Two horses, galloping at full speed, raced toward them.

"Indeed, it is!" Kade said. "Othana and Larken!"

The Shalhalans pulled their horses to a stop.

Kade looked them over. "It is done, then?"

Othana grinned. Raelyn had never seen her so cheerful. "Yes, the egg is safe."

"We will call on Herlov to join us in blessing the Echelon Caverns, so the egg cannot be touched or taken."

"There're other dragons?" Gabe whispered and glanced into the sky.

Othana dismounted and took his hand. "The tremor we felt in the mountains before we reached Shaldon?" She cocked an eyebrow at Avery.

"I'd hoped that was the dragon Joshua killed just out for a stroll," Avery said.

Othana shook her head. "I do not believe so. But dragons, as a rule, are not evil. But under Cosyn's command, they wielded much destruction."

"While the egg is in stasis," Larken added, "the dragons cannot breed."

"Unless we can be confident Cosyn will never exert his power over them," Othana continued as she led Gabe to her horse and indicated he should ride.

"Oh, no," Gabe laughed awkwardly. "I wouldn't, you know, without . . ." he gestured to Jinny.

Larken was already swinging his leg over his saddle.

"She can take mine."

At the castle gate, Kade hailed the captain of the guard, who lowered the drawbridge. The grounds were a frenzy of marching soldiers and scurrying townspeople.

"Much has changed," Kade said as he led them through the commotion. "Kingdoms can now reorder their affairs without the ever-present threat of Cosyn and his horde."

They entered the castle, and a short man with snowy hair and a white beard hurried to Kade.

"King Ellioner," Kade said. "I present to you the Cord of the Periferie."

"Welcome, friends!" he boomed. "You are our honored guests!"

"Cheers," Avery said. "When can we go home?"

***

"So, who was Lima?" Joshua asked. He looked over the rim of a wine glass as he sat at a stone table with the rest of the Cord in a tapestried room on the third floor of the castle. They had agreed to a farewell banquet before entering the Silom Pool, through which they would return to the hadron collider in Silo. As anxious as Raelyn was to go home, Altizara, Tilman, and Emaline still hadn't arrived, and she couldn't leave without saying goodbye.

It had taken much convincing for Avery, but in the end, he had agreed a final farewell was in order.

Kade swirled his goblet, staring into the contents.

"Does it matter?" Avery asked. "Whoever—whatever—she was, she's gone."

Gabe set his glass on the table. "I didn't think anyone was really"—he used air quotes—"gone."

Kade continued to study his wine.

"She was more powerful than Cosyn," Raelyn said, watching Kade's face carefully.

Kade looked up and met her gaze. "Lima returned to Velare, her power greatly diminished."

"What'll keep her from trying this nonsense again?" Avery asked.

"What convinces anyone to do, or *not* do, anything?" Gabe muttered.

Kade nodded thoughtfully. "She will be reluctant to gather her forces for another assault. The temporals proved a greater adversary than she had imagined. But we will watch for signs of her presence. And we are keeping a close watch on Cosyn." He sighed. "I am the leader of Alnok and Guardian of Earth Apparent. I do not have authority over Velare or any of the other realms. To that end, I will take extra measures to separate Alnok from Velare. I will not risk Lima entering our realm again."

"Can she attack Earth?" Gabe asked. "Is there a connection like the LHC that links her dimension and ours?"

Kade sighed. "If I close the Silom Pool, I might minimize that chance. But she may find other means. But I never knew of Lima. She is not the only evil in Velare."

Jinny sat up. "But there's someone like you in Velare, right? Someone to keep her in check?"

"I may have a Velarian counterpart," Kade said, his brow furrowed as he studied the table. He glanced at Othana and then Altizara before his eyes swept the Cord. "The prophecy that spoke of your coming is incomplete."

"But we accomplished the task written in it," Jinny said.

"What more could there be?" Raelyn said. Already, a new burden weighed on her shoulders.

"I do not know," Kade said, "but I believe the lost prophecy will declare a wholly different quest. And perhaps"—he looked pointedly around the table—"new champions."

"What does that mean?" Jinny narrowed her eyes, but, rather than fidgeting with the hem of her blouse, her hands rested on the table.

"I believe it means"—Raelyn finished her wine in one swallow—"we may have another choice to make. Someday."

EPILOGUE

"**J**oshua! The door!"

Raelyn scooched to the edge of the couch, hefting her enormous belly, struggling to get up. But at the pounding footsteps thumping down the stairs, she sank back down.

"Coming!" Joshua shouted.

Lily looked up from the blanket where she was pretending to fit a plastic arrow with a suction cup at one end into a pretend bow. "Daddy?"

The doorbell rang again.

Raelyn smiled and held out her arms. "It's okay, sweetie. Mommy and daddy are having friends over."

Lily nodded. She hadn't yet called Raelyn "mommy", but the bond was growing. And she was thrilled to have a little sister on the way.

The door opened.

"Hey, c'mon in!"

"Ey up, Joshua!"

Lily's eyes lit up. "Unky Avewy!" She scampered to the front door.

"There's my bonnie lass!" Avery's voice boomed in the entryway.

"Rae!" Joshua called.

"Coming," Raelyn said, grunting as she stood.

Avery set Lily down as Raelyn rounded the corner to the entry and grinned. While Joshua had kept a short version of his beard and left his hair slightly shaggy, Avery was clean shaven, and his hair perfectly trimmed. Next to him stood a beautiful woman, a few inches taller than Avery, with short blonde hair and kind blue eyes.

"This is Penny."

"So good to finally meet you!" Raelyn rushed forward and hugged her as best she could around her belly.

"Right, good of you to put us up," Avery said as he bustled through the door out of the cold.

"Just glad it's finally happening," Joshua said, taking Penny's coat.

"I've got a roast in the oven," Raelyn said. "Get comfortable in the dining room."

"Let me help," Penny said, following Raelyn to the kitchen.

"Me too, me too!" Lily cried as she skipped after them.

Soon they were settled, finishing off the last of the potatoes, sipping on cabernet and Raelyn her Sprite.

"How are the renovations coming?" Joshua asked Avery.

Avery shrugged. "Slow. Between the volcanoes and the near world annihilation, it seems lumber is hard to come by in Yorkshire."

"But the floors are in, and Avery's had time to do some of the work hisself," Penny said.

"Oh, really?" Joshua sat back and gave Avery an incredulous stare.

Avery rolled his eyes. "She said time, not talent. Working at the local bank doesn't afford us much to pay contractors." He relaxed and fiddled with the stem of his glass. "But we love it. Feel like the changes are scrubbing off the bad memories of me dad. But we're leaving just enough to remind me of some of the good."

Lily rubbed her eyes.

"Babe," Raelyn said to Joshua, nodding to the little girl. "You want to tuck her in?"

"Yep." Joshua stood and scooped her up. "Let's go, Liliput."

Avery watched him go, then turned and beamed at Raelyn. "A whole year! I can't believe we let so much time go by!" He stood and began clearing the plates.

Raelyn smiled. "No one could've traveled before now. Not with the world still getting back on track."

"Gabe did," Avery countered.

Raelyn raised her eyebrows as she handed him her plate. "You know Gabe wouldn't have ever asked without meeting her parents first."

"She wouldn't've said yes without her family's blessing," Avery chuckled and took the plates into the kitchen.

"She did most of the planning from Seoul, with her mom," Raelyn explained to Penny. "But she wanted to get officially married in the states."

"They're having a ceremony in Korea?" Penny asked.

"Already did. In fact . . ." Raelyn glanced at the clock.

"What?" Avery narrowed his eyes in suspicion as he come back into the dining room.

The doorbell rang, and Joshua's thumping footsteps came down the stairs.

A slow smile of realization spread across Avery's face as Raelyn struggled to her feet.

Joshua poked his head into the dining room. "We should get that." He was grinning from ear to ear.

It was a fight to the door. But Avery got there first and threw it open. Gabe and Jinny stood beneath the porch light. Raelyn nudged Avery out of the way and hugged Jinny's neck.

Avery laughed as he shook Gabe's hand, but Raelyn saw the tear slip from his eye.

Joshua ushered Jinny and Gabe inside as they were each introduced to Penny. Jinny held tight to Gabe's arm. To anyone else, she might have looked particularly devoted. But Gabe's limp, the scars on his hands and face, were stark reminders of all they had suffered in Alnok.

Raelyn poured two more glasses of wine as they settled around the table. "It's getting cold out there!" Raelyn said, easing into her seat.

Gabe sipped his wine, then nodded. "Reminds me of . . ."

"Alnok," Avery finished.

"Yeah."

"How d'you think Kade's doing?" Joshua looked at Jinny. The habit of seeking out her discernment hadn't diminished.

Jinny shrugged. "I think we made both Alnok and Earth safe. In fact"—she glanced around the room—"he might be visiting us right now and we don't even know it."

Avery chuckled. "Hope 'e chooses his drop-ins with discretion."

Raelyn smiled, but it was bittersweet. Knowing he was watching over them only made her miss him more.

"We'll never know," she said. "He closed the portal from the Silom Pool to the B & K LHC."

Avery turned to Gabe. "What happed to the company? They still at it?"

Gabe shook his head. "No idea. When we came back, thankfully after hours, I explained away why the collider had been fired up two different times in a year with no documentation. They seemed satisfied, but the owners came in and made some changes to the company. I didn't like the direction they were going. It was less about science and more about philosophy. When I started teaching at the community college, I sort of lost touch with everyone there."

"Philosophy?" Raelyn asked.

Gabe shrugged. "To some people, science is a religion." He nodded at Raelyn's neck. "You left the Durinial in Alnok."

Raelyn touched the new necklace that had replaced the every-present talisman. "Each of our families has an amulet made from parts of the original one brought here by Moses and Nahor. I didn't see the need to keep Kade's."

Avery took a deep breath and looked at Joshua. "How's work after the Army?" he asked, bringing their conversation out of the past.

Joshua took Raelyn's hand. "After the discharge—"

"Honorable discharge," Raelyn corrected.

Joshua nodded. "Right. I went to work for a security company."

"You're a guard?" Penny asked.

"No, I've had enough conflict. I design security software for big companies."

"Ah," Avery said, "still keeping everyone safe."

"Plus," Joshua continued, "Rae started writing again. She's got a publisher interested in her manuscript."

"That's wonderful!" Penny exclaimed.

The phone rang. Joshua squeezed Raelyn's hand and stood. "I'll get it."

After he'd left the room, Gabe leaned toward Raelyn. "Is your book about"—he shrugged—"you know, Alnok?"

"Sort of," Raelyn said, "I wanted to include what happened in Alnok and Earth Apparent. I've spent the year doing interviews. No one will believe what happened in a fifth dimension they're only beginning to understand. I wanted to show the connection in a way people might accept."

"Speaking of people's understanding," Avery said, "how's your dad?"

"Recovering. He was in bad shape for a while. When he protected Peter while he faded to Alnok to close the Plye . . ." She shook her head. "It's a miracle he and the other NGI soldiers managed to fight off the World Alliance Force." She heaved a sigh. "Let's just say he barely made it."

"We wouldn't have succeeded without him," Jinny said with a soft smile.

Raelyn nodded and blinked back stinging tears. "I think the amulet might have had something to do with that."

"Well, look at us now!" Avery boomed and stood. He seemed determined to keep them in the present.

Joshua reentered the dining room with a frown.

"Back together, healthy and whole!" Avery continued and raised his wineglass. Penny joined him.

Joshua stood next to Raelyn and picked his glass up, but his expression was grim.

Raelyn tugged on his hand. "Everything okay?" she whispered as Gabe slowly rose to his feet with Jinny's help.

Joshua nodded. "I'll tell ya later." He took a deep breath and turned his attention to the toast.

Gabe and Jinny raised their glasses. "To Kade," Gabe said.

Joshua lifted his glass high. "To the reunion of the Cord."

Raelyn stayed seated, tipped her glass toward them and offered a small smile. "Not quite."

***

Raelyn needed to pee. She eyed the end of the pew in which she sat dead center. Joshua sat on her right, bouncing Lily on his knee. Avery and Penny sat on her left. She was stuck.

"You never did say what your brother wanted," she whispered to Joshua. After the phone call and the toast everyone had filed out and they had gone to bed. She wanted anything to take her mind off her discomfort. "What's it been? Five or six years?"

"Ten. He said he found something he wanted to show me. I'm meeting him next week."

Raelyn didn't press. This wasn't a day for bad memories.

She'd arrived early and had joined Jinny in the bridal suite. She wasn't much help with getting her ready, being unable to bend down. But with Jinny's parents unable to fly in, and having not made many friends since returning from Alnok, Raelyn had become her de facto Matron of Honor. They'd opted to forgo a bridal party and many of the formalities and extravagance. Jinny's wedding dress, a snow-white, fitted lace gown, was her own design and one exception. But it was the Seon, perched on Jinny's head with a long veil trailing from the back, that made up for any lack of grandeur.

"You made sure everyone brought their weapons?" Jinny asked as she adjusted the circlet.

"Yep," Raelyn said, then cocked her head. "But I don't understand why."

Jinny grinned. "You'll see."

Now, with the Bokar tucked inside an oversized purse, Raelyn waited in the pew, fanning herself with a program as a distraction.

"You warm?" Joshua whispered, patting her knew. "Don't worry, your dad and brother will be here."

She shook her head. Truth be told, she hadn't felt well all morning. "I'll be fine. Just excited to see Jinny walk down the aisle."

Avery leaned close. "More like eager to watch *Gabe* see her walk down the aisle."

At that moment, Gabe shuffled out to stand next to the altar.

"Excuse me! Raelyn?" A shrill voice came from several pews back.

Raelyn sank into her seat.

Aunt Betty.

"Here!" Joshua turned and gave a quick wave as he stood, pecking Raelyn on the cheek before exiting the pew.

Aunt Betty, dressed in a watermelon-colored jacket and skirt complete with matching hat, gave Joshua an enthusiastic hug. Then she grabbed Lily's cheeks and kissed her all over her face as Lily giggled and squirmed.

Fulton shook Joshua's hand and scooted into the pew, followed by Peter. Raelyn's heart beat a little faster. Even after a year since Alnok, seeing her father and brother still sent a wave of comfort and peace. But even now, those warm feelings couldn't overcome the ache in her back.

Her dad gave her a delicate hug and Peter kissed her cheek.

They were all finally settled, just as the music began and they all stood again.

Jinny strolled past the rows of people, It seemed appropriate, somehow, for her to walk down the aisle alone. She had spent a lifetime looking to others for approval. Now, she breezed past with a wide, relaxed smile, her eyes focused on Gabe.

"Please be seated," the pastor said when Jinny had linked arms with Gabe.

"Our Heavenly Father," the pastor began and Raelyn bowed her head with everyone else.

"We gather as friends and family in your presence," he continued, "to bear witness to the union of Gabriel and Chin-sun. We ask for your blessing and grace for their marriage and for the lives of everyone here. Amen."

"For the valor of Arkonai," the Cord murmured.

The ceremony finished with many happy tears. The pastor invited everyone to the reception in the ballroom at the hotel three blocks away. As the photographer shooed the remaining people from the sanctuary, explaining to a protesting Aunt Betty that photos were to be taken of the newlyweds before heading to the reception, Jinny waved Raelyn and the others over.

She looked at each of them. "You have them?"

Raelyn patted her purse. Joshua handed Lily off to Fulton and disappeared with Avery, Gabe, and Peter. They returned with the sheathed Ruah, the Leohfaet, the Cieskild and Peter's staff, the Staebor.

Jinny looked at Fulton. "Could you do the honors?" She made a motion as though taking a picture.

Raelyn smiled and nodded. "Okay, Dad." She handed Fulton her phone. "This button here."

He nodded. "Got it."

They arranged themselves: Raelyn and Joshua—Lily asleep in one arm, the other gripping the Ruah, tip planted on the step—at the center, two steps down from the altar. Gabe and Jinny, all smiles, stood shoulder to shoulder a few steps down, Gabe holding the Leohfaet high. Though it no longer lit up, the sunlight streaming through the upper windows flickered on it, giving the illusion of a white flame.

None of the weapons functioned. The sword, simply a blade. The Seon, a beautiful tiara. The shield might block a carefully aimed arrow, but nothing more. The Bokar a special, but uninspiring, journal.

Avery held his shield in front of him on Joshua's left and Peter, the staff in his left hand, stood on Raelyn's left. He reached into his collar and pulled out their family's amulet, now on a long, silver chain.

"Ready?" Fulton called. "Say, Kade!"

"Kade!" they sang.

Peter waved, the red mark bright and clear on his palm, the only otherworldly element that remained from Alnok.

Raelyn gasped as a pain shot through her back, worse than the others that morning.

Joshua grabbed her arm. "What's wrong?"

Raelyn forced her grimace to a smile. "I think we're about to add one more to the Cord."

ACKNOWLEDGMENTS

Gratitude can never be understated, though it is often underrated. Finishing the Portal Slayer trilogy was exciting, exhilarating and very, very hard. Without my support network girding my every word, I might still be writing *Beneath the Shadows*.

I know I don't say thank you nearly enough. And while the back of the book doesn't seem to be the place of highest honor, the placement doesn't render my gratitude any less. Please understand, my words of appreciation could fill every page.

My heart sings over each review and encouraging word from every reader, but ardent fans I hold dearest. My kids, all four of them: my son and daughter, Joshua and Jessica and my daughter-in-law and son-in-law, Mariah and Michael, are the leaders of my fandom. The story world and characters would never be fully developed without their input.

A book is always special, but every story needs readers. My sweet friends Gloria and Rhonda are my own personal publicity committee. They're the first to "like" my social media postings and I can count on these two steadfast friends to help me arrange a booksigning, a release or just spread the word.

My biggest fan, my husband, Wil, is the perfect example of sacrificial support. He cheers on my writing, but more than that, he supports *me*. He doesn't always have to understand to be totally on board for every crazy idea. There's a song, *Better Than I Used to Be* by Mat Kearney, that captures the way we build each other up.

I been chasin' this dream

I'm so glad you understand

Climbing up a mountain,

would it leave you hardly standing

Things don't go just the way you planned it

But I never thought we'd have so much to take for granted.

Perfection is never the goal. Forward motion is. But on those occasions when the next step seems not just daunting, but impossible, that's when my crew rallies, and we all get the work done together.

LAUNCH TEAM

Wil Dooley
Joshua Dooley
Jessica Dooley
Mariah Dooley
Michael Freeman
Rhonda Revels
Gloria Sinquefield
Jessica Baker
Jenny Lees
Linda Woessner

ALSO BY SL DOOLEY

COMMUNITY AND RESOURCES

Torn Parchment is more than books. It's a community of nerds. When you sign up, each month you'll receive an email full of fandom and fantasy lore. Not to mention free books, exclusive sneak peeks, and updates on the next book. Sign up now and don't miss an issue.

***

SLDOOLEY.COM

***